Sassy Saturdays

BOOKS BY JUDITH KEIM

THE HARTWELL WOMEN
The Talking Tree
Sweet Talk
Straight Talk
Baby Talk

THE BEACH HOUSE HOTEL
Breakfast at the Beach House Hotel
Lunch at the Beach House Hotel

FAT FRIDAYS GROUP
Fat Fridays
Sassy Saturdays

CHILDREN'S BOOKS BY J. S. KEIM
Kermit Greene's World

THE HIDDEN MOON SERIES
The Hidden Moon
Return to the Hidden Moon
Trouble on the Hidden Moon

Sassy Saturdays

A Novel

Judith Keim

LAKE UNION
PUBLISHING

Published by Lake Union Publishing, Seattle

www.apub.com

Amazon, the Amazon logo, and Lake Union Publishing are trademarks of Amazon.com, Inc., or its affiliates.

ISBN-13: 9781503940673
ISBN-10: 1503940675

Cover design by Danielle Christopher

Printed in the United States of America

For my cousins, with fond memories of being together,
Sue, Ellen, Christie and Bruce

CHAPTER ONE
TIFFANY

Who knew a pregnant torch singer would be in such demand?

Tiffany Wright waited behind the velvet stage curtain, hoping she could get in a couple of more Saturday-night performances before her baby girl arrived. Then she could get on with her life, away from the druggie who'd once been the sweet young guy she'd married.

The chatter of customers, the clinking sound of glasses, and the growing sense of anticipation from the crowd increased her usual pre-performance jitters. She was lucky to have the job. The Glass Slipper was a newly opened, upscale lounge in the town of Williston, Georgia, outside of Atlanta.

Tiffany's thoughts drifted to Beau. From a wealthy, well-known family, he'd had a childhood that had been anything but normal. He'd been spoiled, then reprimanded unreasonably for not behaving the way his parents thought suitable for someone of his background. He'd once told her it made him angry that he could never satisfy his parents. When they continued to eat away at the very same self-confidence she encouraged in him, his frustration grew. Then, when things began to fall apart for him at work, he started using drugs. His anger at her and everyone exploded. At that point, Tiffany decided she wasn't going to be the one he abused.

She drew a troubled breath. She'd never have had the courage to leave Beau if it hadn't been for the women in the Fat Fridays group. They met every Friday for lunch—no calories counted—and though they were of different ages and backgrounds, they'd become best friends. Their friendship meant so much more to her than having fun lunches. It gave them all the opportunity to support one another as they faced their individual problems.

Tiffany took a peek at her friends sitting in the audience, waiting for the show to begin. Loyal as always, they were gathered at one of the round tables, and they were laughing—probably over one of Betsy Wilson's silly sayings.

Filled with affection, Tiffany studied the group. Betsy was the oldest member and the one who'd brought them all together. Karen McEvoy, her partner, was a computer geek and sweet as pie, as Carol Ann would say in her Southern drawl. Carol Ann Mobley was sipping a bright-blue martini, their favorite drink at these gatherings. Two years older than Tiffany, she had a lot to learn about men. Beside her, still recovering from a tragic shooting, Grace Jamison sat with her arm in a cast and studied the empty stage. Tiffany's gaze rested on Sukie Skidmore, her favorite. A young new grandmother in her midforties, Sukie was, in many ways, the leader of their group. She'd recently landed the hottest man in town, eight years her junior. Tiffany couldn't help smiling at the whole romantic idea.

"Ready to go?" asked Sly Malone, coming up behind her. An older man, he was the manager of the Glass Slipper, and if Tiffany wasn't mistaken, he was a little bit in love with her.

She gave him a thumbs-up. She was as ready as she'd ever be. Tucking her long blonde hair behind her ears, she grabbed the portable mic and walked out onto the stage. Sassy Saturdays is what she called these nights.

The crowd quieted and waited for her to begin.

Her gaze swept over the sea of faces. "This is for the ladies of the Fat Fridays group," she said, nodding to her friends.

The small jazz trio played a brief introduction and then Tiffany started off with an oldie. "Only You" fit the tastes of the summer crowd in this small town.

Amid applause she moved on to other songs, soon becoming lost in the notes and the lilting lyrics. Singing was something she loved to do. It sometimes made her forget that, according to her husband's family—the well-known Beauregard Wrights—she was a nobody from western Kansas. They'd attempted to take her in and change her by dictating her life. Instead, they'd all but taken away her soul.

After several numbers, Tiffany announced a break. As usual, the loudest applause came from her friends' table. She walked over to them and sat down.

"Wonderful, Tiffany," said Sukie, beaming at her.

"I wish I could sing like that," Carol Ann said wistfully. With her newly streaked brown hair and more stylish clothes, she was attractive, but she lacked a poised, outgoing personality. Tiffany and the other women were trying to help her gain a little more self-confidence.

"Good job," said Karen. "I love your singing." Quiet by nature, she was a great match for fun-filled Betsy.

Betsy smiled at Tiffany. "To quote an old Chinese proverb, 'A bird does not sing because it has an answer. It sings because it has a song.' And you, my dear, sing sweeter than anyone I know."

Tiffany returned her smile. Betsy was such a dear woman. When Tiffany had first met her, she never would have dreamed that beneath Betsy's jolly, grandmotherly appearance was an unhappy woman who didn't realize she was gay. It was only after her husband died that Betsy began to question herself and what she wanted out of her life.

Sukie gave Tiffany a hopeful look. "When the time comes, you'll sing at my wedding, won't you?"

Tiffany patted her round stomach. "You bet. We two girls wouldn't miss it for the world."

She loved the idea of having a daughter. But Beau and his family had considered the baby's sex another failure of hers. They'd wanted a boy to carry on the family name. After a fight about it, Tiffany couldn't hide her misery any longer. When she'd gone to Sukie to talk about it, Sukie had reminded her that a girl is made up of two *X* chromosomes, not just one chromosome from the mother, so she shouldn't have to take the blame on that one.

Carol Ann clasped her hands together, a dreamy expression on her face. "So when is this wedding going to take place?" The pitch of her voice grew whimsical. The other women smiled. Carol Ann was a hopeless romantic.

"I don't think it'll happen for a while," said Sukie. A pinkish tint crept into her cheeks. "I want to enjoy every moment of being engaged."

"Oh, sort of like those movie stars." Carol Ann stared at the ring and lifted Sukie's hand to study it. "I can't wait until I have a diamond like that." She sighed. "If only . . ."

Grace (who had until recently been living under the assumed name of Lynn) rolled her eyes and let out a puff of disgust. She wasn't the man-hater she'd once been, but she was definitely not a romantic. With her background, it was understandable.

"It's beautiful," said Betsy, coming to Carol Ann's defense. In the midst of the noise of the revelers surrounding them, Tiffany noticed Betsy and Karen exchanging looks that spoke of many things.

Sukie held out her hand in front of her. "Cam did a really nice job of picking out a ring." Her eyes sparkled with happiness. "He's such a sweetheart."

"He sure is," said Karen, and the others murmured their agreement.

The eyes of the women at the table suddenly widened with surprise. They stared at the entrance. Tiffany turned around to see who'd entered the club.

Oh, no!

She gripped the edge of the table.

Looking very out of place and wearing a frown that spelled trouble, Judge Beauregard Wright was headed in their direction. Tall and handsome, he had a shock of white hair and a distinguished presence few could ignore.

With him in the room, the red-velvet booths and small round tables with starched white tablecloths looked . . . cheap.

The judge approached and bowed to her friends. "Good evening, ladies. I've come to talk to Tiffany." When he faced her, his blue-eyed stare drilled into her. "Won't you join me at one of the other tables, my dear?"

Regard's courtly manner and silky smooth Southern voice didn't fool Tiffany one bit. Behind that velvet-tongued speech was a cutting meanness she'd experienced more than once. She shot Sukie a helpless look.

"Would you like company?" Sukie asked her.

Regard's cheeks turned dark red with displeasure. He glared at Sukie.

Hesitant to make matters worse, Tiffany shook her head. "No, thanks. Wait for me here."

She followed Beau's father to a table out of earshot of her friends. She wondered what he had to say that hadn't been said before. He still couldn't accept the fact that she'd told Beau she wanted a divorce.

Regard held a chair out for her.

Feeling about five years old, Tiffany took a seat. Conversations with Regard were more like lectures.

He sat opposite her. "Tiffany, this is no place for you." He shook his head. "Imagine how Muffy and I feel about our daughter-in-law singing in a place like this—singing anywhere, for that matter. It does not fit the Wright image."

Tiffany smirked at his unintended pun. His idea of the right image for the Wright family was such a pseudo-existence that she couldn't buy into it. What she couldn't understand was why their son wasn't allowed to get the help he needed. According to them, such help didn't fit the image the public had of the family.

Determined to be strong, Tiffany lifted her chin. "I'm going to support myself and my baby the best way I know how. After the baby is born, Beau will send a small monthly check to help pay for her care. That's the only thing I've asked for."

Regard was silent for a moment. "Is this because Beau lost his temper that one time and hit you?"

She remained quiet. It had been more than once.

"Or is it because of what he did to the nursery? Writing those ugly words on the walls?" He lowered his voice. "I admit I was disappointed in him for doing that, but it won't happen again, I assure you."

That wasn't the only problem. Though Regard wouldn't admit it, Beau wasn't just taking drugs occasionally. He was hooked on them big-time.

She let out a sigh. It was the same old story. "Why won't you allow him to get the help he needs? A good psychiatrist can help him work out some of his problems."

"Psychiatrist?" Regard's eyes rounded with indignation. "They're all quacks. We Wrights don't need help from them. My father and his before him would roll over in their graves if that ever happened. Beau just has some growing up to do."

The whole thing was pathetic—this belief that they somehow were not ordinary people prone to the same troubles as everyone else. She'd had such high hopes for a happy life together when she'd agreed to marry Beau. All she'd hoped for, all she'd lost, cut through her like a knife. "I'm sorry, but I've made my decision."

"Now, little lady, don't you be going teary on me." Regard waggled a manicured finger at her. "Just come to your senses and get back home where you belong. Beau, blast him, wants you back, and we've got our reputations to protect."

Her stomach churned. She felt her baby's foot kicking at her ribs, as if to get her attention. Determined, she rose to her feet. "Beau knows I'm never coming home unless he gets help and works things out. I'm sorry, Regard, I really am."

The color in Regard's cheeks deepened. Tiffany knew the battle wasn't over—he was used to winning.

Trembling inside, she turned her back to him and walked away from the table. Still overwhelmed by the judge's presence, she made her way backstage, past tables of laughing, smiling, happy people, to get ready for the second half of the show. She prayed Beau's father would leave. She wasn't sure she could squeeze a note out of a throat gone dry.

When Tiffany returned to the stage, Regard was gone. Relieved, she took up the microphone and began to sing. After crooning a few romantic numbers, she let the music bring back happy memories to a time two and a half years ago when she and Beau first met.

The bar in the Atlanta airport had been crowded when she and a friend waded through the gathering and nabbed a high-top table. They were on their way to Savannah for St. Patrick's Day weekend. After ordering drinks, her friend elbowed her.

"What a hottie!"

A tall, well-built, blond-haired guy was standing by the entrance to the bar, looking for a place to sit. Dressed in khakis and a blue golf shirt that showed off his trim body, he looked like he'd just stepped from the pages of *GQ*.

He noticed her watching him, and his lips curved into a smile. As they stared at each other, the din around them faded. A shiver went through Tiffany when she realized her smile was as wide as his.

He walked over to their table.

"Want to join us?" her friend asked.

"Sure." He studied Tiffany.

They introduced themselves. Caught off balance by the immediate emotional connection she felt with him, Tiffany sat silently while her friend quizzed him. "Beau Wright? You're not from that family I just read about in *Southern Living*, are you? You know, the one with the whole family history of judges?"

Beau's expression shifted to neutral. "Why?"

"Omigod! You are!" The shrill of her friend's voice indicated she'd discovered something wonderful.

Tiffany sat there wondering what her friend was talking about.

Beau noticed her confusion. "No big deal. So my father's a judge."

Tiffany shrugged and smiled. It didn't matter to her. She'd never met her own father. He'd taken off before she was born.

They talked about everything and nothing.

She checked her watch, finished her beer, and turned to her friend. "Ready to go? We've got to catch our plane to Savannah."

Beau got to his feet and helped her with her leather jacket. "So? Am I going to see you again?"

Tiffany shook her head. "Probably not. Your family is from Charleston and I live in Georgia." She knew her place in the world. It wasn't with some rich guy from a famous family.

"Hey, wait! Don't go!" He grabbed his duffel bag. "I've decided to go to Savannah with you."

"Are you crazy? You said you're on your way to Florida." She couldn't believe he'd just change his mind like that.

"Not anymore," he said, giving her a cryptic look.

And that was the beginning of the end of her world.

She finished the last song to a startling quiet in the room.

Alarmed, she opened her eyes.

Focusing on the audience, she realized there was hardly a dry eye in the place. As applause rang out, her friends rushed up onto the stage. They shared a group hug with Tiffany, right in front of everybody.

Tiffany clung to them. She loved them. She really did.

Afterward, as people left the building, she gathered her things and prepared to leave.

Sly came over to her and handed her an envelope. "Thanks. Everyone had a great time tonight. Good job, sugar," said Sly. "Love that sass of yours." He gave her a quick hug. "See you next Saturday unless that baby of yours decides to disappoint my customers and appear ahead of schedule." His smile was sweet.

She laughed, waved good-bye, and walked out to the empty parking lot. Alone, the high she'd enjoyed while singing ebbed away.

In silence, Tiffany drove to the small apartment she'd sublet from Karen after Karen had moved in with Betsy. Tiffany enjoyed her new independence, but it didn't erase her sorrow at the changes in her life.

She entered the apartment and closed the door behind her with a lonely click. The apartment was nice, clean, and affordable—nothing like the large, luxurious house Beau's parents had given them for a wedding gift. She didn't miss that house, though. Betsy once said a house is not a home without love inside. Somewhere along the way, she and Beau had lost their love. She was certain their present situation had arisen from dealing with his parents' expectations, the family's notoriety, and trying to be people they were not. It had exhausted her to live a lie.

So tired she could hardly stand, she slipped out of her clothes and pulled on an old T-shirt of Beau's over her panties. After washing her face and brushing her teeth, she collapsed on the double bed. She looked to the empty space beside her. It was sometimes hard for her to believe what had begun as so wonderful had turned so ugly.

She let out a sigh and pulled up the lightweight blanket she used to keep away the chill from the air conditioner. Her thoughts turned to Regard. She'd been shocked to see him at the club. He might think it was terrible of her to sing there, but she loved it and the money was good. Sly called her a singer with sass. And everyone had loved her performance.

Tiffany turned onto her side and cradled her stomach. "So there, Beau Wright and your awful family," she muttered. "I'm somebody after all."

CHAPTER TWO
SUKIE

Sukie Skidmore left the Glass Slipper with the rest of the Fat Fridays group, pleased to have been part of such a pleasant evening with friends. As always, Tiffany's performance on stage was wonderful. Her sweet soprano voice seemed a musical gift from the angels, and even obviously pregnant, she had an alluring beauty that both men and women appreciated.

She checked her watch and wondered if it was too late to call Cam. He'd had a busy week at work. Maybe he was sleeping as soundly as his three-year-old daughter, Chloe. Thinking of their situation, it seemed foolish to Sukie for her to live apart from them. Cam had asked her to move in with him and she'd accepted. But it hadn't happened yet. Her house was on the market, and she didn't want to leave it unoccupied or try to sell it without her furniture in it. She knew, and the real estate agent had confirmed, that it was important if she wanted a quick sale and a good price.

As Sukie drove her car into the small enclave of upscale homes, she noticed lights on in Cam's house and smiled. Instead of heading into her own driveway, she pulled into his. He'd left the front porch light on for her.

She parked the car and hurried up the walkway to the front door. Opening it, she called out, "Hi, sweetie!"

Cameron Taylor emerged from the den.

Sukie's pulse quickened at the sight of him.

Tall and fit, he grinned at her. Above finely defined features, his rich golden-brown hair met his ears and swept his brow. But it was his intelligent, kind, blue-eyed gaze that had drawn her in from the beginning. Now it was focused on her.

"I was hoping you'd stop by." He hurried to her and wrapped her in his arms. Drawing her close, he said, "How'd it go? Tiffany great, as usual?"

Sukie settled against his strong chest and listened to the beat of his heart grow faster. "She was wonderful." She looked up at him and smiled. "The whole time she was singing those romantic songs, I was thinking of you."

He chuckled. "Good. I've been thinking about you too." His eyes darkened with desire. "Will you stay?"

"Yes." She leaned into him, loving the feel of his hard, virile body. After twenty-seven years of being married to Ted Skidmore, she'd forgotten what lust was all about. Being with Cam, making love to him, was unlike anything she'd ever known. There was something magical between them. She knew it, and so did he.

Cam lowered his lips to hers. His sweet kiss was full of the promise of something better.

Heat flared inside Sukie. She wanted much, much more of what he had to offer.

When they finally pulled apart, she and Cam grinned at each other, aware of all the sensations that lay ahead.

It never failed to surprise Sukie that of all the women who practically swooned every time Cam appeared, he'd chosen her. The Fat Fridays group, bless their hearts, had helped her understand that she should enjoy her unexpected happiness and, better yet, that she deserved it.

"Chloe's asleep?" she asked.

Cam winked. "We have all the privacy we need." He took her hand and led her toward the stairs.

Sukie's heart pounded with anticipation of the delicious moments ahead of her.

The ringing of Cam's landline phone stopped them.

Cam's brow furrowed. "Who'd be calling here at this hour?" He picked up the receiver and checked caller ID. His frown deepened. Without saying a word, he handed the phone to her.

"H-hello?"

"Sukie, it's Ted. Bad news."

Her heart stopped beating. "Is it the kids? Elizabeth? Rob? What?"

"Emmy Lou and I have split up."

Sukie was silent. She was so surprised she didn't know what to say. Her ex-husband had dumped her for Emmy Lou, and she was supposed to be sorry the relationship had ended?

"Thought maybe you and I could talk about getting back together." Ted's words were slurred. "Uh . . . Sukie? You there?"

Struggling with her emotions, she found it difficult to form words. "I'm here in my fiancé's home, as you very well know, or you wouldn't have called this number. Where are you?"

"At the house. Thought we could talk here."

Surprise changed to fury. "That is no longer your house, Ted. It's mine. And I'm not going to talk to you about any reconciliation. The idea is . . . is . . . laughable."

Astonishingly, he continued, "I know you got together with Cameron Taylor just to get me back. So let's move on." His smooth-coated words turned barbed, grew more slurred, and Sukie realized he was very drunk.

"I'm serious, Sukie."

Okay, now that qualified as more than drunk—stupid. He must have had a brain injury. Or had the dye he'd been using on his thinning hair leaked through to his half-witted brain?

She fought to find the right words and make herself clear without antagonizing him. "Ted, you and I have done just that, moved on. Our days together are over. I'm happier than I've ever been. Please leave the house. Someone is coming to look at it first thing tomorrow morning. I don't know how you got in unless you got the key from Rob."

"I'm not going to sign any papers agreeing to sell the house. Not now."

Her hands clenched. "Dammit, Ted, don't start any fights. I'm tired of you backing out of agreements. I'll go to court if I have to."

"What a bitch!" he screamed. The venom in his voice sent shivers of fear down her back. He was totally out of control. And she wasn't a bitch. She'd been a good wife, a good mother.

Cam gave her a worried look and put an arm around her shoulder. Sukie realized there was no use arguing with Ted in his condition. "Good night, Ted," she said and lowered the phone to its cradle.

Shaken, she stood a moment, trying to understand the situation and all its implications. Ted hadn't mentioned Emmy Lou's baby—the baby he'd been so proud to claim as his. Lately, there'd been rumors that the baby might not be his after all. Was that why they'd broken up?

"What's going on?" Cam asked her.

Sukie shook her head. "Ted and Emmy Lou have broken up. He thought we should get back together. Can you believe it? Of course, he was drunk when he said it." She covered her face with her hands and took a deep breath. When she lifted her eyes, Cam was studying her.

"I feel better that you're staying here tonight. Ted can get out of control."

She nodded. "I think his whole life is out of control, and that scares me."

They climbed the stairs hand in hand. At the top of the stairway, Sukie tugged Cam over to the door of Chloe's room. They peeked inside.

Chloe lay stretched out across her bed. Her curly blonde hair looked almost white against the pink princess sheets. One hand clung to the long worn ear of a stuffed rabbit she adored. Her favorite doll, Sally, lay beside her.

"She's so darling," whispered Sukie, her voice soft with affection. She'd come to love this bright-eyed, cheerful toddler. Cam had done a good job of raising her alone. It was one of the many reasons she was attracted to him. She herself had had little help in raising her own two.

She and Cam silently closed the door, leaving it open a crack, like Chloe wanted.

Desire built inside Sukie once more as she walked into Cam's bedroom. One of her female friends had once asked her how it was, being with a younger man. Taken aback by such a direct question, Sukie had paused and then had said the one word that described it best—*wonderful*.

Cam wrapped his arms around her and hugged her to him.

Leaning into him, inhaling the spicy aroma of his aftershave lotion, she became aware of how eager he was to make love. Sukie smiled and lifted her lips to his. Yes, she thought happily, being with Cam was wonderful.

All ugly thoughts of Ted evaporated as Cam began to give her many more reasons to enjoy being with him.

◆ ◆ ◆

The following morning, Sukie felt something soft land on top of her as she lay in bed. She jolted wide awake.

"I love you, Sukie," whispered Chloe, throwing her arms around Sukie's neck.

Sukie smiled, blinking away the sleepiness that stubbornly clung to her. She drew Chloe up against her body and cuddled her, inhaling the flowery smell in her hair. "Love you too."

Beside them, Cam stirred. "What time is it?"

Sukie checked the bedside clock and sat up with alarm. "It's eight o'clock. I've got to get going. The house is being shown this morning at ten. I need to make sure everything is all right after Ted called from there last night."

Cam frowned at her. "I don't like the idea of you going into that house alone. Chloe and I will accompany you. Right, pumpkin?"

"Yes, but I'm hungry," Chloe said. She held up her doll. "Sally's hungry too."

Sukie climbed out of bed, grateful for the pajama top Cam had lent her. "I'll get dressed and make a quick breakfast."

"I'll help Chloe get dressed, then join you." Cam lifted his daughter up into the air and then pulled her into a bear hug before setting her down on the floor beside the bed.

Sukie grabbed her clothes and hurried into the bathroom. She was relieved Cam would accompany her home. Before he'd ditched her and their marriage, Ted had been a pretty stable guy—obnoxious at times, but consistent. But with his drinking and Emmy Lou's possible infidelity and demands for material things, Ted was falling apart.

Though Sukie felt sorry for Ted and all that had happened to him, there was no way she'd ever consider going back to him. With Cam she'd found a sweet, kind, passionate love she never knew existed.

After eating a quick, cold breakfast of yogurt, fruit, and granola, Sukie helped Chloe into Cam's car and climbed into her own.

As she drove down the street to her house, she wondered how long it would be before it sold. She wanted to move in with Cam. It was becoming harder and harder to be away from him and Chloe.

Thankful Ted's BMW was nowhere in sight, she pulled into her driveway and parked the car in the garage.

Cam pulled into the driveway behind her.

Sukie waited for him to get Chloe out of the car, and they all walked into the house together.

At the doorway to the kitchen, Sukie came to a shocked stop. Her favorite pottery canister set lay in pieces on the floor. Flour and sugar coated the marble countertops and spread onto the wooden floor. Milk sat in a puddle atop the kitchen table and was dripping onto the chairs and floor.

Sukie clamped her jaw together to keep from swearing in front of Chloe. She glanced at Cam and blinked away the sting in her eyes.

"Why is it so messy?" asked Chloe.

Sukie stared at the damage, certain of who'd made it and why.

Cam's look of dismay tightened into one of anger. "You think Ted would have done something like this?"

Sukie nodded. After being spurned by her and knowing the house was about to be shown, she could well imagine Ted doing this in a fit of rage. He was used to having things go his way. In their marriage she'd worked hard to make sure he was happy so he wouldn't become temperamental. But that wasn't the kind of woman he'd left her for.

"C'mon, I'll help you clean this mess up." Cam's words were clipped with annoyance. He went to the kitchen closet and pulled out a broom and a mop.

"Can I help too?" Chloe asked.

Sukie forced herself to speak calmly. "Sure. Why don't you hold the dustpan for Daddy while I check the rest of the house?"

Cam shot her a worried look. "Want me to come with you?"

Sukie shook her head. "I'll call down to you if I find anything terribly wrong." Seeing her home defiled, she felt as if she, herself, had been violated.

She fought off the sick feeling in her stomach and went upstairs. Going from room to room, the only thing she found out of place was the bed in the master bedroom. It had been slept in. Seeing a few traces of flour and sugar on the sheets on Ted's old side of the bed, she knew she'd been right to think Ted had made the mess.

She lifted the phone on the bedside table to call her son. At twenty-seven, Rob was a joy to her. He and his wife, Madeleine, were a stable, loving couple who'd recently welcomed a baby, Jonathan, her first grandchild, a little boy she adored.

Rob answered the phone after a couple of rings. "Hi, Mom. What's up?"

She steadied her voice. "Did you give Dad the key to the house?"

"Yeah. Why? He said he had to pick up a few of his things and that you knew all about it."

"He lied to you, Rob. I did not give your father permission to enter the house."

"Really?"

"Yes, there's no need for him to be here without me. He knows he's welcome to pick up anything of his whenever he makes those arrangements with me, no one else. And now he's made a mess here at the house, and it's due to be shown this morning."

"You're kidding! I'm sorry, Mom. I never would've given him the key unless I thought you knew about it." Rob paused. "What is going on with him anyway? He's not the same person I knew as Dad before all this embarrassing stuff with his affair."

Sukie wondered how much she should say, then couldn't hold back. "I'm really worried about your father's mental health. Is there any way you and Madeleine can try to get him to see a therapist? For him to mess up the house for revenge isn't at all normal. And now he thinks we can get back together again. After all that's happened, that's not the least bit possible. Besides, I'm in love with Cam. I'm afraid your father's losing touch with reality."

"Whew! That bad? I'll talk it over with Mad and let you know. Again, I'm sorry, Mom. Good luck with the sale of the house."

"Thanks, Rob. I'll see you soon. Love to everyone there."

"Thanks. Back at you."

They hung up and Sukie stared at the empty bed, disgusted. She wouldn't have time to change the sheets. She quickly made up the bed, fluffed the pillows on top of it, and went downstairs to the mess that awaited her.

Cam looked up at her with a questioning look when she entered the kitchen.

"No real damage done in the other rooms," she softly announced. "But Ted obviously slept here last night in my bed."

Cam shook his head and continued working with Chloe on sweeping up the stuff from the floor. Sukie grabbed a dishrag and went to work on the kitchen table. *How, in a little over a year, has my life changed so completely?*

CHAPTER THREE

TIFFANY

Tiffany awoke, still dreaming of that weekend in Savannah when she and Beau had first met. Then, seeing the empty bed beside her, reality hit her like a blow to the gut. A softer blow followed, one more to her liking. Her baby girl was kicking. Smiling, Tiffany rubbed her stomach and sang a little lullaby to the baby, a song she'd made up one day when the little one was especially restless. She'd called the song "Moonbeam Ride." Someday she hoped to record it.

After the baby settled down, Tiffany stretched. Thank goodness it was Sunday. She'd have the whole day to herself.

She got out of bed, padded over to the bedroom window, and peered out. The sun streamed through the slats of the blinds in lemony stripes, landing on the soft bedroom carpet like bright butterflies. Outside, the clear blue, cloudless sky told the story of another hot summer day in Georgia.

Tiffany made her way into the kitchen to turn on the coffee maker. After it began to perk up, she carried a glass pitcher of water outside to the small balcony off the living room. The three potted pink geraniums lined up against the wrought-iron railing bobbed their heads in a breezy greeting.

"There, a refreshing drink for you," she said, pouring water onto them, letting it seep down into their pots. She loved flowers.

"What about me?" asked a deep, low voice.

Tiffany whirled around in surprise, almost dropping the water pitcher.

A tall, dark-haired young man smiled at her from the balcony next door. He wore a pair of jeans and nothing else. It was obvious he worked out. He was slim and buff—a real male specimen.

Hot. Very hot.

Tiffany smiled and tugged her T-shirt down over the bulge of her stomach. She knew nothing could help the blonde hair hanging in clumps at her shoulders. "Good morning."

"Hey. I'm Kevin Bascombe. I rented this apartment yesterday, but my furniture doesn't arrive until today. Any chance you've got a cup of coffee? I can't leave the building because the truck should be showing up any time. I'm desperate."

She laughed. "You're in luck. I have a fresh pot brewing."

"Great!" He grinned. "I'll be right over."

The doorbell rang as Tiffany walked back through her apartment. She grabbed a robe and hurried to answer it. She normally wouldn't let a stranger into the apartment, but he'd looked like a nice, clean-cut guy.

"That was quick," she said, smiling and waving him into the kitchen.

After pouring him a cup of the hot brew, she turned to him. "How do you like your coffee?"

He smiled. "Straight up and strong."

"Oh, I'm sorry. It's decaf . . . because of the baby."

"Not a problem," he said, glancing at her belly. "I'll take it."

He accepted the mug from her and took a deep swallow. "Ahhhhh, now I can see, hear, and think."

Tiffany laughed, knowing exactly how he felt. She didn't drink much coffee, especially with the baby on the way, but she loved that cup of java in the morning, decaf or not.

"When's your baby due?" Kevin asked between sips of coffee.

"In another month or so. I can't wait."

"Does your husband play golf?" Kevin said. "I heard the course at the country club is pretty decent."

Heat rose to Tiffany's cheeks as she wondered how to explain her situation. She was planning on divorcing Beau but hadn't filed yet. She was waiting for him to agree to a few simple terms without a lot of fuss. So far he'd refused to talk to her about it.

"My husband and I are divorcing," she finally said.

Kevin glanced at her stomach. "Sorry." He handed her the empty mug. "Thanks. You saved my life."

"You're welcome." She showed him to the front door.

She was starting to close the door behind him when he put a hand out and stopped her. "Wait! What's your name?"

"Tiffany Wright."

His eyes rounded. "You're kidding me! Beau Wright's wife?"

She nodded, wondering how he knew Beau. She didn't recall seeing him at their wedding, but then the wedding itself was a social whirlwind of Muffy Wright's doing with people she'd never met or cared about— all she and Beau had wanted was a small ceremony.

"Beau and I were at prep school together," he explained. "That's why I'm here. He has some business he wants to do with me."

"He does?" She knew she sounded stupid, but she'd heard nothing about it. Come to think of it, she hadn't heard anything about Beau for weeks now.

"Yeah," Kevin continued. "It's some kind of hush-hush deal. Don't say anything about this to him, okay?"

Too stunned to speak, she nodded.

Kevin went on his way, and Tiffany shut the door. Leaning up against it, she wondered what Beau was up to now. He hadn't been happy with his job. Maybe he'd gotten up the courage to leave it. She hoped so. That had been one of the reasons they'd fought.

Tiffany glanced around the apartment. It was furnished mostly with Karen's hand-me-downs. The other women had filled in blank spots of the décor with a chair or a rug or any other small item as needed. Beau had allowed her to have some things from the house, though she kept that to a minimum because she didn't want Muffy to know. His mother was nasty when someone defied her, and she'd done that big-time.

Tiffany went into the bathroom. After undressing, she studied herself in the full-length mirror. Her belly looked as if she'd swallowed a huge melon. She caressed the skin that stretched over the bulge and laughed when she felt the tap of the baby's foot against it.

"Baby girl," she said, "I can't wait to see you!" She hoped the baby would have Beau's good looks and her temperament.

"I'll always love you and protect you," she whispered, and gave her stomach a loving pat.

◆ ◆ ◆

When she'd finished doing the laundry, Tiffany stretched out on the couch to read the baby book Betsy had given her. Reading about all the things a mother needed to know was intimidating, especially because she was alone. Her Fat Fridays friends would help her, but there would be many hours in the night when she'd be totally on her own.

The doorbell rang. Thinking that Kevin must need something else, she hoisted herself off the cushions. Feeling enormous and awkward, she waddled to the door and opened it.

She staggered back, blinking in surprise.

Beau stood before her as handsome as ever. Gazing past her into the apartment, he rocked from one foot to the other, looking like a cornered rabbit about to run.

"Hi!" was the only word she could manage. She hated that he still had the ability to make desire build inside of her. But then their relationship had always had a sexual energy.

"A friend of mine is moving in next door. I'm helping him," he explained. He swallowed hard. "My therapist told me I should apologize to you for what I've done. So, uh, I thought I'd take care of it now, as long as I'm here."

She couldn't hide her surprise. "Whoa! You're going to a therapist? Do your parents know?" They'd always refused to even discuss it.

Beau shook his head. "I'm doing it on my own. Look, Tiff, I'm really sorry about all that went down. I'm learning to work things out differently. The good thing that came out of our marriage was you deciding to leave me. That's given me a chance to deal with a lot of stuff."

Tears sprang to her eyes. "The one good thing?" She'd thought they had something special between them. Especially in the beginning, before his parents ruined everything.

He avoided looking at her. "I've gotta go. See you around."

Without so much as a glance in her direction, he walked away.

Tiffany shut the door, leaned against it, and let the tears that had filled her eyes roll down her cheeks. Beau apparently didn't remember the times he'd told her he loved her, that she was the best thing that had ever happened to him.

◆ ◆ ◆

Tiffany was in a blue funk when Sukie called to remind her she'd agreed to come to her house for an early dinner. She debated whether to tell her she couldn't make it, then decided anything was better than hanging around the apartment regretting she'd ever met Beau Wright.

As she prepared to leave the building, she checked the parking lot. Beau's BMW was no longer in the visitor's spot. Relieved, she went down the stairs and climbed awkwardly into her SUV, taking extra care with her belly before settling behind the wheel. If she got much bigger, she'd have trouble driving.

When Tiffany entered Sukie's neighborhood, she noticed several cars parked at Betsy Wilson's house and wondered if she and Karen were throwing a party.

As soon as she pulled into the driveway, Sukie appeared on her front steps.

"Good! You made it!" she called to her as Tiffany got out of the car.

Moving awkwardly, Tiffany made her way to the porch.

Sukie gave her a hug. "Hi, glad you're here. Chloe and I have been waiting for you."

Chloe peeked out at her from behind Sukie's blue-striped sundress. "Hi, Tiff'ny."

Tiffany smiled at Chloe and followed Sukie inside.

"Surprise!"

Shocked, Tiffany came to a stop.

The living room was filled with her Fat Fridays friends and other women from work.

Amid clapping, her friends rushed forward to give her hugs.

After the hurtful conversation with Beau, the sweetness of their gesture touched her heart.

Chloe tapped Tiffany's arm. "'Prise, Tiff'ny! 'Prise!"

Tiffany ruffled Chloe's curls. "It sure is," she managed to say, dabbing at her eyes with a tissue that Sukie handed her.

Betsy beamed at her. "We had to give your baby a proper welcome. After all, she's a future member of Fat Fridays."

Tiffany laughed and allowed Betsy to lead her to a comfortable chair. Carol Ann handed her a yellow paper crown.

Sukie and Chloe placed the sparkly crown on her head. "You're our royal guest this afternoon," said Sukie, smiling at her.

Getting into the spirit of the party, Tiffany grinned and gave a Queen Elizabeth–like hand wave to everyone.

It felt like Christmas Day times ten as she opened one gift after another. Chloe took the ribbons from the packages and handed them to Sukie, who pushed them through a hole in a paper plate to form a colorful ribbon bouquet.

Each gift brought murmurs of approval. Tiffany lifted a little pink smocked dress out of a box and held it up.

"Let's see it closer," said Grace.

The dress, like the more practical items of onesies, flowered sheets, blankets, and appliquéd bath-towel sets, was passed around the room.

After all the gifts were opened, Carol Ann took care of the wrapping paper and Sukie handed Tiffany the ribbon bouquet.

"There you are, a bouquet of love for the baby," said Sukie.

Tiffany sat back, overwhelmed by all that had been given to her. She'd been too proud to ask Beau for money.

"Now?" said Chloe, tugging on Sukie's hand.

Sukie nodded and gave Tiffany a sly smile.

Chloe left the room and returned, pushing a combination carriage and stroller.

Tiffany gasped. It was exactly what she'd wanted—lightweight and easy to fold.

"Thank you so much!" She pushed to her feet to take a closer look.

"Now?" asked Chloe again.

Sukie nodded and left the room with her, followed by Betsy and Carol Ann. She returned carrying a car seat. Chloe dragged a musical infant seat along the carpet behind her. Betsy followed, carrying a baby swing. Carol Ann trailed her, a diaper genie in her hands.

Tiffany's vision blurred. She'd bought a secondhand crib and a dresser whose top surface served as a changing table, but that was all she'd managed so far.

"Love you guys," Tiffany said, going to each woman and giving her a hug. It felt so wonderful to be part of a sisterhood of women of all ages and backgrounds.

"Have you decided on a name for the baby yet?" asked Lynetta Greene, a fairly new employee at MacTel. A smile, typical of her friendly, fun nature, spread across her face. Her curly dark hair ringed a face whose pleasant brown features were enhanced by her bright eyes. Tiffany had always liked her. On the short side, Lynetta carried herself with an assurance that came from the strength inside her. Tiffany glanced across the room at Grace. A true heroine, she'd pushed Sukie aside and taken a gunshot to the chest to save her.

"I'm naming her Savannah Grace," Tiffany announced, smiling at Grace. "Savannah is where I first dated Beau and Grace is for *our* Grace."

Grace's look of surprise and the tears of emotion that followed brought deep satisfaction to Tiffany.

Betsy beamed at her. "That's so sweet, Tiffany. Savannah Grace. I love it." She wrapped her arm around Grace's shaking shoulders.

"Nice gesture," Karen agreed, giving her a thumbs-up.

"Yes, I'm so touched," murmured Grace. She clasped a hand to her chest and gave Tiffany a shaky smile.

Tiffany was happy her friends were pleased with her choice. Both names meant a lot to her. Aside from Grace and what she'd done for the group, Tiffany would always remember the wonderful time she and Beau had experienced walking the quaint streets of Savannah with the rowdy crowd celebrating St. Patrick's Day. Even more special was the memory of the quiet days that followed with just the two of them together. It seemed like ages ago.

Sukie clapped her hands for attention, softening the buzz of conversation. "Time for refreshments. Our guest of honor will lead the way."

Tiffany rose to her feet, unable to remember ever having felt so clumsy.

Chloe tugged on Tiffany's hand, her eyes shiny with excitement. "Hurry, Tiff'ny! I want cake!"

Everyone laughed.

"Please, everyone, help yourself to the food. There's plenty." Sukie caressed Chloe's blonde curls with obvious affection and smiled down at her. "And afterwards, not before, there's cake."

Tiffany led the group into the dining room. Dainty tea sandwiches, assorted salads, rolls, and a bowl of cut-up fresh fruit beckoned from the dining room table. On the nearby credenza, fruit punch glistened in a cut-glass bowl. Bottles of water nestled together in an ice bucket. Tiffany realized everyone who'd come to the party had brought not only a gift, but food too.

Touched by their sweet gesture, she wondered if they'd ever know how much their friendship meant to her, especially now that she'd begun to cut herself free from Beau's family.

After the guests had finished their lunch, Sukie urged everyone to return to the table for cake.

"Yay! Cake!" cried Chloe, tugging on Tiffany's hand, urging her to get up out of the chair.

"Oh, how darling!" Tiffany exclaimed when she saw the cake shaped like a baby carriage. Tiny strips of licorice formed the spokes of the round, silver wheels made of cake that were attached to the body of the yellow carriage. A pink bow accented the light-green hood of the carriage and a silver rattle formed the handle.

Tiffany and Sukie handed out slices of cake to everyone before returning to the living room.

"Yummy!" said Chloe, licking icing off her fork. She sat on the rug at Tiffany's feet, wearing the paper crown Tiffany had taken off.

Tiffany took a bite of the chocolate cake, and though she'd been trained from childhood to count every calorie, she took another bite. For once she was not going to worry about her weight. Making a child suffer for gaining weight was one of her mother's sick ideas. Her mother had been a high school beauty queen in the small Kansas town where she still lived and had badgered Tiffany about her perfectly thin figure all her life.

As people began to depart, Sukie approached her. "After everyone else has left, Cam will help us load your car. I'll follow you home in mine so I can help you carry the things inside."

"Thanks." Tiffany stood and, with her belly in the way, gave Sukie an awkward hug. "Thanks for everything."

Sukie gave her a squeeze of affection. "You're welcome, Tiffany. We're all so excited for your baby to arrive. She's going to have a lot of doting aunties."

At that thought, Tiffany smiled.

Cam arrived as the last guest left the house. Sukie's face lit with pleasure before greeting him with a kiss. Watching their obvious chemistry, Tiffany grew wistful. She and Beau used to have that same magical connection.

In his late thirties, Cam was handsome, strong and steady, used to being on his own with a child to tend. Sukie, in her midforties, didn't look or act her age. Maybe it was their innate kindness, but to Tiffany, the two of them seemed beautiful together.

Chloe tugged on her father's arm. "Me, too, Daddy."

Cam swung Chloe up in his arms, gave her a kiss, and then tossed her up in the air.

Watching them, hearing Chloe's shrieks of laughter, Tiffany hoped Savannah Grace would know such joy. Beau and his family had been so unhappy, so cruel to her when they'd learned the baby was a girl—a fact Tiffany never wanted Savannah to know. It was one reason she was so insistent about being on her own. She wanted Savannah to grow up in a loving, kind environment where she always knew she was wanted.

"Ready?" Sukie asked her.

Tiffany nodded, pushing away bad memories.

Cam and Sukie helped load the gifts into her car. Tiffany thought of Santa's sleigh as she gazed at the number of gifts that filled every nook and cranny of the space inside her SUV.

Sukie said goodbye to Cam and, after helping Chloe into her car, took off to help Tiffany unload. The drive to Glenview Apartments, filled with Chloe's excited chatter, was short.

Parking as close as she could to the entrance, Tiffany helped Sukie unpack the car and carry the gifts inside. Even Chloe did her share, like a helpful little elf, carrying a few stuffed toys up the stairs.

They placed everything in the second bedroom, which already contained the crib and dresser Tiffany had purchased, along with a rocking chair Sukie had given her.

"Let's get everything put away," suggested Sukie, "so you won't have to worry about it later."

The sparse look of the room quickly disappeared as they placed a mobile over the crib and laid a new quilt and musical pillow inside. Over the bureau, Tiffany hung a whimsical painting of fairies in a flower garden that Lynetta had given her. Stuffed toys—monkey, lamb, and elephant—softened the straight, wooden lines of the crib's railings. Sukie hooked a second mobile above the changing area.

Together, Tiffany and Sukie folded onesies, nightgowns, and little shirts and placed them inside drawers. Then they hung clothing on hangers, lining up fancy dresses, ruffled overalls, and play outfits according to size.

"I can't believe how generous everyone has been," Tiffany said, deeply moved by all they'd done.

Sukie smiled. "We all enjoyed doing this for you, believe me. We can't wait for this little one to arrive."

Tiffany patted her stomach. "Neither can I. You have no idea . . ."

Sukie's laugh cut her off. "Oh, yes. I remember very well what those last few weeks were like."

"Listen! It's music," said Chloe, rattling the colorful rubber teething keys that had adorned a package.

Their clacking sound was a melody to Tiffany's ears. A few more weeks and this baby girl would be hers to hold.

CHAPTER FOUR
CAROL ANN

Carol Ann returned home from the baby shower more than a little depressed. Living with her parents was so not cool, but she had no choice. After being scammed out of a whole lot of money, she was back to saving her dollars and hoping and praying to be able to buy a place of her own or, better yet, find the guy of her dreams—someone handsome and rich.

She sat in her car in the driveway, trying to build a willingness to go inside. Once a heavy smoker, her father was hooked to an oxygen tank and struggled to breathe. Her mother was a born nagger who harassed her father for being a nuisance and Carol Ann for not doing enough around the house.

As she often did, Carol Ann thought of running away to a kingdom where a prince would discover that she, Carol Ann Mobley, was really a princess in disguise as a plain, hardworking woman at MacTel.

Carol Ann was brought back to reality by the sight of her mother peering out the living room window at her. Gritting her teeth, she got out of the car and headed into the world she apparently couldn't escape.

As she entered the house, her mother stood before her, hands on hips. "What were you doin' out there, Carol Ann? Dawdling?"

Carol Ann shrugged. "Just resting, Mama."

Her mother clucked her tongue. "We've got work to do here. Your father's bed needs to be changed. I can't do it because of my back."

Carol Ann bit back a retort. Her mother's back was a convenient excuse, one of many.

In a year or so, Carol Ann figured she'd have enough saved to put down on one of the condos at the edge of town. Not one of the ones by the lake, which she dearly loved, but a smaller unit in the woods on the way to Millville. At this point, she'd willingly live in a tent. Almost.

She went into her bedroom. The king-size bed barely fit into the room, but she'd bought it on Craigslist, waiting for the day when she'd have her own place. The quilt on the bed had cost a lot originally, but she got it for a bargain price at an outlet store. In a large box hidden beneath the bed, she stored the things she bought from time to time for her new place, in anticipation of the day she'd leave her parents' house.

"Carol Ann? You coming?" Her mother's voice came through the closed door to her bedroom.

She let out a sigh that came from the very core of her. "Yes, Mama."

CHAPTER FIVE
TIFFANY

On Friday, Tiffany entered Anthony's with Carol Ann. The Italian eatery was one of a few restaurants in their small town and their favorite spot for Fat Fridays luncheons.

The aroma of garlic, tomatoes, and sausage met Tiffany's nose in a pleasing way. Anthony's was known for its pizza and delicious sauce. Her mouth watering, Tiffany followed Carol Ann through the noisy crowd to the back room. There, in a large booth, Betsy, Grace, and Sukie were waiting for them.

Meeting with her four best friends every Friday had become one of Tiffany's favorite things to do. It was a wonderful way to relax. They ordered anything they wanted—no calories counted—and they talked, really talked, with one another about what was going on in their lives.

Without the support of this group, Tiffany wasn't sure what would've happened to her. She'd come close to being broken by Beau's family. And she wasn't alone in her gratefulness for the group. Each of the women had her own issues and had found the others willing to provide support. It's what made their friendship so special.

"What does everyone want to eat?" Grace asked, as soon as Tiffany and Carol Ann were seated.

"Let's order the special veggie pizza," said Sukie. "With extra cheese, peppers, and tomatoes."

"Sounds good to me," said Betsy. Her eyes sparkled with humor. "And then I'm going to have tiramisu. I'd like to have a thin body, but not until after I have dessert."

They all laughed. Betsy was known for her crazy sayings.

When the laughter had died down and the waitress had taken their order, Betsy's expression turned somber. "I have an announcement to make."

Betsy's seriousness alarmed Tiffany. She straightened in her seat as best she could with the bulk in front of her.

"Is everything all right, Betsy?" Sukie asked, frowning with concern.

"Yes . . . no . . . I don't know," said Betsy. "Nothing has changed between me and my daughter-in-law. Because of my loving relationship with Karen, Sarah still won't allow me to see my grandchildren."

"Yeah, what a bitch," said Grace, shaking her head with disgust. "Sarah shouldn't be so judgmental."

Everyone around the table nodded.

"Well, I've done everything I can to convince her and Richie that I won't apologize for being who I am, that my being with Karen will not hurt those children in any way." Betsy's eyes filled. "I love my grandchildren more than I can say. To be kept from them has been pure torture for me."

Sukie reached across the table and clasped Betsy's hand. "We understand. It's such a mean thing for Sarah to do to you after all the time you've spent babysitting those children. And I know they love you."

Betsy let out a shaky breath. "Well, the harsh fact is I'm not allowed to see them. And I don't know when that's going to change."

"So what are you going to do about it?" Grace asked in her brisk manner. With her arm in a cast, still healing from the shooting that had affected her shoulder, she was as tough looking as her voice sounded. Her tall, muscular body and no-nonsense style were sometimes intimidating.

"Karen has been offered a job in Miami. We're going to move there. Together." Betsy clasped her hands. "It's a great job. Karen's so excited about it. She's going to be running the whole IT department for one of the cruise lines. It's a big deal. I'm very proud of her."

"Cruise line? Does that mean you'll get to take free cruises?" Carol Ann's face glowed with excitement.

Betsy held up her hand. "No, no." Her lips curled into an impish grin. "But maybe we'll get discounts. And maybe someday we can all take a cruise together."

"Oh, my! That would be wonderful," exclaimed Carol Ann. "Just wonderful."

Tiffany smiled with the others. Carol Ann had never traveled beyond Georgia.

"Betsy, I'm happy for you and Karen, but we'll really miss you," said Sukie. "You're the heart of this group and one of the dearest friends I have." Her face flushed with emotion.

As Tiffany knew, Sukie and Betsy had been neighbors and friends for years.

"Yeah," added Grace. "Fat Fridays won't be the same without you, Betsy. You're the one who got this whole thing going."

Betsy's eyes moistened. "That's just it. This is an exciting opportunity, but it means leaving you, Williston, my family." She wiped her eyes. "Don't tell Karen I got all weepy. If she knows I'm miserable, she won't take the job and she really, really wants it."

Tiffany studied Betsy. In her midfifties, she was the image of everyone's grandmother—gray hair cut short, a round and comfy body, a pleasant smile always on her face, and a natural warmth about her. As she listened to the sacrifice Betsy was willing to make for Karen, Tiffany realized that kind of generosity had been missing in her failed marriage.

"So when are you leaving?" asked Grace.

"As soon as possible," said Betsy. "My house is going on the market tomorrow."

"This is happening so fast. What does Richie think about it?" Sukie asked. They all knew Betsy's son Richie was too weak to insist his wife treat his mother differently.

Betsy grimaced. "He doesn't know. I'm going to call him tonight."

"Who are you going to recommend to replace you at work?" Tiffany asked. "With my going on temporary maternity leave, it'll leave another opening on the exec floor."

"The usual procedure is for them to post the job internally before posting it elsewhere." Betsy paused. "I was thinking that Lynetta Greene might be interested. I know she's not that happy in the accounting department."

There was a moment of silence at the table; then everyone spoke at once.

"She'd be great," said Grace.

"At the baby shower, she seemed so nice," Sukie said. "Is she nice at work?"

"What do you think, Tiffany?" asked Carol Ann. "I like her."

Tiffany nodded. "I've heard she does a good job. So, if she's willing to work on the floor with us and our bosses, I say ask her to apply for it."

When the waitress came with their pizza, Betsy took on the role of hostess, sliding the slices onto plates and handing them out.

"This group will never be the same without you, Betsy," said Grace, her voice uncharacteristically soft. "I can't imagine you not being here."

They all grew quiet.

Everyone picked at their food. No one, it seemed, was very hungry after all.

Tiffany wandered into the nursery. She lifted a onesie out of one of the drawers and held it up. It looked impossibly tiny. She couldn't imagine holding a baby that small or caring for such a little one all by herself. What if something went wrong? As anxious as Tiffany was for her baby to arrive, she was overwhelmed by the notion that the little girl inside her would be her daughter forever and ever. It was such a huge responsibility.

As she refolded the tiny article of clothing and placed it back in a drawer, Tiffany thought of her own childhood. She hoped she'd be a better mother than her own. It was sometimes hard to believe they were even related. Their beliefs, their desires, were so different. One of the few times her mother had been pleased with her was when she'd found out the young man Tiffany was about to marry was rich. Her mother and other people didn't understand it wasn't Beau's money that had attracted her to him—it was his need for her to love him like she'd always wanted to be loved.

She left the nursery and walked over to the computer desk in the corner of the living room. Her mother had sent her an email that morning that said it all. Tiffany reread it: "I was surprised to get your change of address. I didn't expect you and Beau to move so soon, but I suppose Muffy and Regard wanted an even bigger house for you and the baby."

Tiffany shook her head at her mother's lack of genuine interest in her and her life. With all the changes going on, Tiffany would have a lot of explaining to do. But right now she didn't see the need to go to all the trouble. Her mother had already made it clear she wasn't about to come east from Kansas to help take care of the baby after Savannah was born. Tiffany didn't care. After managing to keep her mother away from the wedding, she'd only suggested that her mother visit out of guilt. Besides, she had the women in the group to help her. They were already fussing over the baby like normal, kind, interested grandmothers would do.

After deleting the email, Tiffany stepped out onto the balcony. Though it was still hot, cloud cover and a few light showers had cooled the temperature a little. She stood by the railing and gazed out at the woods beyond the apartment complex. The fresh scent that followed a newly fallen rain touched her nose and smelled of promise. Breathing deeply, she reminded herself that the mess that had become her life would soon straighten out. She and Beau would officially end their relationship and she'd go on alone. At the thought, sadness curled inside her, burrowing down deep.

"Hey there, neighbor!"

She turned to find Kevin Bascombe standing on his balcony looking over at her.

Tiffany returned his smile. "Hi."

"Looks like it might turn out to be nice after all," he said, tilting his head toward the brightening sky.

She nodded. "Maybe." She was dying to ask him about his new work project, but with Beau being a part of it, she didn't want to appear overly interested.

"Say, I understand you sing at the Glass Slipper on Saturday nights," Kevin said. "Are you going to be there tonight?"

Tiffany patted her stomach. "As long as the baby cooperates, I will be."

He smiled. "Great. I'm planning on coming. Gotta go, but I'll see you tonight."

She gave him a little wave, feeling unusually nervous. Maybe she'd try to do something different with her hair, dress up a bit.

◆ ◆ ◆

From behind the Glass Slipper's stage curtain, Tiffany watched the tables in the small club fill up. She was pleased to see, among new faces, the Fat Fridays group sitting at their usual table and a few other regulars in the crowd.

Sly Malone came up behind her. "I'm going to introduce you and Charlie. You ready?"

She nodded and swallowed her nervousness as Sly stepped onto the stage and spoke into the microphone.

"We're happy to have Tiffany Wright, our sassy singer, back with us. On the keyboard tonight is our guest from Atlanta, Mr. Charlie Easton, along with two members of the jazz trio. Please give them all a hand."

Approaching her from behind, Charlie gave Tiffany a salute and walked onto the stage to join the drummer and the bass player.

Tiffany followed and stood by while they played a short opening number. When the last few chords of his original song died away, Tiffany lifted her mic. Loud applause followed. With the sound of approval ringing in her ears, all thoughts of being unable to measure up to anyone else's standards disappeared. On the stage, she felt like a star.

As had become her custom, she started out with "Only You." Quickly she became lost in the lyrics and the music. Closing her eyes as she hit the high notes at the end, she let the melody soar. When she opened her eyes, her throat tightened at the sight of Beau and Kevin entering the club.

At her missed note, Charlie gave her a quizzical look and played louder, covering her mistake.

Tiffany tried to ignore Beau as he and Kevin squeezed their way through the crowd to the bar, where they found seats on two bar stools.

Prompted by Charlie playing a few opening notes of a new song, she clutched the microphone and began to sing "My Love." Once she had started, Tiffany didn't know how she'd get through the song without breaking down. The phrases of undying love filled her with emotions she couldn't hold back.

She faced away from the bar so Beau wouldn't see how she still felt about him. It wasn't until she was finished with the song and accepting applause that she realized Beau had left the club.

She signaled to Charlie that she needed a break. While the trio played a solo number, she hurried backstage to the dressing room to try to gain control of her emotions. She loved Beau, but she couldn't live with him. And now he had been acting as if he'd never wanted her or their baby.

CHAPTER SIX

CAROL ANN

Carol Ann bustled around the house. On the weekends, she liked to get everything set for the workweek ahead. Working at MacTel was a job she adored. Not only did it get her out of the house, it also gave her a chance to be with her friends.

On this particular Sunday afternoon, she worked especially hard to get all her chores done in time to attend a farewell party for Betsy.

This next week would be Betsy's last one at work before leaving for Florida to find a new place to live with Karen McEvoy. To everyone's surprise, Betsy's house, in the same upscale neighborhood as Sukie's, had sold within a week. It was all happening too fast for Carol Ann.

"Carol Ann? Before you leave for that party of yours, I want you to get all the cleaning done, like you promised." Her mother's voice was like a fingernail screeching across a chalkboard.

Carol Ann gritted her teeth and took a deep breath, wondering as she often did in times of stress just when her life would turn around. She'd been doing well saving her money to move out—until she met that guy online, John. He'd swept her off her feet and ended up swindling her out of her savings. If he hadn't taken her money, she might already be living elsewhere.

Sighing with despair, Carol Ann plugged in the vacuum cleaner and got to work. She'd discovered it was best to simply do as she was told and avoid days of silent scorn from her parents—days during which she prayed for a winning lottery ticket.

A couple of hours later, Carol Ann checked herself in the mirror and gave herself a critical review. The women in the Fat Fridays group had encouraged her to frost her brown hair. They said it softened her features. That and the subtle new makeup she wore. They told her she had beautiful eyes. A green-blue, they were one of her best assets—her eyes and her bust.

Her hefty bosom caused her mother dismay. Coming from a strict church background, her mother had always told her that displaying herself in any way was sinful—a thought that secretly thrilled Carol Ann.

"I'm off," Carol Ann announced, breezing through the living room and out the door before she could be stopped. Enough was enough.

The going-away party for Betsy was going to be both a happy and sad occasion for her and everyone else in the group. Carol Ann wished her well, living in Miami, but no one could ever take her place. Betsy had formed the group and had made sure Carol Ann was included. Carol Ann would always be grateful to her for that.

Carol Ann pulled up to Sukie's house and turned off the motor. Once more, she checked her hair in the mirror. Satisfied, she carefully lifted her gaily wrapped package off the seat, climbed out of the car, and headed up the walk to Sukie's house.

Lynetta Greene called out to her from behind.

"Hi, Lynetta!" Carol Ann stopped and waited for her, and they walked up to Sukie's door together.

As they waited for the doorbell to be answered, Carol Ann studied Lynetta out of the corner of her eye. Short and a little on the chunky side, Lynetta had a ready smile that easily lit her face. With her quick wit, she loved to make the people around her laugh. Everyone in the office agreed she was the perfect choice to fill in for Betsy on the exec floor.

Sukie greeted the two of them with a smile. "Come in. Good to see you both. The guest of honor is already here. Tiffany's on her way. She's picking up Grace."

"Still no baby?" asked Lynetta. "She looks like it could happen any moment."

Sukie nodded. "I know. She couldn't finish performing last weekend."

Carol Ann was silent. Watching Tiffany that night and seeing the way she'd looked when Beau came into the club, Carol Ann was pretty sure he was the reason Tiffany had ended up cutting her performance short.

"Here she is now," said Sukie, moving forward to greet Tiffany and Grace.

Grace was wheeling a bright red suitcase behind her.

Carol Ann helped Grace lift the luggage onto the front porch. At the moment, they all had to help Grace with many of the things she normally would do for herself.

Inside, Carol Ann happily took a seat on the living room couch. Sukie offered wine and sodas to those who wanted them. After everyone had been served, she left the room and returned carrying a large plastic pink flamingo.

Sukie handed it to Betsy with an impish grin. "We all thought this would be a perfect way for you to remember us. Place this in your yard or on your patio so that when you relax with your evening wine, we're with you in spirit."

Accepting it, Betsy chuckled good-naturedly. "Wait until Karen sees this! Too bad she had another commitment today." She turned to the group. "A friend is like a book: you don't need to read all of them, just pick the best ones," she said, choking up. "You're the best friends anyone could have."

Carol Ann felt her own eyes water as Betsy dabbed at hers.

Grace rolled the suitcase over to Betsy. "This is for all the flights between Atlanta and Miami we hope you'll make to come back and see us."

"Thanks, this is the perfect size. You know what they say about travel—take half the clothes and twice the money!" quipped Betsy. She beamed at them. "Traveling is a new adventure for me. Rich never wanted to do much of it. He always said he was content to stay home."

After everyone else had presented their gifts, Carol Ann handed Betsy hers. Unlike the others, she was never sure what to give someone. She'd taken a chance on this one.

As Betsy undid the ribbon and unwrapped the paper, a smile spread across her face. "Perfect!" She held up the oversized, colorful beach towel. "I'll get lots of use out of this. Thanks, Carol Ann!"

Carol Ann beamed her pleasure. She'd done all right this time.

Betsy cleared her throat. "Now I have a surprise for everyone. When Karen found out you were having this party for me, she sent me a ticket for a free three-day cruise from Miami to the Bahamas! We'll have a drawing and one of you will win."

Amid the sound of excited chatter, Carol Ann clasped her hands in her lap and said a silent prayer. A trip to the Bahamas was something she'd never be able to do on her own.

"All your names are in here," continued Betsy. She held up a little wicker basket. "Sukie, go ahead and pull out a name."

"Make it me," said Lynetta. "It's been ten years since I took any trip like that."

"It would make a nice after-the-baby trip for me," said Tiffany. "But wait! That would mean buying another ticket for Savannah, so it better not be me."

The voices of the other women faded into the background as Carol Ann stared at the small wicker basket in Betsy's hands, willing her name to come up.

"Here we go," said Sukie. "One, two, three." She pulled out a slip of paper and handed it to Betsy.

Carol Ann held her breath.

"The winner is . . . Carol Ann!" said Betsy, beaming at her.

Carol Ann sank back against the cushions on the couch and covered her face with her hands. When she lifted her face to Betsy, her eyes filled. She'd never won anything like this in her life. "Thank you! Thank you!"

"Here's to Carol Ann!" said Betsy. "Now aren't you glad we made you get a passport last year so you could be ready to set one of your dreams in motion?"

Carol Ann nodded. It had been a big step for her to spend money on what her mother would say was pure foolishness.

"Bon voyage!" said Sukie, lifting her wine glass in a toast.

The others lifted their glasses and cheered.

Accepting their congratulations, Carol Ann had a feeling that maybe, for once in her life, things would change for the better.

CHAPTER SEVEN
TIFFANY

Following the farewell party for Betsy, Tiffany returned to her apartment to prepare for her last week of work before taking her maternity leave. She wondered if she'd been foolish to wait so long. Each day had gotten harder and harder to carry her baby. And she'd already felt twinges of what people told her were Braxton Hicks contractions, precursors to the real thing.

Exhausted, she lay down on the couch. After a while, she decided to get into her pajamas.

She climbed into bed with a book. It had begun to rain, and with severe thunderstorms forecast, she was becoming uneasy. As a girl, she'd witnessed a number of such storms rolling across the prairie, their black clouds boiling in the sky like a witch's brew. She'd watched bolts of lightning streak to the earth like bright fingers pointing directly at her, their jagged points a dire warning from above.

As the front edge of the storm moved into the area, Tiffany curled up as best she could in her condition, hoping to ease the pain in her back. Beneath the covers, she shut her eyes against the blinding flashes of lightning and listened to the rain pound against the bedroom windows in windy waves, like trouble knocking, impatient to get in.

Weary, she finally slept. Tiffany awoke from a dream in which she'd stood in front of her college classmates, mortified at wetting her pants. Still hearing their gasps of horror in her mind, she sat up and tried to get her bearings.

She looked down and discovered she was lying in a puddle of liquid.

A rolling pain started in her lower back and traveled around to the front of her body. Growing cold, then hot with fright, Tiffany wrapped her arms around her belly. Holding back a sob, she instinctively knew the baby was coming.

The wind howled outside, matching the terror she felt. She worked to control the panic rising in her like a stormy sea. The tap-tapping of hailstones against the glass caught her attention. She glanced at the windows, seeing nothing but darkness beyond them. She reached over to turn on the bedside lamp and tried the switch again and again.

The room remained dark.

Tiffany grabbed her cell phone. Sukie was her birthing coach for the delivery room. She needed her help now.

Fingers shaking, Tiffany searched for Sukie's number. She was forced to stop when another pain rippled through her. Groaning from the pain, she tried to calm herself by breathing deeply, like she'd been told. She felt so alone, so vulnerable.

She found Sukie's contact information and clicked the name. The phone rang and rang. Finally, Sukie's voice-mail message came on.

At the sound of Sukie's voice, Tiffany's eyes flooded. Struggling to control the wavering in her voice, she left a message for Sukie, telling her the baby was on the way and she needed a ride to the hospital, like they'd planned.

As she hung up, fresh pain racked her body. She sat on the edge of the bed, wondering what to do. She was alone in a darkened apartment with no electricity and a storm raging outside. Her birthing coach was not available. She had to find someone to help her, but she didn't know anyone in the apartment building. Then she recalled her new neighbor. Maybe, she thought hopefully, Kevin Bascombe would help her.

Tiffany yanked off her wet pajama bottoms and slipped on a clean nightshirt. On the way to her closet to get a robe, she was forced to stop. Doubling over with pain, she could hardly breathe.

Shit! Shit! Shit!

She put on her robe and, afraid to be alone, found her way through the darkness to the front door. She opened the door and stepped into the hallway. The emergency exit sign at the stairway lit the area with a pale red that in that moment reminded Tiffany of blood.

In a panic, Tiffany hurried over to the apartment next door. Another pain rippled through her. She pounded on the door, praying Kevin would be home.

After what seemed like hours, Kevin appeared at the door and stared at her sleepily. Through a skylight above them, a flash of lightning illuminated her in the hallway. Noticing her condition, Kevin stared at her with a look of shock.

"Kevin, it's me, Tiffany Wright, from next door. You've got to help me. Call 911, my baby is coming and I don't want to be alone."

"Oh, God!" he said, taking a step backward. "Don't have the baby here. I don't know a frickin' thing about babies."

"Call 911!" She handed him her cell and groaned as another pain shot fire through her abdomen. "Hurry!"

"Come on in. I'll get a flashlight. I think I can find it in all this mess." He called 911 and took her arm. As if from a distance, she heard him give the operator the address of the apartment building.

His voice grew high with anxiety. "Hurry! I think she's having the baby now!"

Tiffany spread her robe on the living room rug and lay down. She could hear Kevin rifling through moving boxes, searching for a flashlight.

"I found it!" he cried. A beam of light landed on her face.

Tiffany squinted against the brightness and brought her knees up as an overwhelming need to push took over.

"Jesus! Hold on! They said they're coming! You're not going to have the baby here, are you?" Kevin knelt beside her, his face a mask of horror. "Hold it in!"

"I can't, dammit!" she cried, furious with him. "Oh, God! Here comes another pain!" She grabbed his hand and squeezed.

Kevin waited until the pain had passed, then jumped to his feet and ran to the front door of his apartment. "I hear them! Hold on! They're coming! Hang on, Tiffany!"

"Help me!" she cried.

His face white, Kevin reappeared at her side and took hold of her hand. She squeezed it so hard, he winced.

The electricity suddenly came back on.

Tiffany was dimly aware of the stacked boxes around her. "Some welcome committee, huh?" she managed to gasp out before grunting and bearing down again.

A man and a woman in dark blue uniforms appeared at the open doorway. Relief poured through Tiffany at the sight of the EMTs.

"I'm having a baby," Tiffany said.

The woman examined her and then took her hand. "You sure are, honey. I'm Linda and this is Bill. Now listen to me. When the next pain comes I want you to bear down. The baby's crowning."

She helped move Tiffany onto a sheet-covered gurney Bill had rolled in and lowered.

Kevin turned to leave. "No! Don't leave me!" Tiffany murmured, clinging to his hand.

Though she could tell he didn't want to, he stayed at her side. Tiffany promised herself she would thank him properly when she could. Right then, her breath was coming out in painful bursts. *To hell with breathing exercises!*

She gave in to a loud, long scream.

"Steady now. Good. Good," said Linda. "Oooh! It's a girl! A beautiful baby girl."

Tiffany rose up on her elbows and watched as her baby began to cry in a high-pitched howl. Tears of joy streamed down her cheeks. They placed the baby in her arms, and Tiffany held her to her breast. When she glanced over at Kevin he was swaying on his feet.

"Better put your head down between your knees, dude," Bill warned him. "Better yet, why don't you go into the kitchen and see if you can boil up some water." He winked at Tiffany. "That's a good way to keep him busy, away from here. Now we're going to take care of the cord and the afterbirth."

Linda took Savannah from her. The EMT cleaned the baby up a bit and swaddled her in a small lightweight blanket she produced, then handed her back to Tiffany.

In the euphoria of holding her baby, Tiffany paid little attention as they continued to work on her and clean things up.

"Okay, hon, we're going to get the two of you to the hospital," said Linda. They covered her with a blanket and prepared to wheel her out of the apartment.

"She's leaving?" Kevin appeared at her side. Color had returned to his cheeks.

"Are you going with her?" Linda asked.

Kevin shook his head. "Better not. It's not my place. Her husband, or I should say, her about-to-be ex-husband is a friend of mine."

Linda's eyes widened, but she remained silent, just gave him a nod.

"Thanks, Kevin, I really mean it." Tiffany was suddenly aware of all he'd seen and gone through with her. Her cheeks grew hot with the realization. "I'll see you soon."

He leaned down and gave her a chaste kiss on the cheek. "Good job, Tiffany. I'm sure Beau would be real proud of you."

Too emotional to speak, she nodded, wishing things were so different from how they were.

◆ ◆ ◆

At Northwest Regional Hospital near Roswell, Georgia, Tiffany was quickly settled in the maternity ward. Dr. Davis, her obstetrician, came in to see her. Her baby girl was checked out by the resident pediatrician. Satisfied that all was right with both of them, Tiffany settled back against the pillow on her bed and slept so deeply she wasn't aware of anyone else in the room until Sukie squeezed her hand.

"I'm so sorry, Tiffany," Sukie said. She leaned over and gave Tiffany a kiss on the cheek. "I wanted to be there to help you."

Tiffany smiled. "I think I scared the crap out of the guy next door."

Sukie laughed. "I heard you delivered Savannah in his apartment. I had my cell phone charging overnight which was why I didn't get your call. Is everything all right?"

Tiffany couldn't hide the smile that emerged from the very heart of her. "My baby is beautiful, Sukie. Did you get a look at her?"

"Yes," said Sukie. "She's the prettiest baby of them all. Her hair is a strawberry blonde and her features are dainty. Like yours."

"I couldn't believe the feeling when I held her," said Tiffany, her voice full of awe. "It really is a miracle, isn't it?"

"Always." Sukie squeezed her hand. "Have you talked to Beau?"

Tiffany shook her head sadly. "I had to leave a message on his cell. In a way, I'm just as glad he didn't answer. I don't want his parents down here yet. You know how they are. But I'm hoping the women in our group will come see me. Sukie, I've decided to call Savannah Grace by a nickname. "Vanna" for short. Do you like it?"

"Very cute," said Sukie. "She'll like it too." She turned toward the doorway and then faced Tiffany with a smile. "I believe they've arrived."

Betsy, Grace, and Carol Ann burst through the doorway.

Betsy tied a bunch of pink balloons at the end of Tiffany's bed. "I'm so proud of you, Tiffany. A baby is such a sweet beginning."

Grace handed her a book. "It tells all about the baby's first year. Thought you could use it, though I'm betting you'll have more than enough advice from all of us. Especially Betsy, even if she has to do it long-distance."

Tiffany grinned.

"I brought you flowers," said Carol Ann, placing a basket of daisies on the bedside table. "Aren't they sweet? Perfect for a baby girl."

A knock at the door made them all turn toward the sound. Kevin stood there awkwardly, holding a bouquet of pink roses.

"Sorry, don't mean to interrupt anything." His gaze settled on Tiffany. "I wanted you to have these. I've never seen a baby being born and well . . ." his voice trailed off.

Sukie went over to him. "Come in. You must be Kevin Bascombe. I understand you took my place as Tiffany's birthing coach! Sorry I wasn't there to help." She led him inside the room. "Kevin, these women are all part of what we call the Fat Fridays group. This is Betsy, Grace, and Carol Ann."

Amused, Tiffany watched each of them shake his hand—Betsy, smiling and open as usual; Grace, reserved; and Carol Ann, all but drooling over him.

Moments later, Kevin left. Tiffany had the feeling that if he could, he would've sprinted out of the room.

"Wow, Tiffany! What a hunk!" said Carol Ann. "Is he married?"

Before Tiffany could answer, a nurse knocked on the door and entered, carrying a little pink bundle with a very loud cry. Tiffany held out her arms.

"The tests were fine." The nurse handed Vanna to her.

The tiny baby stopped howling and stared up at Tiffany.

"Ah," said Sukie with a note of satisfaction. "I think little Vanna already knows her mother."

"Oooh, let me see." Betsy leaned over Tiffany's shoulders. "She's beautiful. Just beautiful."

Tiffany opened the pink blanket, and everyone gathered around. Eagerly, Tiffany showed off Vanna's perfect body, her ten little fingers and ten adorable toes. Sharing her baby with the others, Tiffany was filled with such love that her vision grew misty. The room swam around her.

"Need any help with breastfeeding?" the nurse asked.

Tiffany smiled happily. "I think I've got all the help I need."

Any embarrassment at her fumbling was quickly dismissed by the looks of pride on the women's faces when Vanna began sucking.

"Good job," said Sukie.

"She's so lovely," gushed Betsy. "I can't wait to hold her."

"Reminds me a bit of my Misty," said Grace in an unnaturally soft voice.

Tiffany glanced up and noticed Carol Ann's wistful look. She was the only one among them not to have a child of her own. A rush of sympathy swept through Tiffany.

"Carol Ann can be the first to hold her."

"Really?" The smile that crossed her friend's face was rewarding, but Tiffany wondered if Carol Ann would ever know the joy of having a baby of her own.

CHAPTER EIGHT
CAROL ANN

Carol Ann left the hospital in a funk. She was the first in the group to hold little Vanna and what did the baby do? She screamed until Betsy took over. Feeling like a failure, Carol Ann made her way to her car. Why couldn't she seem to do anything right? She tried so hard to be as sophisticated as Tiffany, as funny as Betsy, strong like Grace, and warm like Sukie, but it seemed impossible.

When she'd met John Vaughn online, she'd thought she'd finally be able to leave home, get away from her bickering parents, out of the run-down, two-bedroom house where they lived. Even now she felt stupid about how John had ended up stealing a lot of money from her, money she'd been saving up to buy a place of her own.

In a way, it was the fault of her Fat Fridays friends. They'd encouraged her to try online dating. She'd had a ball dating a number of guys. The problem was, one date with a guy hardly ever led to two. She knew she wasn't ugly. She just couldn't seem to get herself together, come up with a cute way of talking, a sexy way of walking, anything to make her stand out. And when the guys realized she was living at home with her parents and wasn't about to go to bed with them, they backed away so fast it hurt.

Carol Ann drove home and parked in the driveway. Behind the wheel of her car, she studied the house her parents had owned all their married life. It was on the wrong side of town, needed a coat of paint, and there was absolutely nothing special about it. She shivered. For those very reasons, she was holding out until she could move into a decent place that would never remind her of this one.

Her sister was the lucky one. She'd eloped with her boyfriend the day after she graduated high school. Her mother had been furious about it and had informed Carol Ann that *she* had to stay home and help take care of her father. Thinking of her life now, Carol Ann vowed that once she left this existence, she was never going back.

Aware that she had no alternative, she climbed out of the car and dragged herself into the house. She couldn't believe she'd won a free cruise to the Bahamas at Betsy's party. Her spirits brightened. Maybe on the cruise she'd meet the guy of her dreams.

As soon as Carol Ann stepped inside the house, her mother called out from the kitchen, "Carol Ann? That you?"

"Yes, Mama." She paused in the front hall, wondering what her mother wanted now. She'd already taken out the garbage and vacuumed and dusted the whole house—all her usual chores.

Frowning, her mother met Carol Ann in the hallway. "Betty's Boutique called. Somethin' about a dress. Since when do y'all buy clothes from that fancy place?"

Carol Ann rolled her eyes. "They had a sale, Mama. Don't worry about it." Why, she wondered, should she have to explain herself? If she were living alone like she wanted, no one would quiz her on such things.

Wondering how they could be so different, Carol Ann studied her mother. She was wearing a button-down blue floral housecoat that had a large coffee stain across the front of it. And though it was midafternoon, her mother's hair was still in curlers.

Her mother frowned and shook a finger at Carol Ann.

"Don't use that snippy tone of voice with me, Carol Ann. Honest to God, ever since you started working at MacTel with those women, y'all think you're so high and mighty."

"Mama, please. It's just a dress, and I want to look nice at work."

Carol Ann left her mother standing in the front hall and went into her room. Though she wanted to slam the door so hard it would shake the walls, she quietly, but firmly, shut the door behind her.

She plunked down in the rocking chair and let out a sigh. She had to get out of this godforsaken house. Her parents treated her like a servant.

The chair squeaked a little as she rocked back and forth, but Carol Ann ignored the sound. Her mind raced. Her boss Ed had once told her he might know of a special program for first-time home buyers.

Maybe, just maybe, there was hope for her.

CHAPTER NINE
SUKIE

Sukie drove into the World Foods parking lot intent on getting in and out of the store quickly. It was the meeting place for a lot of women who had nothing better to do than troll for newsy tidbits. Katy Hartmann was the worst of the lot. Sukie spied Katy's powder-blue Cadillac in one of the spaces closest to the door and let out a groan. She had no choice but to go in. She was on her way to the hospital to pick up Tiffany and her baby and she didn't want to be late.

Inside the store, Sukie hurried into the produce section. She knew from past experience how difficult it was going to be for Tiffany to get out for a while, so she wanted to stock Tiffany's refrigerator with lots of fruit, veggies, and easy prepared meals.

As she stood in front of the fresh romaine display, Sukie felt, rather than heard, Katy's presence. Reluctantly, she turned around.

Katy smiled at her, a dangerous smile that reminded Sukie of a feral cat about to pounce. "Why, Sukie, bless your heart! How are you and that handsome boyfriend of yours? I swear, I haven't seen you around town in a dog's age. He must be keeping you busy."

Sukie ignored the innuendo and pasted a smile on her face, determined to give nothing away. "How are you, Katy? Still president of the neighborhood women's association?"

Katy nodded. "Debbi Warren and I decided to keep our slots as officers. It's so hard to find women who don't have to work. But, Sukie, you sly thing, I heard you're staying home now, taking care of that cute little girl of Cameron's. So, maybe you'd like to become active in the club again."

Sukie's smile slid a little. "I couldn't possibly find the time," she said truthfully, grateful for an excuse. "Now that I'm not working there, I'm going to head the volunteers for the library. I promised Julie Garrison I would."

"Ah, yes. How does Edythe Aynsley feel about that?"

Sukie's temper flared. "I don't know, and as Rhett Butler would say, 'Frankly, my dear . . .'" She let the rest of the sentence hang in the air.

Katy's eyes widened.

A sense of satisfaction rolled through Sukie. Let Katy spread that little tidbit, she thought viciously. Edythe Aynsley, who served on the library board, had fought to get her fired from the temporary job of children's librarian from the moment she'd met her. Julie said jealousy was behind it. Sukie didn't care. She'd needed that job, and it had hurt to be treated that way.

"Well, good luck . . . with everything," Katy said. "I've got to go. There's Debbi now." She hurried away.

Sukie knew Katy couldn't wait to spread that latest bit of news. Bless her heart!

Quickly, Sukie moved through the aisles, picking up the items she needed. She'd have just enough time to get out of the store and to the hospital.

At the stroke of eleven, Sukie pulled into the front circle of the hospital. Tiffany sat outside in a wheelchair holding the baby. A nurse's aide stood beside her.

When Tiffany saw Sukie, a smile lit her face.

Tenderness filled Sukie. Tiffany looked so eager, so brave, so ready to face the future.

Sukie got out of the car and stood by while the nurse's aide helped Tiffany place the baby in the car seat Sukie had temporarily installed in her car.

When Tiffany straightened, Sukie gave her a hug. "Ready to go home, Mom?"

As she nodded, Tiffany's lips quivered.

Well aware of Tiffany's painful situation, Sukie worked to keep her voice cheerful. Tiffany had been right to leave Beau until he got some help, but at a time like this, his absence understandably hurt. "Okay, then, let's get you settled, and we'll take off."

When they reached the apartment complex, Sukie helped Tiffany inside her apartment. Then she made a couple of trips to the car and back with bags of groceries while Tiffany put the baby down for a nap.

Sukie was unloading the groceries, when Tiffany entered the kitchen. Her eyes rounded. "Thanks so much, Sukie! It looks like I won't have to go to the store for a month!"

"If I missed anything, give me a call," Sukie said, smiling. "The others will be stopping by on a regular basis. And if you need a break, you can always call one of us. Now, what can I do for you?"

"Can you stay while I take a real shower and wash my hair?" Tiffany asked hopefully. Her eyes widened. She clapped a hand to her mouth. "Oh, my God! I left my bedroom in a mess. I'll have to clean that up."

"No worries." Sukie smiled. "Betsy already did that for you."

Tiffany plopped down in a kitchen chair and covered her face with her hands. Her shoulders shook. When she looked up, her face was wet with tears. "What would I do without y'all? What am I going to do on my own?"

Sukie went over to Tiffany and patted her back. "Every new mother feels the way you do, Tiffany. I know it seems scary right now, but you're going to be fine. And remember, we're here to help you."

Tiffany sniffed into a tissue. "I was hoping I'd at least hear from Beau."

"Maybe there's a reason he hasn't called," Sukie said. Tiffany's message to him was over a day old.

The sound of the doorbell broke through the silence in the kitchen.

"Can you get it?" Tiffany said. "I look such a mess."

"Sure." Sukie went to the door and opened it.

From where he stood in the hallway, Kevin Bascombe smiled at her. "Uh, I saw that Tiffany was home. How's the baby? Just thought I'd come and see."

At the sound of Tiffany approaching her from behind, Sukie stepped aside.

"Hi, Kevin." Tiffany gave him a smile. "Thank you again for helping me out. Vanna is doing just fine. Would you like to see her?"

He nodded. "Uh, sure."

Tiffany signaled Sukie to follow them.

The three of them entered the nursery and approached the crib. Wrapped in a pink swaddle, Vanna lay sleeping peacefully.

A look of wonder crossed Kevin's face as he stared down at the baby.

"She sure is tiny," he whispered, lingering by the crib for a few seconds before turning to go.

While Tiffany said good-bye to Kevin, Sukie returned to the kitchen. She didn't know what, if anything, would become of Tiffany's friendship with Kevin, but she supposed they'd always have a bond because of Vanna's birth.

Tiffany was smiling when she returned to the kitchen. "He's such a nice guy."

The doorbell rang again.

Tiffany gave Sukie a pleading look. "Will you get it?"

Sukie headed to the door, opened it and faced a huge bouquet of pink roses. "Delivery for Tiffany Wright," the man said, peering at her from behind the flowers.

"Thank you. I'll take it." Fearful of dropping the heavy glass vase, Sukie managed to shut the door by giving it a good bump with her elbow.

"Who was it?" Tiffany walked into the room and came to a halt. Closing her eyes, she let out a sigh. "Muffy and Regard must have heard."

Sukie set the huge vase of flowers on the dining room table and handed Tiffany the card attached to the bouquet.

Tiffany opened the card, read it, and threw the note down on the table. "Go ahead and read it. God! I hate those people!"

Sukie lifted the card: "Best wishes to our new little Wright! Muffy and Regard."

Appalled at the lack of love and warmth in the note for Tiffany, Sukie sighed. "Oh, Tiffany . . ."

"They're so mean. It's always been this way. It's as if I don't exist." Tiffany's face flushed with anger. "But I'm not going to allow them to treat Vanna that way or let them try to make her their own."

Sukie nodded, but she wasn't at all sure Tiffany would be able to do much about Vanna's relationship with her grandparents. They were powerful, nasty people.

CHAPTER TEN

TIFFANY

Spent, Tiffany collapsed on the couch. Before she'd left, Sukie made her a nice lunch and had allowed her time to take a shower and give herself a good shampoo. Now, alone in the apartment with her baby, Tiffany's spirits were low. She sighed and glanced over at the pink roses sitting in their fancy vase on the dining room table. She'd willingly exchange all those fancy flowers for one bedraggled daisy from Beau. She couldn't understand why he hadn't been in touch. The man she loved wasn't that callous.

The sound of the baby's cries brought Tiffany to her feet. She went into Vanna's room and picked her up. The tiny girl had soaked through the pink swaddle and onto the sheets. Trying not to feel overwhelmed, Tiffany changed Vanna's diaper. She did her best to ignore the baby's screaming as she worked Vanna's arms and legs through the proper openings of a new little onesie with fumbling fingers.

"There, little girl," she said. "Now let's try to feed you."

Tiffany lowered herself onto the rocking chair. Opening her robe, she exposed her breast and tried to get the baby to latch on, like she'd learned at the hospital. Vanna attempted to nurse but when little milk came out, the baby howled with frustration. Sure she must be doing something wrong, Tiffany tried the other breast. It was no better.

With the baby screaming and no one there to help her, Tiffany panicked. Nothing was working and she didn't know what to do next.

She got to her feet, grabbed her phone, and punched in Betsy's number. The moment she heard Betsy's voice, Tiffany's throat closed with emotion.

"What's wrong, Tiff?" Betsy asked.

Fighting emotions, Tiffany got the story out in bits and pieces.

"Oh, hon, don't worry. We'll work it out," said Betsy. "I'm on my way."

Relief flooded through Tiffany. Help was on the way.

Vanna's continuous screaming hurt Tiffany's ears and her heart. Shaken, she paced the floor with her baby. It was painfully obvious she couldn't handle a baby alone. But what could she do about it? She couldn't ask her mother to come help and no way would she ask Muffy.

Sick with worry, Tiffany let out a shaky breath. "Okay, baby. Let's try again."

Once more, Tiffany took a seat in the rocking chair and brought the baby to her breast. This time, Vanna latched on smoothly. But after sucking and getting nothing, the baby fussed and eventually cried herself to sleep.

Tiffany gazed down at Vanna's sweet face. Remorse filled her. She wasn't a good mother. She wasn't producing any milk for her baby.

At the sound of the doorbell, Tiffany hastily fixed her robe and got to her feet. Happy to think Betsy had made it there so quickly, she hurried with Vanna to the door.

Tiffany opened the door with a flourish. "Thank God you're here!"

"Hi, Tiffany." Beau stared at her, and then his gaze settled on the sleeping baby.

Mortified by how she must look, Tiffany wiped away the trace of wetness on her cheeks. "Hi, Beau. I wondered if you would come to see your daughter."

"Yeah, I wanted to. Kevin told me he helped you all through it. He was pretty shaken up about it."

"Wanna come inside?" She stood back to allow him room to enter.

Beau hesitated, then he stepped past the doorway into the small entrance area.

"Do you want to see her? She's beautiful." Tiffany's voice quavered. "She has your blonde hair and your mouth. Her eyes are mine though."

Beau smiled at Tiffany. "I'm glad. You've got pretty eyes."

Tiffany opened the blanket around Vanna. "See? Vanna has ten fingers and ten perfect little toes."

He studied the baby and nodded. "Yeah, like you say, she's perfect. Vanna? Is that her name?"

"Her real name is Savannah Grace. Savannah for . . ." She swallowed hard. "For you know what . . . and Grace for my friend who was shot."

His gaze swung to the roses sitting atop the dining room table.

"Your parents sent them," Tiffany said, unable to hide the hurt in her voice. "They never even congratulated me in their note. They just said best wishes to the baby. They're so mean."

A shadow crossed Beau's face. "I'm sorry they're so miserable. I wish . . ." He stopped, looked away, and then back at her. "I'm going away for a while. So I won't be around. Do you want to move into the house while I'm gone? It might be more comfortable for you and the baby."

"No. But thanks." She studied the man she couldn't help loving, even after all they'd gone through. "Are you okay, Beau? You told me earlier that you were in therapy."

"I'm trying to work out a lot of things. That's why I couldn't come earlier. That's all I can tell you right now."

Tiffany knew he was holding back on something. "Are your parents okay with all you're doing?"

He let out a snort of disgust. "They have no idea that we're leaving the country."

"We? Do you have a new woman in your life?" The pain of saying those words felt like a sharp knife twisting inside her.

He shook his head. "Look, I've got to go. If you need to get in touch with me, Kevin will know where he can reach me." Beau leaned down and planted a kiss on her cheek. "Take care."

Before she could stop him, he turned and walked out the door, leaving her to wonder what had just happened. The father of her child had kissed her almost like she was a stranger.

CHAPTER ELEVEN
BETSY

In the midst of packing for the move to Florida, Betsy clicked off the call with Tiffany. Bless her heart, Tiffany had sounded hysterical.

She grabbed her car keys and her purse and hurried outside to her car.

As Betsy pulled into the parking lot of Glenview Apartments, she noticed Beau's Beemer leaving.

She parked her car and hurried inside the apartment building. After rushing up the stairs, Betsy stood at Tiffany's door breathing heavily. The sound of a baby crying reached her ears, and she wondered what she was going to find inside.

Holding Vanna, Tiffany opened the door. Betsy was taken aback by her young friend's appearance. This wasn't the sassy girl who sang at the Glass Slipper on Saturdays. This was a defeated woman whose eyes were swollen and red rimmed.

"Hi, sweetie!" Betsy said gently as she entered the apartment. "I'm here. What can I do for you?"

Tiffany handed the baby to her. "I don't know what to do! I can't get Vanna to stop crying. She won't nurse for long . . . and then Beau was here . . . and his parents . . ." She stopped talking and hid her face in her hands.

Sympathy poured through Betsy. Tiffany's emotions were in tatters. She placed a free arm around Tiffany. "Okay, Tiff. We're going to take it one step at a time. First, we'll have you take a seat on the couch, and then we'll see what we can do to get Vanna to nurse."

Tiffany nodded and wiped her eyes.

Betsy led Tiffany over to the couch. When Tiffany was seated and calmed, Betsy handed her the baby. "Let's try nursing again. Remember, until your milk comes in, the baby won't get much. The more times you try, the better it will be. That will stimulate milk production. Where are the special nursing cookies we gave you to help with that?"

Tiffany shrugged. "I don't know. I forgot all about them. I'm just so worried I won't be good at this mothering thing." She indicated the flowers on the dining room table with a bob of her head. "Beau's parents sent them. They called Vanna *our* princess. I'm afraid they'll want to take her away from me."

Betsy placed a calming hand on Tiffany's shoulder. "Slow down, Tiffany. Let's take care of you and the baby. The rest can wait until later."

It had been years since Betsy had nursed Richie, but it was an experience a woman didn't forget. Carefully, she coached Tiffany.

When Vanna seemed satisfied, Tiffany beamed at Betsy. "Thanks! This was so much better!"

"You're going to be all right, hon. It just takes a few times to get used to it. Now rest. I'll put Vanna down for a nap." Betsy took the sleeping baby from Tiffany.

In the nursery, Betsy deftly changed Vanna's diaper and placed her in the crib. Gazing down at the tiny, beautiful little girl, Betsy was overcome with memories of her granddaughter Caitlin at that age. Now eight, Caitlin was a delight—or had been until her mother convinced her that Betsy was evil for living with Karen. Betsy sighed. It seemed so unfair. All her life she'd tried hard to be the person everyone thought she was. Until she met Karen she hadn't understood why she'd felt so misplaced her whole life.

Betsy tiptoed out of the room and found Tiffany sleeping soundly on the couch. She went into the kitchen and fixed herself a cup of tea. Sitting at the kitchen table, sipping the hot liquid, Betsy's thoughts turned to the situation with her grandchildren. Her son Richie had been shocked by the news of her moving to Miami. But when she explained to him the hopelessness of seeing her grandchildren, he'd given her a sheepish look.

"I'm sorry, Mom, but I can't get Sarah to change her mind. For the kids' sakes, I'm trying the best I can to save my marriage."

It had taken every bit of restraint Betsy had to keep from telling him all the reasons he should let the marriage go. But she'd remained quiet. She couldn't take a chance on losing her only child over his poor choice of a wife.

Betsy's thoughts were disrupted by the sound of a disturbance in the outside hall. She got to her feet and hurried to the front door, hoping the noise wouldn't awaken Tiffany.

She opened the door and stared in surprise at Muffy and Regard Wright.

"We're here to see our granddaughter," said Tiffany's mother-in-law. She held a giant pink teddy bear in her arms. With her perfectly groomed hair, trim body, elegant clothing and jewelry, Muffy was more than just a little intimidating.

"Yes, we've come to see the new little Wright," boomed Regard in his usual commanding way.

Betsy was about to ask them to please be quiet when Tiffany appeared at her side.

"Hello, Tiffany," said Muffy. "We've come to give Savannah a proper Wright welcome." The smile on her face did not reach her eyes.

Tiffany and Betsy stepped back to permit them to come inside.

Muffy gave Tiffany a perfunctory kiss on the cheek and marched into the living room. "Oh, I see you got the flowers. We had them put in a very nice crystal vase. Be careful with it. It's quite valuable."

Tiffany seemed to visibly shrink. She nodded.

"Where is that little darlin'?" Regard asked, looking around the apartment.

"She's in the nursery." Tiffany gave Betsy a helpless look.

"Would you like me to get her?" Betsy asked Tiffany.

"No need for that. Show us the way," said Muffy.

Tiffany led the way into the nursery. Muffy, Regard, and Betsy followed.

Muffy stopped in the center of the room and glanced around it.

With a shake of her head, she said, "Such a small room." She placed the teddy bear in the rocker. "There, that seat will have to do."

Tiffany lifted Vanna from the crib and held her close.

"May I hold her?" Muffy asked in a tone that defied any objection.

Tiffany shot Betsy a worried glance and handed Vanna to Muffy.

"Oh, such a pretty baby. Look, Regard, she has your nose. She has all of the Wright features." Muffy opened the baby's blanket and inspected her fingers and her toes. "She's perfect. But then, of course, she would be."

"Such a little thing," said Regard, peering at the baby over Muffy's shoulder.

"Well, I'm going to see that this little Wright will have everything she needs," said Muffy, glancing at Tiffany. "I've had my designer set up a complete nursery in the house in Charleston for when she comes to stay with us."

"Stay with you? I don't think that's going to happen." Tiffany's voice shook but she gazed steadily at Muffy.

Waving her hands in dismissal, Muffy said, "We're going to see that Beau and we get our time alone with her. She's a Wright, after all."

"You didn't even want her," said Tiffany in a much stronger voice.

"Well, considering all that's happened, we do now," said Regard.

"Visitation is something that Tiffany and Beau will have to work out together," Betsy said in a quiet, firm voice. She knew how upset Tiffany was. All the color had left her cheeks.

"Who are you to speak to me that way?" Muffy said in an imperious tone that made Betsy want to slap her face.

"This is my good friend Betsy Wilson," said Tiffany. "She can say anything she wants." Tiffany held out her arms to Muffy. "I want my baby back."

Muffy drew in a long breath but reluctantly handed Vanna over to her mother.

Betsy couldn't hide her worry. These were no ordinary grandparents. Tiffany had mentioned that Beau was getting some help with his drug issues. Even so, she wondered how he or any other single person could stand up to these two. She moved closer to Tiffany, ready to intercede if she had to.

"We'll be back," Muffy said. "Hopefully Beau will be with us and then we can settle this business about sharing custody and verify that Savannah Grace will often be ours."

Tiffany seemed to shrink even smaller before Betsy's eyes. "I'm sure Tiffany's lawyer will be able to clarify the situation," Betsy said, coming to Tiffany's aid.

Regard's glare made Betsy want to crumple, but she stood firmly beside Tiffany.

"Tiffany's lawyer and I will see that things are done fairly," said Regard in a tone that defied any comment. He turned to Muffy. "Time for us to be on our way. We have an important meeting to attend in Atlanta."

He ushered Muffy out the door without a backward glance.

After the door had closed behind them, Tiffany collapsed against Betsy's side.

"Let's sit for a moment." Betsy was as shaken as Tiffany.

They took seats in the kitchen.

"You see what I'm up against?" Tiffany placed her elbows on the table and gave her a worried look.

Betsy nodded. "Yes, I do. Have you and Beau ever talked about this?"

Tiffany shook her head. "We haven't even settled on the divorce. He said he's working through a lot of issues." Tears welled in her eyes. "He's gone away. I don't know where. He said if I needed him that Kevin, next door, could reach him."

"For the time being, I don't think you'll have any problems with Muffy and Regard," Betsy said thoughtfully. "Wait until Beau comes home and then you two can discuss it. His parents have no need for visitation rights at this point."

Tiffany pounded the table with her fist. "I'm not going to let them take her away from me."

"Of course not," Betsy said in a soothing tone, but she hoped Beau felt the same way. It could be a very sticky situation. More and more often, grandparents were fighting for the right to see their grandchildren.

CHAPTER TWELVE
GRACE

Grace left the office a few minutes early. She wanted to stop by Tiffany's to make sure everything was all right. She'd been having uneasy thoughts about her being alone in that apartment, especially after hearing the story of giving birth to Vanna in her neighbor's apartment. Before the baby arrived, Grace and the others had promised to help in any way they could, but Tiffany had insisted she wanted to try things on her own. Now, she might have changed her mind.

When Grace pulled up to the apartment building, she noticed Betsy's gray Toyota. Pleased, she got out of the car. It would be another chance to see Betsy before she drove down to Miami. And Grace couldn't wait to see Tiffany and her adorable baby girl.

It seemed strange to think of her own baby girl as being sixteen years old. Because of the need to keep her safely hidden away, Grace hadn't seen her since she was ten. But that, she hoped, was about to change soon.

Waiting for someone to answer Tiffany's door, Grace thought of the young girl inside. Sweet and humble, Tiffany was someone any woman would be proud to call her daughter. Any woman, that is, but Muffy

Wright, who was as bad a mother-in-law as any young wife could have. Everyone in the group had had to deal with Muffy's unfriendly ways when she'd tried to have them investigated some time earlier.

Betsy opened the door. Upon seeing her, Betsy's face brightened. She gave Grace a quick squeeze. "C'mon inside. It's been a little rough on Tiffany this afternoon. She'll be glad to see you."

Grace noticed Tiffany beginning to rise from the couch and waved her back down. "Don't get up, hon." She went over to her and gave her a hug. "How're you doing?"

Tiffany glanced at Betsy and gave Grace a sad shrug. "I didn't think it would be so hard. Vanna is waking up every couple of hours. I'm trying to feed her, but my milk hasn't come in. And my in-laws were here. That ruined everything."

Grace held up a hand to stop her. "Okay, I get the picture. Let's give you a break. No more visiting from them until you're rested and things are going smoothly. Understood?"

Tiffany nodded like an obedient child.

Grace let out a sigh. "I'll stand guard if I have to." Her insides warmed at the grins Tiffany and Betsy gave her.

Taking a seat on the couch beside Tiffany, Grace took hold of her hand. "Now, how about me fixing you a light supper? Sukie said she'd stocked your refrigerator."

"That would be wonderful," Tiffany said. "Until you mentioned it, I hadn't realized how hungry I am."

"Thank you, Grace." Betsy picked up her purse and gave each of them a kiss. "Ladies, I'm sorry, but I have to leave. I've got a lot to do before I take off for Florida."

Grace walked Betsy to the door. "Do you think I ought to spend the night here?" she said softly. "I have nothing else planned."

Betsy nodded. "If you can, that would be great. I'm meeting Richie this evening or I'd offer to do it myself."

Grace smiled. "I hope you have more luck with your son than I'm having with my daughter."

Betsy frowned at her. "Misty still doesn't want to meet you?"

Unable to talk through a throat thickened by emotion, Grace shook her head.

Betsy gave her hand a squeeze. "It'll happen."

Turning away, Grace nodded, but she wasn't at all sure it would.

Tiffany was thrilled by the idea of Grace spending the night. "But will you be comfortable on the couch? I'll give you my bed, if you like."

Grace's chuckle held an edge to it. "Your couch will be fine. You have no idea where I've had to spend some nights escaping from that lunatic ex-husband of mine."

Tiffany's expression turned sad. "I don't even know if I have an ex-husband yet. I haven't filed any divorce papers, and I don't think Beau has. All I know is that he's working on something."

Grace studied Tiffany. "You still love him, don't you?"

"Yeah, I do. It would be easier if I didn't, but I can't help feeling the way I do about him. I'm hoping he'll get well enough for us to be together again." She shook her head. "But I don't think he still loves me."

"Has he seen the baby?" asked Grace.

"Yes. He came by earlier this afternoon." Tiffany's lips curved briefly. "He told me he's glad Vanna has my beautiful eyes."

"Hold on to that thought and let things unfold." Considering her personal story, Grace wasn't used to giving others advice about men, but she still remembered what it was like to be in love.

◆ ◆ ◆

The time went quickly. Between the baby's feedings, Grace fixed a light supper for them. And then, when Tiffany announced she was going to bed, Grace made up a bed of sorts on the couch and stretched out. Like she'd told Tiffany, she'd slept in far less comfortable places.

Pushing away memories of her past, she rolled over and hugged the lightweight blanket to her.

Twice in the night, Grace rose at the sound of Vanna crying. Each time, Tiffany was already standing by the baby's crib when Grace entered the nursery. The third time the baby cried, Grace remained on the couch, alert for any call for help.

When morning light sifted through the windows, Grace got up and quietly made her way into the kitchen. She turned on the coffee maker and went into the bathroom to clean up. In the mirror she saw a large, muscular woman with broad features and short, graying hair. Her friends were trying to get her to style and color her hair. Seeing herself in a new light, Grace decided she'd do it. If the time came when she and her daughter Misty met, she wanted to look her best.

Grace was sitting in the kitchen, sipping coffee, when Tiffany walked into the room.

"Good morning," Grace said. "Did you get any sleep?"

A small smile made its way across Tiffany's face. "A little."

"Good. I'll stay until you have a shower then I'll have to be on my way. I can't be too late to get to the office."

After feeding Vanna, Tiffany handed her to Grace, who sat in the nursery, delighting in spending time alone with the baby. The movement of the rocking chair was soothing. Soon Vanna fell asleep. As Grace cradled the baby and studied her sweet, little pink face, she recalled how wonderful it had felt to hold her own daughter.

Tiffany entered the nursery and gave her a bright smile. "I think my milk has started to come in."

At Tiffany's look of relief, Grace returned the smile. She knew very well how wonderful it felt to nourish a baby.

Grace left Tiffany's apartment with one thought on her mind—her daughter, Misty. As soon as she'd left the hospital after surviving her gunshot wound, she'd sent a letter to Misty, asking if they could meet. Instead of the excitement she'd expected, Grace had been shocked by her daughter's cruel rejection.

When Misty had discovered Grace wasn't dead like she'd been told, she'd refused to answer Grace's letter. She wouldn't even talk to her on the phone. Grace's cousin, who'd taken in Misty for her, warned Grace it would take time for Misty to come around, that she was furious she'd been lied to and felt that her mother had abandoned her for all those years.

Grace was shattered by the way the situation had been portrayed to Misty. Her ex was a sick bastard who'd ruined her life and that of the daughter he refused to believe was his. She needed Misty to understand that in order to keep her safe from a crazy man intent on killing them both, Grace had had to hide Misty from him. Didn't she remember how he'd attacked them? Threatened them? Tried to kill them? Grace still had the gunshot wound, the scars, and healed broken bones to prove it.

More painful than the physical and psychological scars was what it had cost Grace emotionally to leave Misty behind. She could never get back the years she'd missed with her daughter. She had to make Misty realize how much love she'd always had for her. If not, Grace's life would be completely ruined.

Wrapped in fresh misery at the memory of her daughter's total rejection, Grace drove home to quickly change before heading to the office.

CHAPTER THIRTEEN
SUKIE

Before she and Cam left to go out to dinner, Sukie called Tiffany to see how she was doing. She'd thought about Tiffany all afternoon, wondering how she was doing on her first day at home with the baby. When Betsy had showed up, Sukie had left for the library to see why Julie Garrison wanted to speak to her.

Grace answered the phone. "Hi, Sukie," she said softly. "Tiffany's napping. Anything I can do for you?"

Sukie let out a sigh of relief. "I'm so glad you're there. I hated to leave Tiffany earlier this afternoon, but Julie Garrison at the library called to ask me to stop by, that she needed to speak to me about something. So, how's Tiffany doing?"

"I guess it was a pretty tough afternoon. Muffy and Regard were here for a visit."

Sukie's heart clenched. The Wrights were such cold, self-absorbed people. "Is she all right?"

"Yes," Grace said. "But I've decided to spend the night. Betsy was here and we both thought it was a good idea for me to stay."

"Oh, great. Thanks for doing that. Let me know if you need anything. I'll check in with Tiffany tomorrow." Sukie disconnected the call much happier with Tiffany's situation. She and Cam had planned a special night out and she didn't want to disappoint him. It had been a long time since they'd had a real date.

"All set?" Cam asked.

Sukie grinned. "Ready."

She bid the babysitter and Chloe good-bye, and walked outside.

Cam held the door while Sukie climbed inside his SUV. Then he raced around the car and slid in behind the wheel. Turning to her, his lips curved happily. "Just you and me, huh?"

She returned his smile. "For a few hours, anyway."

Having a three-year-old in your life meant little time for romantic dinners. Once in a while they fed Chloe early and enjoyed a nice adult meal together. But it wasn't the same as a night out on the town.

"I can't wait to try Glenn's new place," said Sukie. The man who'd opened Glenn's Gourmet store a few years ago in nearby Millville had recently gone into business with a chef from Atlanta. Together, they'd opened a small gourmet restaurant near the store called Escapes.

They drove through town, into the countryside. On this summer evening, the fading light gave an interesting dimension to the scenery. The browns of the fields and greens of the trees met in soothing tones. It wouldn't be too long before the colors of fall would form a brighter palette. Enjoying the scenery and the quiet time alone with Cam, it seemed in no time at all to Sukie that they were pulling up to Escapes.

From the outside, the restaurant looked like an ordinary large brick house with a sweeping porch lining the front of it. A large patio and flower garden, enclosed by a decorative wrought-iron fence, sat alongside the house.

A valet hurried over to the car and held the door open for Sukie. She stepped onto a brick sidewalk and waited for Cam to join her. Cam took her elbow and they went up the front walk together. On the wide porch they took a moment to look around. Chairs and tables had been placed in small groups. Several guests were enjoying cocktails outside on the porch. Their chatter added to Sukie's anticipation.

She entered the restaurant and glanced around with interest. She'd heard the interior had been gutted. What a beautiful job they'd done, she thought, staring at the elegant old brass wall sconces lining the walls of the hallway. To the left of the marble-floored entrance area was a room that contained a small wooden bar and comfortable chairs strategically placed for intimate conversations.

"Look at the crown molding," said Cam, standing beside her.

She admired the carved wooden trim that added to the restaurant's elegance.

The hostess, an older woman dressed in black and wearing a gorgeous pearl and diamond necklace, approached them. "Mr. Taylor?"

Cam nodded.

"I'm sorry your table isn't ready," she explained. "It should be all set for you in another fifteen minutes or so. May we offer you something to drink in the bar?"

"That will be fine," said Cam. He took Sukie's elbow and led her into the softly lit room.

The Oriental rug in shades of red and blue was perfect with the overstuffed chairs covered in tiny prints whose colors matched those in the rug. They walked over to a couple of chairs in the corner. Sukie took a seat, pleased to find this private space available.

A waitress immediately came over to them and took their order. Settling back against the cushions of the comfortable chair, Sukie let out a sigh of contentment.

Cam took her hand in his and, lifting it to his lips, kissed it. "You look lovely, Sukie."

A warm feeling spread throughout her. She'd once thought her lackluster marriage to Ted was what all couples went through after a number of years of being together, but Cam had made her realize what she'd missed all those years.

As they were discussing Chloe's preschool, their drinks arrived.

Sukie lifted her glass of pinot noir to toast Cam and gasped, almost spilling the red wine.

Cam turned around to see what had startled her.

Emmy Lou Rogers, looking very pregnant, was standing in the hallway. With her was a young man Sukie had often seen at the gym months ago, when she'd been taking Pilates lessons from Emmy Lou. She frowned in confusion. She'd thought Jordan Smith had moved away.

As if watching a movie, Sukie observed Emmy Lou smile at Jordan in a way that lovers do. Sukie felt her body grow tense. Was this why Emmy Lou had broken up with Ted?

Unaware of Sukie sitting in the corner, gaping at them, Emmy Lou and Jordan swept into the bar.

"Darling," Emmy Lou was saying, "you know I can't drink alcohol with the baby and all." She caught sight of Sukie and let out a little squeal of surprise. Then she turned and hurried out of the room.

"Hey, where are you going? Are you sick?" Sukie heard Jordan say as he rushed out of the room behind her. "Hey! Don't leave!"

From her chair by the window, Sukie watched Emmy Lou and Jordan having a discussion outside. Emmy Lou looked scared. Jordan looked pissed.

Cam gave Sukie a puzzled look. "What was that all about?"

Sukie's stomach knotted. "I'm not sure, but I suddenly have an awful suspicion about the situation with Emmy Lou and Ted." She shook her head. "I don't know what to do about it."

Cam took hold of her hand. "Let's not let talk of them ruin our evening."

Sukie gamely nodded, but a shiver crossed her shoulder.

The hostess came to them. "Your table is ready now. Please follow me."

Following the hostess through the restaurant, Sukie observed rooms on either side of the hallway. Each room was decorated differently from the others. She noticed paintings of vineyards and prints of the old masters of Italy in the green room. In another room, painted a cheery yellow, she glimpsed prints of Monet's works hanging on the walls among photographs of Paris. She loved the idea that diners could escape to different countries.

The hostess led them into a small room with just six other tables in it. "This is what we call our London Room."

Photographs of famous London landmarks were mounted on the soft-gray walls, alongside painted portraits of stiff-faced people who could very well have come from British royalty. The tables were covered in crisp white tablecloths. Crystal goblets and heavy silverware adorned the table, along with gold-rimmed china. The effect was lovely, Sukie thought, taking the seat offered to her at the only empty table in the room.

"Nice, huh?" said Cam, after he'd been seated. "Smells good, too."

Sukie smiled. Cam loved a good meal as much as she did.

After perusing the menu, Sukie ordered the Dover sole. Cam went with the beef Wellington.

Sipping her fresh glass of white wine, a sauvignon blanc to accompany the fish, Sukie's thoughts turned to Ted. No wonder he was losing it. If her suspicions were correct, he'd been played for a fool.

"You okay?" Cam asked.

Her concern for her ex-husband was real. It could very well affect her children. But Sukie pushed aside her worries and nodded at Cam.

After their meal, Cam and Sukie walked out of the room hand in hand. Sukie glanced in each room for Emmy Lou and Jordan but saw no sign of them. The fight she'd seen brewing must have happened.

Not sure what she'd do with the information, Sukie turned her attention to Cam. Like he'd said earlier, she couldn't let thoughts of them ruin an evening that still held a lot of promise.

As if reading her thoughts, Cam squeezed her hand and gave her a smile that spelled *s-e-x*.

Chuckling happily, Sukie tugged him out the door.

◆ ◆ ◆

Sukie loved any opportunity to spend time with her son and his family. On this Saturday, she stood outside Cam's car, waiting for Chloe to unbuckle her car seat. Chloe wouldn't let anyone else do it: "I'm a big girl now and can do it all by myself."

"C'mon, sweetheart, let's go." Sukie swung Chloe to the ground and took her hand. They followed Cam up the front walk to the small brick ranch house where Rob and Madeleine lived with their son Jonathan.

Rob stepped out onto the porch to greet them. "Right on time. The Falcons are playing, Cam. Hurry."

Sukie smiled. In the beginning of her relationship with Cam, Rob had had to work hard to accept it. But now the two men were close.

Inside the house, Sukie glanced around with satisfaction. Madeleine had a knack for using cast-offs to create an interesting, eclectic look in the rooms. It was a talent Sukie envied. With the arrival of the baby, Rob and Madeleine had talked about moving to a bigger house, but money was an issue.

"Hi there!" said Madeleine, emerging from the kitchen.

Sukie embraced her daughter-in-law affectionately. "Hi. Where's the little man?"

Madeleine's eyes sparkled. "Jonathan's upstairs napping. If we're lucky we'll be able to get through lunch without him waking up."

"I brought Sally," Chloe said, holding up her favorite doll.

"Oh, I'm so glad she could come," Madeleine said sweetly before turning her attention to Sukie. "While the guys watch the football game, want to come help me?"

"Sure," said Sukie, pleased to be asked. She wanted to talk privately with Madeleine too.

Chloe left them to find her favorite uncle in the whole wide world—a title Rob coveted.

"What can I do to help?" Sukie asked.

"In a minute you can toss the salad," said Madeleine. "I'm prepping the special grilled cheese sandwiches Cam requested."

"Nice. It's your secret mustard that makes them so wonderful." Sukie hesitated, then blurted out, "I'm worried about Ted. He seems to be losing all sense of reality. I think I know why." She told Madeleine about seeing Emmy Lou at the restaurant with Jordan Smith.

Madeleine set down the knife she'd been using to slice the ham for the sandwiches. "I'm worried about him too. He told Rob that Emmy Lou thinks she should get the condo."

"Whaaat?! She's not married to Ted. And there are rumors the baby isn't his. In fact, after seeing her with Jordan, I'm wondering if the baby is Jordan's. Emmy Lou took up with Ted right after Jordan left town, so the timing could be right."

Madeleine nodded. "It would make sense. Ted's got money. Maybe she decided to make the best of a bad situation and go after him."

Sukie's sense of fairness forced her to be honest. "Maybe *he* went after *her* and it worked because she was in a vulnerable situation. I realize now our marriage wasn't that great." She'd been heartbroken when Ted had left her for Emmy Lou. But after being with Cam, Sukie understood what she'd been missing all those years. No doubt, Ted had felt the same way—at least in the beginning of his relationship with Emmy Lou.

Madeleine gave Sukie a steady look. "We can talk about our concerns all we want, but I can't say a word to Ted. He won't listen to anyone but Rob. He's so angry, so depressed, that he refuses to be reasonable about his drinking, his job, his financial problems with Emmy Lou."

"Thank God he didn't buy the house on the lake like she wanted," said Sukie.

Madeleine nodded. "That would've been a total disaster. On a brighter note, what do you hear from Elizabeth?"

Sukie smiled. Her daughter was a dynamo. "She's doing well with her law courses and still loves living in the city. Though I miss her terribly, New York is a great place for her. She loves the ethnicity of it—the food, the people, everything."

"Do you think she'll ever come back here?"

"Probably not. She's dating someone at school from Boston." Sukie couldn't hide the depression she felt. She and Elizabeth had grown even closer in the last year. But it was that very closeness that kept Sukie from telling Elizabeth she should come back to Georgia, that she owed it to her family to do so. Her job as a parent was to let her children go.

"Rob told me you have the job back at the library." Madeleine grinned at her. "And what does Edythe Aynsley have to say about that?"

"Absolutely nothing," Sukie said with glee. "Julie called me into the library to tell me that the board overrode Edythe's request to turn me down for the job. It's just a part-time position until they find another permanent replacement, but I feel great about it. I was all set to become head of the volunteers, but this is so much better."

"Good, I'm glad it all worked out. Edythe is such an unpleasant person." Madeleine checked the sandwiches. "Oh, it's getting late. Let's get ready to serve."

Sukie tossed the salad, then helped Madeleine carry plates into the den so the guys could eat while watching the football game. Afterwards, she and Madeleine and Chloe sat up at the kitchen bar. They'd just started to eat when the sound of Jonathan's cries came through the baby monitor.

Sukie waved Madeleine back to her seat. "I'll go get him. I need a little time with my grandson."

"Can I be a grandson?" asked Chloe wistfully.

Sukie laughed and gave her a hug. "No, but you can be my favorite little three-year-old girl."

Placated, Chloe beamed at Sukie.

As she rushed upstairs to get Jonathan, Sukie felt very grateful to have her family close by.

CHAPTER FOURTEEN

TIFFANY

Vanna's cries reached Tiffany. She let out a groan and rose from the couch. All the baby books said that it wasn't unusual for newborns to require so many feedings, but to Tiffany it felt like a never-ending session of feeding the baby, changing her diaper, and starting all over again. Besides that, she was getting sore from all the attempts at nursing when her milk supply seemed so low.

Tiffany went to get Vanna and found her daughter's little face red from screaming. Tiffany gingerly lifted her up out of the crib and held her close. "Shhhhh," she whispered. "I'm here."

She changed Vanna's diaper and then took a seat in the rocking chair with her.

Tiffany had just laid her little girl down for a nap when the telephone rang.

Expecting a call from Sukie, Tiffany hurried to answer it. She snatched it up and spoke into the phone. "Hi! I'm going crazy here. That little monster of mine is hungry all the time."

The silence that followed alerted Tiffany that something was wrong. She checked the phone number on the screen.

Shit!

"Tiffany? I'm concerned about you. Why would you ever call *our* baby a monster?"

At the sound of Muffy's voice, Tiffany grew queasy. "You know I didn't mean it. I love Vanna."

"It sounds to me like you have too much to handle on your own. Why don't you think about bringing the baby here?"

Muffy's words set Tiffany on edge. She drew herself up. "Vanna and I are doing just fine."

"We'll see. Regard has a meeting in Atlanta tomorrow and I thought I'd stop by to see for myself."

"I'll . . . I'll be out part of the day. I have a doctor's appointment at eleven," Tiffany said, glad for any excuse to keep her mother-in-law away.

"Well, in that case, I'll babysit for you. That will give me a chance for some alone time with Savannah Grace."

"Oh, but . . ." Tiffany began.

Muffy cut her off. "No buts about it. It'll work out just fine. I'll see you tomorrow."

Tiffany stared at the disconnected call and let out an angry puff of air. Muffy had a way of making her feel so inadequate, so powerless.

Sukie called a moment later. "How are you doing?" she asked innocently.

"I can't do this baby business by myself, and I refuse to have Muffy help me," growled Tiffany. Catching her breath, she uttered, "Oh, Sukie, I'm so sorry to take my frustration out on you. Muffy just called. She insisted on staying with Vanna tomorrow while I go to the doctor's office."

"But I said I'd do that for you," said Sukie.

"Yes, I know, but I didn't even get the chance to tell her that." A sob caught in Tiffany's throat. "Muffy wants me to bring the baby to their house. I'm so afraid they're going to treat her like they treat me—just a showpiece for the family reputation."

"Tiffany, I'm going to come over for a little while. We can talk then. I'll bring lunch. How does that sound?" Sukie's voice was so soothing that Tiffany wanted to cry.

"Perfect. It sounds perfect," she managed to say, getting the wobbly words out with effort.

◆ ◆ ◆

Even though she knew nothing would make Muffy appreciate her efforts, Tiffany vacuumed and dusted, trying to make the apartment look more presentable.

She selected a cute outfit from the baby shower and carefully dressed Vanna in it before settling down to nurse her. They'd just finished, when the doorbell rang. Putting her blouse back together, Tiffany carried Vanna to the door.

Full of trepidation, she opened it.

Muffy stood in the hallway, holding a number of shopping bags. She beamed at Tiffany. "I'm here, ready to take over."

Tiffany's stomach clenched. Muffy's words were exactly what she feared. "A friend of mine, Sukie Skidmore, is going to drop by as well. You didn't give me a chance to tell you that yesterday."

Muffy straightened her back. Her nostrils flared. "I don't need anyone else here."

Not about to be baited into an argument, Tiffany waved her inside. "What do you have in the bags?"

Her mother-in-law's sour expression immediately changed to one of satisfaction. "Wait until you see the darling dresses I bought Savannah Grace. I got a number of different sizes so when her formal Wright photographs are taken, she'll look appropriate. I told you about the photographer we've hired, didn't I?"

Tiffany shook her head. Muffy had never mentioned it.

"Well, you see, Regard and I thought having some formal photographs taken of Savannah Grace every three months would be a good idea. It would make for nice images of the family."

"What about Beau?" Tiffany said.

"What about him? He'll be included in the pictures, of course. When I spoke to him, he agreed to it."

Tiffany's heart fluttered. "When did you speak to him?"

Muffy waved her hand in dismissal. "Right after the baby was born." She sighed. "We had a little tiff, so I haven't been able to reach him since then. I thought I'd try to meet up with him later today."

Tiffany's mind spun. Apparently Muffy didn't know Beau was out of the country.

Muffy held up a white smocked dress, covered with little pink rose buds. "Isn't this adorable?" she gushed.

Tiffany nodded. Muffy might be mean and pushy and very judgmental, but the woman had good taste.

As Tiffany was about to leave for the doctor's office, Sukie arrived.

They traded hugs and then Tiffany reintroduced Sukie to Muffy. After exchanging hellos, the two women faced each other as if they were boxers about to spar.

Smiling to herself, Tiffany left them and headed out into the fresh air.

CHAPTER FIFTEEN
CAROL ANN

During a quiet moment at the office, Carol Ann clicked onto the Internet. She'd been thinking about the cruise she won and all the things she'd need. She'd decided that if she spaced her purchases over a couple of paychecks, she could come up with exciting additions to her wardrobe—things her mother might not approve of. Things like a bikini and a couple of dresses with plunging necklines.

At the thought Carol Ann grew giddy.

"What are you doing?" Grace asked, coming over to her desk. "You're grinning like the Cheshire Cat. Is it a new joke from Betsy?"

Carol Ann quickly switched computer screens. "No, no, nothing like that." Grace was almost as bad as her mother about the need for Carol Ann to dress conservatively. But what girl had a barrel of fun on a cruise ship dressed like a nun?

For her lunch break, rather than going down to the employee cafeteria, Carol Ann stayed at her desk. Once the idea of new clothes for the cruise had come to her, she couldn't wait to go ahead and splurge on some. End-of-summer sales were happening and she didn't want to miss out. By ordering on line, she could have her purchases delivered to her office and her mother need never know.

Carol Ann nibbled on a few of the crackers she stored in her desk and went to work. Her excitement grew as she ordered more and more. She'd just finished placing her last mail order when Lynetta and Grace returned to the exec floor.

"We missed you at lunch," Lynetta said. "They had your favorite—chicken parmigiana."

"Thanks for letting me know, but it's too late." She didn't mention that for the next several weeks she'd probably be forced to bring a sandwich from home instead of spending money in the cafeteria.

Ed Pritchard, Carol Ann's boss, stuck his head out of his office. "I need you to take down some notes for my upcoming meeting."

Carol Ann grabbed a notebook and pen and quickly got to her feet. At one time, after she'd gone to him for help when John stole her money, she thought she and Ed might have something going. But then she realized he was right. Working in the same department in the same office meant they couldn't date. And she couldn't do anything to jeopardize her job. Besides, he wasn't the handsome, rich guy she really wanted to find.

But as she took a seat in Ed's office, she couldn't help wondering how he liked the condo he'd recently purchased—the very same condo she'd thought she'd be living in with John.

Carol Ann brushed aside those thoughts and focused on getting the job done. Ed was a good guy to work for—particular about what he wanted but easygoing about getting it done. Still, she wanted to do the best job she could for him.

The rest of the day—and then the entire week—sped by as Carol Ann worked on projects for the seminar Ed was putting on. The bright spot of each day was when mail deliveries were made and boxes were handed to her. Then she'd rush into the ladies' room to open them.

Though she'd spent more than she should have, Carol Ann loved all her purchases. Not one single item she'd bought could be found at Betty's Boutique.

As she sneaked the boxes into her bedroom at night, Carol Ann decided she couldn't hold on much longer before moving out. Maybe, she thought, she wouldn't wait so long to go on the cruise. It could change her whole life.

CHAPTER SIXTEEN

SUKIE

Sukie pulled into the parking lot of Bea's Kitchen. A landmark in the area for years, Bea's was known for its down-home Southern cooking. Their collard greens, butter beans, and fried chicken were Sukie's favorites.

With her mouth watering in anticipation, Sukie entered the restaurant. She couldn't wait to tell the others in the group about her meeting with Julie Garrison, the director of the Williston Library. It was such a sweet turn of events.

Carol Ann and Lynetta were sitting at one of the round tables covered with red gingham vinyl.

"Hi there!" Sukie said. "Where's Grace?"

Carol Ann shrugged. "I don't know. She took the day off. And Tiffany said she couldn't make it today. Vanna was fussy and still a little too young for this."

A waitress appeared at the table and handed them menus. "Just the three of you?"

Sukie smiled. "It looks that way." Betsy had left for Florida. Out of the corner of her eye, she saw a figure approaching them and blinked in surprise. "I guess it will be four of us, after all."

Carol Ann turned around. "Wow! Grace is that you? You look so . . . so . . . different!"

Grace beamed at them. "Do you like it?" She patted her hair. "Henri cut and colored it."

"You look great!" Sukie grinned. "I never would have thought of it, but auburn suits you perfectly." The new style and color made Grace seem much younger.

"It's what my hair color was as a kid. Misty's hair was about this same color, too. I thought I'd do a little something to spruce myself up before I meet her."

Sukie's jaw dropped. "Misty has agreed to see you? How wonderful!"

A shadow crossed Grace's features. "We're not actually meeting. But my cousin told me she's agreed to talk to me on the phone sometime over the weekend."

"Good. That's a beginning," said Carol Ann happily.

"Yes," Sukie agreed. "One step at a time."

Grace took a seat, and they quickly ordered. Bea's fried chicken special was everyone's favorite, and because of their no-calories-counted rule, they often ordered it for Fat Fridays.

"Thank you for including me," Lynetta said shyly. "I love the whole idea of having a little extra time on Fridays for a long lunch hour. And being with y'all makes it extra nice."

Sukie studied Lynetta. With her ready smile and sparkling eyes, she seemed like such a fun person. But since Sukie was the only one in the group not working at MacTel, she didn't know much about her.

She leaned forward. "So, Lynetta, tell me a little about yourself. We didn't get a chance to really talk at Tiffany's baby shower."

Lynetta drew a deep breath. "There's not much to tell. I moved out of Atlanta a few months ago. I have two teenage boys, fourteen and fifteen. I had to get them out of the city. I figured a small town would be a better place for them—a place where they couldn't get into so much trouble."

"So you're a single mom?"

Lynetta nodded. "I have been for about ten years now. It hasn't been easy, but it's better than living with their father. He's never grown up. I got tired of taking care of him too."

Grace gave Lynetta a look of approval. "You were smart to dump him."

"I guess so," said Lynetta to her. "Unlike your situation, he couldn't have cared less about seeing either me or the boys again. I'm sorry about that for them, but not for me. I say good riddance."

"Amen," said Grace with feeling.

Sukie had the distinct impression Lynetta wouldn't be a pushover for anyone. Behind that pleasant demeanor was a strong woman. "How are the boys doing here? Do they like the schools?"

"The schools are good, but thank goodness they're big boys. The high school football coach signed up both of them." Lynetta chuckled. "They're usually so tired when they come home, it's all they can do to finish their homework. The coach, bless his heart, insists that the members of his team have good grades."

Sukie smiled. Sports had been a good thing back when Rob was in school. He was no football player, but he'd done fine on the basketball team, and he'd had no problem getting into Georgia Tech.

The waitress brought their food, and when everyone had been served, Sukie waved her hand for attention. "I've got some exciting news!"

"Great! Spill!" said Carol Ann, leaning forward eagerly.

Sukie couldn't help the smile she felt spreading across her face. "Julie Garrison has asked me to come back to the library as head of children's programs. The woman they hired to take my place is unexpectedly moving out of town because of her husband's job."

Grace frowned. "What does Edythe Aynsley think about that? She was a real bitch to you."

"That's the sweet part. Edythe tried to get the board to vote against it, but nobody would do it. Julie told me they all thought I'd done a superb job in the spring and they wanted me back."

Carol Ann clasped her hands together. "Oh, Sukie! I love stories like this. Good for you!"

Sukie nodded. It had pleased her no end to have that kind of support from the library board. She knew Edythe would continue to be a problem, but it didn't matter as much anymore.

"So Cam is okay with all this?" Grace asked, one eyebrow raised in a teasing manner.

Sukie chuckled. "Yes. He said he was all for it because he knew how happy I'd been there. Actually if Chloe hadn't taken part in the Nighty Night program I started, we might not be together. She's the one who'd insisted on coming to the program when I thought the relationship was over between Cam and me. Seeing each other again, we realized it wasn't over after all."

"Say, I'd love to volunteer at the library when I have some free time," Lynetta said. "Books are my escape."

"When you're ready, let Julie or me know," said Sukie, admiring Lynetta more and more.

"So what books should I take on my cruise?" said Carol Ann. "I can't stop thinking about it. I'm going to have so much fun." She grinned. "Actually, I might not have time to read because I'll be so busy. I just might be dancing with a handsome stranger."

Grace groaned. "Don't even go there!"

Sukie shot Grace a warning look.

"Still, it'll be a fun cruise," Grace quickly added.

"So, did you buy clothes for it?" said Lynetta. "I've noticed you getting a lot of packages delivered. I've never been on a cruise but I hear that the dinners can be fancy."

Carol Ann's eyes widened. "Really? I ordered a cocktail dress . . ." she hesitated, then blurted out, "And a bikini!" Her cheeks turned pink. "And some other stuff too."

"That sounds nice," said Lynetta pleasantly.

"Yes," agreed Sukie. But secretly she wondered if she and the other women in the group had been right to encourage Carol Ann to dress differently, to allow her figure to show a little more. At her mother's insistence, Carol Ann had been dressing like a prim schoolgirl, not an attractive young woman. But after the group had talked to Carol Ann, her appearance was sometimes over the top, figuratively and for real.

"I can't wait to go on the cruise," gushed Carol Ann. "I'm thinking of going pretty soon."

"We'll have to give you a bon voyage party," said Sukie. Of all the people who could have won the cruise, she thought Carol Ann was the one person who would enjoy it the most.

Discussion turned to Tiffany and the baby.

"That baby sure does cry a lot," said Carol Ann. "I don't know if I could do well with so little sleep. She needs to be fed every few hours. How does Tiffany do that alone?"

"You do what you have to do," said Grace. "Tiffany is a natural mother."

"She's very good with her," agreed Lynetta. "And that baby is a dear little thing."

Grace checked her watch. "Hate to put an end to this, but it's time to go."

They quickly paid their bill and prepared to leave.

Sukie followed the others outside and decided to check on Tiffany. As Carol Ann had mentioned, handling the baby on her own had to be tough for her. Besides, like everyone else, she was smitten with Tiffany's beautiful little girl.

CHAPTER SEVENTEEN
LYNETTA

Lynetta Greene left the luncheon pleased she'd been invited. She'd been in Williston for only four months, but she already felt at home. Working at MacTel had a lot to do with it. She'd quickly moved from the accounting department to the executive area—a move she liked a lot. Cynthia Blakely, her boss, treated her well, and she loved the other admins on the floor. Everyone missed Betsy, of course, so Lynetta had made an extra effort to fit in. If it hadn't been for Betsy pushing Lynetta as her replacement, she might still be totaling up numbers.

Later that afternoon, Lynetta left work and headed to the apartment she and her boys recently moved into. At the edge of town, the apartment complex held people of all types and backgrounds. It was there she'd met James Mason, the sweetest guy she'd ever known. The problem was her boys. They hated the idea of having him in their lives and James knew it.

After parking outside her apartment building, Lynetta climbed out of her car and headed inside.

"Hey, Mom! Wait up!" came a cry behind her. She turned to greet her fourteen-year-old son, Jackson.

Tall, like his father, he ran up to her. "I got invited to a party tonight. Can I go?"

"Who's having it? Where is it? Do the parents know?" It was a litany she often repeated.

He frowned at her. "Aw, Mom, why can't you just say yes?"

"Because I'm a better parent than that," she replied. It was an old argument between them. But of her two boys, Jackson was the one she had to keep a sharper eye on.

"Okay. The party is right here in the complex. It's one of the girls in my class. And her mother told her she could have a few kids in tonight. We're going to watch some horror movies."

"And the girl's name?"

"Melissa O'Connell. She's over in D301."

Lynetta nodded. "Okay, we'll talk about it. Let me get inside."

He followed her like an eager puppy dog. "You've gotta let me go. It's the first time I've been included."

She weighed the pros and cons in her mind. Fourteen was a little young for a boy-girl party. She didn't know the mother and hadn't heard Melissa's name crop up until now. But then getting news out of either of her boys was rare. So maybe it would be all right.

Before she reached her front door, she heard loud music inside. She stepped inside and called out to Martin. "Turn down the music."

When it continued to play loudly, she walked into his bedroom. He was sound asleep on top of his bed.

She shook his shoulder. "Wake up, Martin!"

He sat up groggily.

Lynetta's stomach clenched. "Are you all right?" She inhaled the air between them but couldn't smell any grass on his breath. It had been a problem in Atlanta.

He gave her a look of disgust. "I'm fine, Mom! The coach made me do a few extra laps around the track."

"And why was that?" She couldn't hide the suspicion in her voice.

He glanced away and then gave her a sheepish look. "I gave him some attitude when he said I couldn't play in the game tomorrow unless I showed a little more spirit."

"Oh, I see," said Lynetta. She felt a surge of gratefulness for the strict coach. If Coach Bryant wasn't sixty years old and happily married, she'd already be in love with him for the way he handled her boys.

"So, Mom," Jackson said impatiently, "can I go to the party?"

Exhausted after a busy week at MacTel, she nodded, too tired to spar with him. After all, she'd be close by if needed.

CHAPTER EIGHTEEN
GRACE

Grace waited by the phone and tried in vain to calm her racing heart. She'd made arrangements through her cousin, Kate Woodhouse, for Misty to call her after church. Though Grace herself hadn't been to church in some time, she hoped Misty would absorb all the goodness she could from today's Sunday service. The last time Grace had tried to speak to her daughter, Misty had refused to have anything to do with her.

The phone in her hand rang. Panic raced through Grace.

She clicked onto the call. "H-hello?"

"Is this Grace Jamison?"

Grace listened for the sound of a ten-year-old, but the voice she heard was that of a young adult, not the child she'd been forced to send away. "Is this Misty?"

"Yes. My mother said I had to speak to you."

Grace felt as if she'd been kicked in the stomach. "Mother? But I'm your mother,"

"Kate is my mother," Misty said firmly. "She's the one who's seen me through everything, not you."

"Did Kate explain why I left you with her? At the time I tried to tell you why I was doing it, but we were both still pretty traumatized by your father's actions." Tears sprang to Grace's eyes. "It was so very difficult for me to leave you behind, but I had to be sure you'd be safe."

"Do you have any idea how many times I cried because you didn't love me enough to keep me with you?" Misty's words were cold stabs to Grace's heart.

"I don't know how much Kate has shared with you, but I wouldn't be able to talk to you today unless your father was dead."

"Kate tried to tell me some story that he kept trying to kill you, but I'm not sure I believe it. It's like a plot from the worst television show ever."

Anger wove through Grace. She fought the urge to shout. "Do you realize he died trying to kill me, just like he said he would? He promised me no matter how long it took him he'd kill us both. With you safely out of the way, I could keep his attention focused on me. I spent years running from him, but he trailed me every time I moved on. There was nothing the police could do to protect me, not until he did something to me again."

A painful silence followed.

"I'm happy here. I want to stay with Kate and Josh. I want them to go ahead and adopt me." The determination in Misty's voice was shocking.

Grace's breath left her in a gasp of dismay. Her throat closed with pain.

"Did you hear me? I don't want anything to do with you. You're apparently as crazy as my father."

"Why?" Grace choked out. "Why are you saying that?"

"Kate says I have a good life with her. She says I can stay."

"May I speak to her?" Grace spoke through lips turned wooden in disbelief.

"Hold on. Mom? Grace wants to speak to you."

Overhearing Misty call Kate "Mom" was the last straw. Grace's heart tore apart. Her cousin hadn't had children of her own, which was one of the reasons Grace had chosen her to take in Misty. Had it been another horrible mistake of hers to have Misty stay with her? A mistake like all the others?

"Hello?" Kate's voice had the ring of Judas in it.

"Kate, what's going on? What's all the talk of adoption, and why is Misty calling you Mom?" Grace's voice shook with the effort of getting the words out.

"Now, Grace, let's be reasonable. We wanted Misty to feel as if she had a real family, so we encouraged her to call us Mom and Dad. A real mother doesn't leave her child with a relative while she takes off traveling all around. Misty has a good life with us. Leave her alone."

"Don't you understand what I've been through the last six years? If Misty had stayed with me, she might be dead. I'm her real mother. A mother who loved her well enough to fight to keep her safe." Grace's voice rose dangerously. "Don't you understand what I've lost all these years to keep her alive? Her father was a crazy maniac who spent his time trying to find the two of us so he could kill us!"

"Calm down, Grace," said Kate. "It's all such a fantastic story that it's become hard to believe."

"If you don't believe me, you can talk to the sheriff here in Georgia any time you want. He'll explain to you what happened. As a matter of fact, he's using it for a case study on the effect of drugs on an unbalanced mind."

"Let's take it one step at a time. You've talked to Misty. Give her time to think things over."

"I want to come see her," said Grace. "I'll have my cast off soon. And then, Kate, I will see *my* daughter."

"That will be fine," Kate said, her voice as cold as the northern winters Grace had once experienced. "Now I must go."

As Grace disconnected the call, a howl rose from inside her. After six hideous years on the run from a maniac who couldn't be caught, she wouldn't lose her daughter.

She couldn't!

CHAPTER NINETEEN
CAROL ANN

Carol Ann arrived in the office breathless. She'd overslept and had to race through her morning routine.

Lynetta looked up from her desk and smiled. "No worries. Slow down. All the execs are in a meeting."

Carol Ann let out a sigh of relief. Getting settled behind her desk, she took a deep breath.

"Where's Grace?" she asked, looking around.

"In the ladies' room," Lynetta said. She shook her head. "I don't know what's going on, but she looks terrible."

Carol Ann rose. "I'd better go check on her." Though Grace was recovering well enough from the gunshot wound, she was still fragile emotionally. It was astonishing to everyone that she was able to work at all. But she'd told the doctor she had to work. He'd cooperated by making a cast that allowed her fingers to move. And the cast was set at an angle so she could type a little at a time. Any big word-processing projects given to her were quietly shared between Carol Ann and Lynetta.

Carol Ann stepped into the bathroom and called out softly, "Grace? Are you in here?"

The quiet was ominous.

"Grace?"

"Carol Ann, is that you?" One of the doors rattled and Grace walked out of a stall.

Carol Ann gasped, "Are you all right?"

Tears ran down Grace's cheeks. She shook her head. "No, I don't know what to do. My daughter doesn't want to see me. She's calling my cousin "Mom" and my cousin wants Misty to live with her. In fact, she's encouraging it because . . ." She stopped and caught her breath. "Because they say they're going to adopt her."

Carol Ann opened her mouth to say something and slammed it shut, unable to think of the right words to say. She hurried to Grace and hugged her shaking shoulders. They'd often been at odds—a romantic and a cynic. But she and all the other members of Fat Fridays knew what a sacrifice Grace had made to keep her daughter safe. At first it had seemed an improbable story. None of them understood how sick Grace's ex was until he'd sent threatening notes, playing a sadistic game with them. And then when he'd tried to kill Grace, they'd realized that if he hadn't been caught, they might all be dead.

"I'm sorry, Grace. I'm so sorry," Carol Ann said, meaning it with all her heart.

Grace let out a trembling sigh. "You don't know what it's like to love a child. But someday you'll get your man and have a family and then you'll know."

A rush of affection flowed through Carol Ann. It was the sweetest thing Grace had ever said to her. "We need to help you talk this out. I'm going to call a special meeting of the Fat Fridays group."

Carol Ann expected Grace to tell her no. Instead, in a trembling voice, Grace said, "Okay."

◆ ◆ ◆

After work, Carol Ann joined Lynetta and Grace at Sukie's house. It hadn't yet been sold and was the perfect place for this impromptu meeting of the group.

Tiffany arrived with Vanna.

"I came as soon as I could," she explained as she lugged the car seat inside and placed it in the center of the living room.

"Refreshments are in the kitchen, everyone. Help yourself to wine, coffee, or soda," said Sukie warmly. "I'm heating up some hors d'oeuvres. And if you want, we can order pizza from Anthony's."

It was a somber group as Carol Ann returned to the living room with her glass of wine. She found an empty chair and lowered herself into it, wondering how best to start.

"I called this meeting because I thought we might be able to help Grace."

"What happened? Do you want to tell us?" Sukie asked Grace.

Grace sat stiffly on one end of the couch. "It's about Misty and my cousin Kate." She was more controlled than she had been earlier, but Carol Ann noticed the shakiness in Grace's voice.

Witnessing her agony, Carol Ann's heart went out to Grace all over again. She thought about a mother's love. She'd always wanted a family of her own. If that ever happened, she hoped she'd be as good a mother as Tiffany, as strong a person as Grace.

When Grace finished telling the group about the conversation she'd had with her daughter, Sukie cleared her throat. "I think the important first step should be a face-to-face meeting with Misty." She paused. "And I don't think the meeting should take place at your cousin's home, Grace. Not after what you told us."

"Yeah," said Lynetta. "With her wanting to keep Misty for herself, her house is the last place you want to be with her."

"She would make it difficult for both you and Misty," agreed Carol Ann. "Like Lynetta says, she wants Misty for herself."

Tiffany, who'd been pacing the floor with a fussy daughter, stopped and faced Grace. "If Misty has the chance to talk to us, she may be able to understand a little better what you went through. The story of your ex sounds crazy, like Misty says. I wouldn't have believed something like this myself if I hadn't experienced some of it. So, I say bring Misty here. We'll set her straight."

Grace nodded slowly. "Okay, that's what I needed to hear. I was thinking the same thing, but I was worried Kate would make it sound as if I didn't care enough to fly out to Ohio."

"At sixteen, Misty is old enough to make an effort to meet with you, even if she says she doesn't want to," Sukie said firmly. "Your cousin owes it to you to see that Misty does this."

Grace let out a trembling sigh. "I'll call her. Maybe Misty can come for a long weekend."

She gazed around the room. "I don't know what I'd do without all of you. I've been alone for so long and y'all took me in."

"I bet Betsy would come back for that weekend just so she could talk to Misty," said Tiffany.

Sukie nodded. "After all we've been through together, I'm sure she would."

Carol Ann looked around the room. Such good friends. And now Lynetta was part of the group and already loyal to it. As much as she wanted to find a man, Carol Ann would never want to give up this kind of friendship.

CHAPTER TWENTY
TIFFANY

Following the spontaneous supper with the Fat Fridays group, Tiffany went back to her apartment with a deeper sense of motherhood. She'd fight tooth and nail to keep anyone from taking Vanna away from her.

She fed Vanna and, after putting her down in her crib, stepped out onto the balcony. She stood a moment gazing out at the woods beyond the lawn skirting her apartment building. The darker green of the evergreen branches set against the lighter-colored leaves of the sweet gum trees made an attractive pattern. The heat of the day had faded, making it easier to breathe. She drew in the refreshing cooler air. Nights like this were her favorite.

Tiffany opened the sliding glass door a little so she could listen for Vanna. Then she took a seat in one of the folding chairs. Stretching her legs out in front of her, she let out a sigh of contentment. Her thoughts drifted to Grace and all she'd had to endure. Most people would refuse to believe that a man could be so determined to kill an ex, that he'd stalked her for a number of years. But Buck Keeley had been one crazy dude.

"Nice evening, huh?"

Tiffany turned to find Kevin gazing at her from his balcony.

She returned his smile. "Yes, it's finally cooled down. I love evenings like this."

"How's the baby?"

"Vanna's doing fine," Tiffany said. "What are you up to?"

He shrugged. "Just taking a break. I've been doing some research here from home."

Tiffany frowned. "You once told me that Beau asked you here to do some business with him. What's that all about?"

"I'm sorry, but that's privileged information." His look was apologetic.

"You sound like a lawyer. Are you?" she asked, unable to hide her curiosity.

He nodded. "Yes. I do a lot of advising on legal issues."

As they chatted, she realized how lonely she was. "Do you want to come over? I can put on a pot of coffee."

He chuckled. "Instead, how about if I bring a can of cold beer for each of us?"

"Sounds good." She hadn't had a beer in a long time, and she'd read that an occasional beer helped with milk production. If it might help Vanna, she was willing to try it. She still wasn't producing enough milk to satisfy Vanna for long.

Tiffany met Kevin at the door and walked him through the living room to the balcony. Outside, they each took a seat.

Kevin popped open one of the cans of beer he'd brought and handed it to her before opening a can for himself.

"This is really nice," Kevin said, smiling at her. "You've got a better view than I have."

"I was lucky to get this apartment," Tiffany said. "If it hadn't been for my friend Karen wanting to sublet, I'd never be able to live here."

"Really? I didn't have any problem. Beau got mine for me."

Confused, Tiffany said, "How do you know Beau? You said you went to school with him, but I never heard him mention your name."

"It's not exactly true that we went to school together. At least, not in the way you might think. I was the resident dorm leader for the freshman class at his prep school. That's when we met."

"Oh? And what did you think of him?" She couldn't wait to hear more about the man she'd married.

Kevin shook his head. "He was a cocky little brat. You should've seen his face when I told him so."

A chuckle escaped from Tiffany. "I bet he was pissed."

"Totally. Whenever he pulled one of his 'I'm better than you' bullshit stances, I took him to task for it. It took several months before we became friends. And then we were friends only because he knew he couldn't pull any of that shit on me."

"If you were friends, why weren't you at our wedding?"

Kevin made a scoffing sound. "Like I said, we were friends during Beau's freshman year. After that, I went on my way and he went on his. Besides, you know Muffy and Regard. When they quizzed me on who my parents were"—he gave her a wry look—"or weren't, they didn't want Beau to have anything to do with me. I'd gone to the school on a full scholarship. My parents could never afford to send me there on their own. Not with their low-paying jobs and with the care of my five brothers and sisters."

Tiffany let out a sigh. "His parents made a mess of him, but Beau's really a good guy. Or, he was until drugs messed him up even worse than his parents did."

Kevin gave her a steady look. "Sounds like you still love him."

Feeling her cheeks turn warm, she nodded. "Crazy, huh? 'Cause I'm pretty sure he doesn't feel that way about me."

"I wouldn't be too certain of that," Kevin said. He emptied his can of beer and got to his feet. "Guess I'd better be going. Thanks for the company."

Tiffany stood with him. "Thank you. I really appreciated talking with you. Vanna isn't a very good conversationalist yet."

Kevin laughed. "She'll be talking before you know it. By the way, are you going to sing at the club this Saturday?"

"Yes." Tiffany grinned. "My friend Lynetta is going to babysit so I can do it. My friends all know how important it is to me."

He gave her a dazzling smile. "I'll try to make it there."

"Great." Tiffany showed Kevin to the door. "Good night. And thanks again."

He gave her a little salute and left.

Tiffany closed the door and leaned against it with a troubled sigh. She was learning she didn't know as much about Beau as she thought she did.

CHAPTER TWENTY-ONE
LYNETTA

Lynetta had left Sukie's house unable to stop thinking about Grace's situation. Grace was an incredibly strong woman. She herself had never doubted a woman's strength. Her grandmother had been a single mom, her mother as well. Now she was carrying on the family tradition of raising her children alone. But that didn't necessarily mean she liked it. She was ready for a decent guy to share her life. Ten years of raising two rambunctious boys alone was enough.

Her thoughts naturally turned to James Mason. She'd met him the first day she moved into her new apartment. He was a teacher at one of the technical schools nearby. By anybody's standards he was a hottie—a hottie with glasses and a quiet manner, but a hottie nevertheless. She'd been thrilled when he'd asked her out for a date.

Her boys had been anything but supportive.

Pulling into the parking lot of the apartment complex, Lynetta thought it might be time to talk to them about respecting her right to have a little more freedom.

It was quiet when she entered her apartment.

"Hello?" she called out.

No answer.

Lynetta double-checked her cell phone. She'd received no calls or texts.

She phoned Martin. Receiving no answer, she tried Jackson. He didn't pick up her call either.

Setting down her purse, Lynetta ran through all sorts of possibilities in her mind. Maybe, she thought, the coach made them stay late at school. But then she remembered they weren't even having a Monday practice because they'd won their Saturday game. Her thoughts turned to Melissa O'Connell, the party girl in D301. Jackson had raved about the good time he'd had there, but as usual, he'd been reluctant to give details of the evening except to say that everything was cool.

She was about to go check on things there when Martin appeared.

"Hi! Where were you?" she asked. "And where's your brother?"

Martin gave her a "what are you blaming me for now?" look. "I was at school. And who knows where Jackson is? I took the late bus home."

"I'll be back in a minute," Lynetta said, pretty sure her instincts were right.

"Where are you going?" Martin gave her a worried frown.

"I'm going to get your brother."

As Lynetta was crossing the lawn to the D building, James emerged from his building. "Hey, there! Just the woman I want to talk to. I know your boys don't like your dating me, but do you feel brave enough to go to the movies with me sometime this weekend?"

Lynetta's pulse surged with delight. She smiled. "I'm babysitting on Saturday. But I might be able to work something out for Friday. Can I let you know?"

"Sure. You have my number. Give me a call." His sexy smile sent a thread of heat weaving through her.

Feeling like a love-struck teenager, Lynetta went on her way to D301.

The thump-thumping of loud music echoed around her as she climbed the stairs to the third-floor apartment. Unable to stop frowning,

Lynetta continued on her way. She'd tried to stress to her boys the importance of keeping music low so as not to bother their neighbors.

Outside the apartment, she heard the sound of laughter and a familiar voice. Tension drew her eyebrows together. She rang the doorbell.

When nobody came to the door, she opened it and peered inside. "Hello?"

A number of teenagers, sprawled on the furniture in the living room, looked up at her and smirked. Smoke curled upwards in the air. The cloyingly sweet smell of pot drifted her way. Most of the kids held a clear plastic cup filled with some kind of drink. By the collective smell of their breath, alcohol was involved.

Lynetta stepped inside and raised her voice to be heard. "Jackson? Where are you?"

He emerged from one of the bedrooms. His look of surprise changed to one of anger. "What are you doing here?"

She gave him a smile that held no warmth. "I might ask you the same question, but you needn't bother to answer. Do not push me. You're in it deep as it is. You're coming with me, *now.*"

Jackson set down his drink on the living room table so hard some of it splashed out. Without a backward glance, he marched by her, one angry step after another.

Lynetta stared at the kids, memorizing their faces. "Which one of you is Melissa?"

A pretty girl with auburn hair glared at her. "I am. What of it?"

"Does your mother know about this party?" Lynetta knew the answer, of course.

Melissa shrugged. "She's working a late shift."

"I think you should ask your friends to clear out," Lynetta said with as much authority as she could muster under the circumstances.

"Who are you to boss her around?" asked a boy. By the looks of him, he couldn't be older than Jackson.

Lynetta drew herself up. "I'm a concerned neighbor." She turned to Melissa. "I hope you do the right thing."

Silent, Melissa looked down at the carpeted floor.

Lynetta let herself out of the apartment, leaving the loud music and belligerent voices behind. She was glad she'd spoken up because she now knew that, like herself, Melissa's mother was a single mom. Parents like them had to stick together.

Back at her apartment, Lynetta was met with a stony expression from Jackson. "Why'd you have to go and ruin everything? You treated me like a baby. The kids will never let me forget it."

"You're lucky I didn't drag you outta there. If you have so much time on your hands, time for parties you shouldn't be at, I'll find something to keep you busy." Lynetta's anger fled in a flood of worry. She went over to her son and threw her arms around him.

His body stiffened.

"I don't want you to get in trouble, Jackson. And that's where you're headed. We moved to Williston so you could make new, better friends than you had in the city. I want to be able to trust you, but you need to prove to me that I can. Understand?"

Jackson pulled away from her, stomped down the hallway, went inside his room, and slammed the door.

Martin, who'd watched the whole exchange between them, shook his head. "He's just bein' a dumb ass."

Lynetta nodded. "He sure is."

Surprised by her response, Martin grinned at her.

Lynetta could feel her lips curve in response. Martin was a good kid who'd gone through the same stage as Jackson. She just had to have the strength to hold on through these years. And that might mean putting off dating the cutest guy she'd ever met.

CHAPTER TWENTY-TWO
SUKIE

After her friends left her house, Sukie went around straightening pillows and making sure everything was in order. The housing market had taken a sudden tumble, making it more difficult to sell. Though no one was currently interested in buying her house, she kept it on the market anyway, because the sooner it could be sold, the more quickly she could move in with Cam.

Sukie debated going to Cam's for the night and decided to stay home. The library board was meeting the next morning, and she wanted to appear fresh and rested. After locking up, she went upstairs and drew a hot bath.

Undressing, she studied herself in the mirror. At first, it had bothered her that Cam was almost eight years younger than she. But he'd soon proved to her that she needn't be the least bit worried about it. A sigh of gratitude escaped her lips. Cam was such a special man in so many ways.

She dimmed the lights in the bathroom, lit a scented candle, and eased herself into the sudsy water in the spa tub. Stretching out in the hot water, she felt her body relax and let out a groan of pleasure.

Her mind drifted to her children, then to Ted. He was on a path of destruction, and she had no way to stop it. That bothered her. What if his behavior hurt her children?

Her cell phone rang. Sukie picked the phone up off the tile floor and checked the caller ID: Betsy.

Sukie eagerly clicked on the call. "So glad to hear from you! How are you?"

"Great," Betsy answered. "We're getting settled in our condo. It's beautiful. We're within walking distance of the beach. And we have a nice private guest room. It couldn't be better."

"But?" There was a tone to Betsy's voice that Sukie recognized.

"Oh, I miss all you Fat Fridays girls so much. You know what they say—'Friendship isn't a big thing: it's a million little things.' I realize now my days were filled with all that was going on with everyone else in the group."

"We miss you too, Betsy. I hope you can visit often. And when you come north, you know you always have a place to stay with me at my house."

"You haven't sold it?"

Sukie let out a sigh. "You were the lucky one. The market has suddenly gone still."

"I'm sorry to hear that. Does that mean you aren't living with Cam?"

"Not really. I stay there when I can, but it's not the same. It's important for me to protect this house though. At this point, it's my largest investment."

"Oh, there's someone at the door. Sorry, I've got to go," said Betsy, her voice tinged with regret. "Let me know when Misty is coming to Williston, and I'll try to make it."

"Will do. Talk to you soon." Sukie disconnected the call, thinking of her friends as she settled back in the warm water. They all had challenges but time had proved they'd always stick together. After Ted had left her, she'd relied on them for honest friendship. Best of all, they'd helped her realize she deserved someone like Cam.

She was about to get out of the tub when the phone rang again. Thinking it was Cam, she snatched up the phone. "Hi, sweetheart!"

"Sukie. It's me. Ted."

Sukie's stomach knotted. "Yes. What do you want?"

"I need you to come to the police station tomorrow morning to pick me up."

A cold thread of suspicion snaked its way through Sukie's body. She stepped out of the tub and wrapped a towel around herself before taking a seat on her dressing table chair.

"What happened?" She was pretty sure she knew the answer.

"You know how these small town cops are," he grumbled. "They said they saw me weaving down the street as I drove. And then the Breathalyzer test they gave me was all screwed up."

"So you got a DUI," Sukie said, certain the result of the cop's test was accurate.

"Yeah, but I'm gonna fight it," Ted promised.

Sukie was tempted to tell him to call Rob for a ride, but she held back. Maybe this would be the chance for Rob, Madeleine, and her to force him to get help.

"I have a library meeting in the morning, but I'll come directly from there. It'll probably be some time around eleven."

"Eleven? That's too damn late!"

"Then call Rob," she said crossly.

"No. I'll wait for you," he grumped. "I don't want him to see me like this."

Sukie hung up. After Ted's call, her relaxing soak in the tub was wasted. Her neck muscles had knotted with tension.

She quickly got dressed. Before it became too late, she had a few phone calls to make.

◆ ◆ ◆

The two-story, red-brick building housing the town's library sat next to the town hall, Williston's center of activity. White shutters accented the many-paned windows that lined the front of the building, inviting people inside. A double black door served as its main entrance.

Very much at home, Sukie headed inside. Until Edythe had maneuvered her out of the position, Sukie had loved acting as the children's librarian. The job provided an important opportunity to introduce children to the joy of reading books—something she strongly believed in.

From behind the circulation desk, Julie Garrison greeted her with a warm smile. "So nice to have you back, Sukie."

Sukie grinned. "Thanks. I'm really excited to pick up where I left off."

They walked together into the children's section of the library.

Gazing at the pristine arrangement of furniture, Sukie let out a sigh of frustration. "I guess Edythe got her wish to destroy everything I'd done here."

"Don't worry," Julie said. "I saved all the big pillows we bought, and Bill Walters, the custodian, has agreed to move the furniture back to where you had it. The children have missed the cozy reading nooks you set up for them." She shook her head. "The woman who replaced you was afraid of Edythe and would do whatever Edythe wanted."

Sukie nodded. "Edythe can be intimidating, but I'm not afraid of her anymore." Still, she didn't like the idea of having Edythe around to criticize her every move.

Life was so complicated, Sukie thought, as she prepared to go into the board meeting.

When she entered the conference room, Edythe Aynsley was already there, surrounded by three of the board members. Tall and thin, Edythe's posturing as someone important made her impossible to ignore.

Noticing Sukie's appearance, Edythe's lips pursed with distaste.

An unwelcome shiver danced across Sukie's shoulders. The woman's narrow face and small dark eyes had always reminded her of watercolor drawings of a weasel she'd once seen in a picture book. She shook off the bad feelings and told herself not to be so judgmental.

But when Sukie joined the group, Edythe turned her back to her and began a two-way conversation with one of the board members.

Sukie sighed. She and Edythe would never be friends. Edythe was a bitter woman. Some said it had to do with being made a laughingstock in Atlanta when her wealthy husband left her for someone older—a cause for much speculation.

Simon Prescott, head of Citizens Fidelity and Trust and chairman of the library board, approached Sukie. "So glad you're back," he said. They had a cordial conversation, then it was time to begin the meeting.

Julie Garrison took a seat at the long conference table beside Sukie. "Be sure and tell the board all you want to do while you have their support," she whispered.

As the time grew closer for Sukie to make her presentation, her nervousness grew. It would be a face-off. In typical fashion, Edythe had made a suggestion or negative comment over every new issue brought up. The other board members were rolling their eyes, but none spoke up.

"And so, Sukie Skidmore, we thank you for stepping in once more while we look for a permanent replacement for the position of children's librarian," said Simon. "We'd like to hear from you as to what you are planning. We were most impressed with your earlier innovations."

Sukie cleared her throat. "Thank you, Simon, and board members. I appreciate this opportunity. As to what I'm planning, Julie and I have discussed reinstating comfortable reading nooks for the children. Also, I will be starting up the Nighty Night program again, once a month. As usual, Julie and I will be selecting new books together, and I'm working on an idea for a seasonal reading contest for middle school children."

Two dots of red appeared on Edythe's cheeks. "The board previously agreed with me that having pillows thrown here and there and children lounging everywhere is unseemly for a library. When you left, we made sure that kind of behavior was eliminated."

Sukie reined in her temper. "But when I was working here, we found that more books were being read on-site and more books were checked out by children, due in large part, I believe, to the more inviting setting."

"We're not a babysitting service," snapped Edythe. "So many mothers use this place to entertain their children . . ."

"Precisely," said Sukie, cutting off Edythe. "Encouraging children to read is, and should be, one of the jobs of a children's librarian."

"Exactly," said Simon. "I thought the reason the board voted to bring back Ms. Skidmore was because she was aligned with the philosophy of this board."

"Not everyone on the board voted for her," said Edythe.

"That may be the case," said Simon smoothly, "but majority rules in situations like this."

Edythe remained silent, but Sukie cringed at the nasty look Edythe gave her.

It seemed silly, but Sukie knew the kind of power Edythe and her money had in this small town. She'd have to watch her back.

CHAPTER TWENTY-THREE

CAROL ANN

After she left Sukie's house following the impromptu dinner, Carol Ann aimlessly drove around the town, reluctant to go home. She went by the condos on the lake, where she'd once thought she'd live and, slowing down, let out a sigh. At the rate she was saving money, she'd never make it to a place on the lake. And maybe holding out for a condo she owned was a foolish idea.

She parked by the small marina and climbed out of her car. Walking to the end of the boat dock, she stared out at the peaceful setting. Soft wind sent ripples skimming across the deep-blue water's surface. Pine trees dotted the lake's edge and released a refreshing, clean aroma into the air.

At the sound of quacking, she turned. A mother duck swam by, followed by four little ducklings paddling as fast as they could to stay close to her. Their mother slowed and turned to make sure they were keeping up. The mother duck's attention to her babies brought a painful constriction to Carol Ann's heart. Her own mother had never seemed that caring about her.

Deep in thought, Carol Ann headed back to the car. The women in Fat Fridays had encouraged her to be stronger, more independent. It was time for her to do something about her pitiful situation.

Filled with a new determination to be free of the strangling responsibilities her mother had dumped on her, she drove back to her house.

When she entered the house, her mother, as usual, called to Carol Ann from the living room. "Where you been, Carol Ann?"

Trying to control the despair that threatened to drown her intentions, Carol Ann went into her room and closed the door.

Moments later, a knock came at her bedroom door. "Carol Ann? I asked you a question. Where you been?"

Carol Ann held back a scream and went to answer it. "Hello, Mama. I was with friends. And this week or the next I'll be going to Florida. I'm taking a short cruise."

Her mother staggered back. "Going away? But what will I do?"

"You'll get used to it," Carol Ann said. "Because as soon as I can, I'm renting an apartment and moving out."

"Now you listen here, young lady. After all I've done for you, you need to stay home and help me."

Carol Ann shook her head. "Not anymore, Mama. If you need someone to help you, Becky is in town. Call her. Tomorrow I'll find a nurse's aide to come in and help with Daddy. And I'm sure you can find someone other than me to clean this place."

Her mother frowned at her. "What's gotten into you? It's those friends of yours, I bet. Look at you! You've colored your hair and you're wearing indecent clothes. I've tried and tried to raise you to be a proper, God-fearin' woman."

"And when have you ever said, 'I love you'?" Carol Ann refused to cry in front of her mother. "We'll talk in the morning, Mama. I'm going to bed."

Carol Ann quietly shut the door and waited, expecting her mother to pound on it. In the silence that followed, Carol Ann placed an ear to the door and heard her mother walk away mumbling to herself. To Carol Ann it was just another instance of her mother not wanting to bother to build a better relationship.

She walked over to her bed and sank down on it, feeling abandoned. Her mother's only concern had been for herself.

Carol Ann picked up her cell and punched in Betsy's number.

Betsy answered right away. "Hi, hon! What's up? I just got off the phone with Sukie. What are you up to?"

"I'm trying to work out a few things at home," Carol Ann said. "And I thought I'd take that free cruise next week or the week after. And maybe I could stay with you for a couple of days . . ." Her voice trailed off in a spasm of insecurity. She waited for Betsy to say something.

"Why, that would be wonderful!" Betsy gushed.

Tears filled Carol Ann's eyes.

"I was just telling Sukie how much I missed y'all," said Betsy, unaware of Carol Ann's emotions. "Let me check with Karen and see which of the upcoming weeks would be best to take that cruise. I'll call you back tomorrow. Okay?"

"Sure," said Carol Ann in a trembling voice. "And thanks, Betsy. I really, really need this trip. You're such a good friend."

"Hey, hon, no problem. Friends are like the chocolate chips in the cookies of life."

Carol Ann blinked back the threat of more tears. "Thanks again. Talk to you soon."

She hung up the call and leaned back against her pillow. It felt so good to be accepted. As soon as she could, she'd find an apartment. And if she spent some money on the trip to Florida, she wouldn't worry about it; she'd continue saving to rent and furnish her own place so she could leave home as soon as possible.

CHAPTER TWENTY-FOUR

SUKIE

Sukie left the library feeling good about her job. She'd successfully defended her reactivated programs to the board members. The support they gave her meant a lot to her. Especially since Edythe had made it clear she'd challenge Sukie's every move.

As she reached her car and climbed in, her contentment faded. Ted Skidmore was going to be very unhappy with her.

The sheriff's office was in a one-story brick building a block off the town square. Sukie bypassed it and drove straight to Rob's house. She was running a few minutes behind and hoped it hadn't made matters worse for Rob and Madeleine.

As soon as she pulled into their driveway, Madeleine appeared on the front porch, looking distressed.

Sukie scrambled out of the car and hurried over to her. "How's it going?"

Madeleine shook her head. "Ted is furious with you and us. Better come inside. We need your help."

Worried, Sukie followed Madeleine inside, and into the kitchen.

"So there you are," snarled Ted. "I thought *you* were going to pick me up, that we'd agreed *you'd* do it. I didn't want Rob to know anything about this."

"Hold on, Ted," said Sukie as calmly as she could under his penetrating glare. "The three of us are here to help you. I'm pretty sure you understand why we're concerned. And I don't mean just about your drinking, though that, I suspect, is the reason so many other things seem to be falling apart for you."

Ted continued glaring at her. "All this is *your* fault. We'd still be married if you . . ."

Sukie lifted a hand to stop him. "We are *not* going there, Ted."

To his credit, he remained quiet. A guilty conscience, no doubt.

"I've already told Dad he has an appointment at the Spring Hill Rehabilitation Center in Atlanta this afternoon." Rob drew in a deep breath, silently signaling Sukie for her help.

"It's a wonderful program, Ted," Sukie said. "It's covered by insurance, and they say that most companies are willing to work with employees to have the time off."

Ted slammed a knotted fist down on the kitchen counter. "I don't need something like this. I can stop drinking on my own."

"No, you can't," said Madeleine firmly. "My Uncle Nick, the one who walked me down the aisle at the wedding, had a drinking problem that was ruining his life. He lost his wife, his new girlfriend, his job." She gave Ted a steady look. "Sound familiar, Ted?"

Sukie was so surprised by Madeleine's outburst she couldn't think of one thing to add.

Ted lowered his face. His shoulders slumped. "What about my job?"

Rob placed a hand on his father's shoulder. "I called the bank this morning. They're behind you all the way. In fact, Simon Prescott confided to me that he was on the verge of firing you. After hearing this, he said he'd be proud to have you stay on, once you complete this program."

"That's wonderful, Rob," said Sukie. "Ted, this is the way for you to be the kind of businessman you once were." Surprising herself, she leaned over and gave him a kiss on the cheek. "Do this for yourself. You deserve a break."

He looked up at her. Pain shone in his eyes. "I don't know how I could've been so stupid to lose you, Sukie. Any chance . . ."

Before he could finish, Sukie shook her head firmly. "No, Ted."

"So you'll go with Rob?" Madeleine asked him.

Ted nodded. "I guess I have no choice. First, I need to get some stuff from the condo."

"We've already done that for you, Dad," said Rob. "And if you need anything else, we'll bring it in to you."

Ted looked like a broken man as he took the hand Rob offered him and rose to his feet. But in that moment, Sukie was prouder of him than she had been in a long time.

As she later told Cam, it was Ted's only hope to get his life back in order. By the time he finished the eight-week program, he'd know if the baby Emmy Lou was carrying was his. Then he might have a whole different struggle on his hands.

CHAPTER TWENTY-FIVE

TIFFANY

Tiffany stepped out of the shower and wrapped a towel around herself. It almost felt like old times as she dried off. Taking a moment to study herself, she patted her stomach. Movie stars made it seem natural that a woman could be beautifully sleek right after giving birth. It was such a crock of crap! She'd never been heavy in her life, and she wasn't now, but her body would never be quite the same. And why should it? She'd carried what amounted to something the size of a large beach ball inside her abdomen for weeks.

If her mother could see her, she'd be nagging her right now to aim for perfection. Tiffany shook her head. She knew very well she was attractive, even with breasts that were swollen from nourishing her baby and a stomach that wasn't firm.

Quickly dressing, Tiffany slipped on a pair of jeans she'd worn when she first started showing. She sucked in her stomach and closed the snap on her pants with satisfaction. Now that Vanna was a little older and the summer heat was moderating during these September days, Tiffany intended to take her for long carriage rides. And today would be the first time her daughter would attend a Fat Fridays lunch.

Tiffany could hardly wait to show her off. Vanna was growing like a weed and was, Tiffany thought, an exceptionally beautiful baby.

She'd just finished blow-drying her hair when she heard Vanna's cries. Hurrying into the nursery, she went over to the crib and gazed down at her daughter. Vanna was red-faced with impatience, flailing her arms furiously while she waited to be attended. Tiffany shook her head. In this one respect, Vanna resembled her grandmother Muffy.

"Okay, Miss Princess, Mommy's here," Tiffany said softly. She lifted Vanna and carried her over to the changing area.

After cleaning her up, Tiffany settled down with her in the rocking chair. Gazing at her baby kicking happily in her arms, Tiffany was filled with a tenderness she'd never known. She wished Beau could see her like this. But that, she was beginning to understand, might never happen. He hadn't been in touch.

When Vanna was burped, Tiffany took out a smocked dress from the closet—baby-blue fabric adorned with yellow smocking in a duck design. She slipped the dress on Vanna, put a white, ruffled diaper cover over her diaper, and slid little blue socks on her baby's feet.

Tiffany held her daughter out in front of her and then brought her close for a hug. "You look beautiful, baby girl. Even Muffy would be proud of you. Let's go show you off."

◆ ◆ ◆

Thrilled to be out and about again, Tiffany eagerly entered Bea's Kitchen with Vanna and searched for her friends.

They were sitting at a corner table in the back room.

Noticing her, Sukie waved and pulled up an extra chair at the table for Vanna's car seat. "So glad you could make it!"

Tiffany smiled. "For once, Vanna's schedule worked out." She carefully placed the baby carrier atop the seat of the chair and checked the safety of it.

"Can I hold her?" Sukie asked.

Pleased, Tiffany nodded.

The other women gathered around as Sukie lifted Vanna out of the seat and tucked her in her arms. Sukie fluffed the blue dress so everyone else could see its design. "There! So pretty."

"Such a beautiful baby," said Lynetta.

Carol Ann clasped her hands together and smiled at the baby. "She looks like a real doll."

"She did really well at her doctor's appointment," Tiffany said proudly. "Though I'm struggling with nursing her, she's gained three pounds and grew a little too."

"Hold still, Sukie," said Carol Ann. "I'm taking a picture to send to Betsy."

The waitress came to take their order.

"What can I getcha, ladies?"

They placed their orders, and after the waitress left, Tiffany put Vanna in her car seat and turned to the others. "Okay, everyone. Tell me what's going on? I want every newsy little bit. I'm starved for some adult time."

"Can I go first?" asked Carol Ann, looking around the table. With no objections made, she beamed at them. "I've got big news! I'm leaving for Florida on Monday. Ed just gave me the time off. I'll be able to stay with Betsy and Karen for a few days before I go on my very first cruise!"

Tiffany gave Carol Ann a high five. "So exciting!"

The others chimed in with their congratulations.

"Okay, who's next?" said Tiffany.

"I am." Sukie's smile disappeared. "My news is not exciting like Carol Ann's, but it's good." She told them about Ted's decision to go to rehab.

"That's great," said Lynetta, giving Sukie's hand a comforting squeeze. "I wish my ex had done something like that." An impish grin spread across her face. "Or better yet, been admitted to a mental institute."

Tiffany joined in the laughter.

"What about Emmy Lou?" Tiffany asked. "How is she taking Ted's decision?"

Sukie shook her head. "I have no idea how that situation is going to end up. Once the baby comes, we'll know more."

"Yeah," said Carol Ann. "I bet that baby isn't even his."

"We're thinking it might not be his after all," admitted Sukie. "I think it might be Jordan Smith's baby." She told them what she'd observed at the Escapes restaurant.

"I think you're right," said Grace. "Hard to trust a woman like that."

Between bites of food, Tiffany said, "How are things at the office, Lynetta? Are they still keeping my place open?"

Lynetta nodded. "Carol Ann, Grace, and I are making sure they do." She hesitated. "On another note, I'm looking forward to babysitting for you tomorrow evening, but I'm wondering if I might ask a favor."

Tiffany shrugged. "Sure."

Lynetta cleared her throat. "May I bring my fourteen-year-old, Jackson, with me?" She gave Tiffany a helpless look. "I need to keep an eye on him."

Tiffany nodded. "It's okay with me. Why? What's up?"

Lynetta told the story of the parties at her apartment complex. "He needs to understand what trust is all about. He has to know that he must earn mine. Until then, I'll keep him busy and within reach."

"If you're looking for ways to keep him busy, he can do some volunteer work for me at the library. I've started up the Nighty Night series again and would love to have him read a couple of books to toddlers. They'd love it and I'm trying to get more teens involved in library projects."

Lynetta nodded. "Maybe he'd agree to do it. He likes kids, and it would be a good way for him to stay out of trouble. I'll talk to him about it and get back to you."

As soon as they finished their meal, the MacTel women prepared to go back to work.

Tiffany gave each one a hug. She was so happy to be part of the luncheon group again. Watching them leave, she hoped Vanna would someday have female friends as wonderful as these.

◆ ◆ ◆

Tiffany paced the backstage area of the Glass Slipper, surprised by a sudden case of nerves. She went into the tiny dressing room in back of the stage to try and calm herself. Her hair looked fine, and her outfit was sexy for a new mother. So what was the problem?

A tap at the door caught her attention.

Sly Malone stuck his head into the room. "Ready, hon? The crowd is getting restless. The rate we're goin', we might need to add a second show on the nights you sing."

Tiffany took a deep breath and willed her nerves to untangle. No need to be worried, she told herself. She'd sung at the Glass Slipper a number of times. Was this about Kevin showing up and possibly bringing Beau with him? She straightened her dress and patted her hair and headed for the stage.

As she stepped onto the stage, she saw the Fat Fridays group, minus Lynetta, sitting at one of the tables nearby. Her gaze swept the audience. Neither Kevin nor Beau was in sight. The tension that had pinched her shoulders eased a bit.

She nodded at the keyboard player to begin "Only You." After singing a couple of songs without an appearance by Beau or Kevin, she relaxed and settled into "Always You," a crowd favorite. As she sang the lyrics, she closed her eyes and thought about Beau. Why had he left the country? Would they ever get back together? Did he still love her? None of it made sense.

She ended the song and, taking a deep breath, opened her eyes.

Amid applause, she glanced at her friends' table and blinked in surprise. Kevin Bascombe was sitting with Sukie, Grace, and Carol Ann. He clapped his hands and smiled broadly at her. She acknowledged him with a nod and began her next song, something lighter.

At intermission, Tiffany joined the group at the Fat Fridays table.

"Super job!" said Sukie, giving her a pat on the back.

"Yeah." Kevin's eyes shone with admiration. "It was great."

Carol Ann gave him a bright smile. "We asked Kevin to join us. The place was packed and we didn't want him to sit alone."

"Wonderful as always." Grace lifted her blue martini in a toast. It had become the favorite drink of the group on these Sassy Saturdays.

"Thanks," Tiffany said. "I just wanted to say a quick hello to everyone. I can't stay. I've got to check in with Lynetta to see how Vanna is doing."

Sukie smiled. "I'm sure Lynetta's got everything in control, but I know how anxious a time it can be for a mother with a new baby."

Tiffany nodded and left the table, glad for an excuse to leave the group. Kevin had told her he'd try to come to the show, so why, she wondered, was she feeling so let down? He'd never promised to bring Beau.

CHAPTER TWENTY-SIX
CAROL ANN

Carol Ann paced inside her bedroom, waiting for Sukie to pick her up. Sukie had offered to take her to the Atlanta airport for her flight to Florida. As astonishing as it seemed to others, Carol Ann had never flown, and her hands were cold as ice. But there was no way she would let nerves jeopardize this trip. She meant to keep her vow to be braver, to be more independent, and to get more fun out of life.

Going to the window, she peeked outside. No luck.

Like she'd told her mother, as soon as she could save money for the first and last month's rent on an apartment and fill it with the basic furniture she needed, she was out of her childhood home. She'd already informed her sister she was no longer going to be in charge of their parents. At the news, Becky had been furious, claiming she had a lot to do for her own family. But Carol Ann would not allow Becky's anger to change her mind. Enough was enough.

The moment Sukie's car drove into the driveway, Carol Ann picked up her carry-on suitcase and rolled the larger one toward the door. "Bye, Mama! Bye, Daddy. See you in a week!"

There was no answer. Carol Ann knew there wouldn't be. After their confrontation, her mother had continued to be in a major pout. And her father found it difficult to talk through the oxygen mask he was required to wear.

Once, their silence would have hurt her feelings. Now, with the weight of the household easing from her shoulders, Carol Ann felt light enough to fly on her own. She shut the front door behind her and rolled her new suitcase to Sukie's car.

Sukie greeted her with a hug. "You're going to have a wonderful trip! I'm so happy for you!"

Turning, Carol Ann saw her mother peeking at them from behind the living room curtain. She waved to her gaily.

The curtain fell back in place.

Carol Ann climbed into the car and buckled herself into the passenger's seat. No more head games with her mother.

Sukie turned to her with a smile. "You'll have to tell us all about Betsy and Karen's condo. And take pictures of the cruise."

Carol Ann's pulse pounded. This trip was the most exciting thing she'd ever done. "I'm going to take as many pictures as I can and send them to all y'all."

The Atlanta traffic progressed in stops and starts. Carol Ann began to stir anxiously in her seat. She'd heard the airport was an especially busy one.

"What'll I do if I miss my plane?" she asked Sukie.

"We've got plenty of time," said Sukie. "I'll drop you off out front and you can check in there."

When, at last, she saw the first signs to the airport, to the south of the city, Carol Ann drew an easier breath. As Sukie entered the line of cars heading into the airport, Carol Ann clutched her purse closer. The boarding pass and the money she'd pulled out of savings were inside.

"Here you are," said Sukie, pulling up to the curb at the airline's departure area. With trembling fingers, Carol Ann unbuckled her seat belt and got out. Sukie helped with her luggage and then hastily pulled away.

Bravely, Carol Ann waved her off and entered the hustle and bustle of the Hartsfield-Jackson Atlanta International Airport. In the security line, she fumbled with her paperwork and awkwardly lifted her carry-on suitcase onto the conveyer belt. It seemed such a confusing mad rush.

After making her way through security, Carol Ann entered the throngs of people heading to a train to take her to the proper gate.

Waiting at the gate for the boarding announcement, Carol Ann leafed through a home-decorating magazine.

An elderly gentleman sat down beside her and smiled pleasantly.

Pleased to be noticed, Carol Ann returned his smile. She hoped people on the cruise would be as friendly. Maybe she'd be one of the lucky women she'd read about who'd met the man of her dreams while traveling.

She boarded the plane and made her way to her seat. Hefting her suitcase into the overhead bin, she wondered at the impatience of the people behind her and quickly sat down.

It seemed to take forever for everyone to board. She checked her watch, certain the plane was going to leave late. Finally, the pilot announced they were next in line to take off.

With engines roaring, the plane lifted into the air like a giant bird. Aloft, Carol Ann gazed out the window and let out the breath she'd been holding. She could hardly believe how tiny Atlanta looked from the air. Carol Ann watched the scenes on the ground for as long as she could before clouds blocked her view.

She pulled out her magazine and pretended to read it. But in her excitement the print seemed illegible.

Drinks were handed out.

She checked her watch again. She'd been told it was a short trip, but the flight to Miami seemed to take forever.

When the plane finally landed, Carol Ann applauded with the other passengers who happily clapped their hands for the captain and crew. Then she joined the line of people waiting to disembark.

Inside the airport, she followed the signs toward the baggage claim area. As she made her way, Carol Ann listened with fascination at the cacophony of Spanish and other languages she'd never heard before. Her body hummed with excitement. It felt as if she was in an entirely different country. The thought thrilled her. This was the beginning of her chance to break free of a life she'd grown to hate.

She entered the baggage claim area and looked for Betsy. Crowds bumped by her as she continued her search, growing more and more panicky until she noticed Betsy rushing into the airport.

They hugged as if they hadn't seen each other a few weeks ago.

Betsy stepped back and beamed at Carol Ann. "You're a sight for sore eyes. I've missed you and all the others in our group."

Too emotional to speak, Carol Ann simply nodded.

◆　◆　◆

In the backseat of the cab Betsy had hired, Carol Ann stared out the window. As she studied the palm trees and the bright blue skies, traffic sped by them. Latin music blared from the radio, giving her a sensation once more of being in a foreign country. She couldn't help smiling.

Betsy's gaze settled on her. "I hope this is the beginning of many happy memories."

Carol Ann gave Betsy's hand a thankful squeeze. "I hope so too."

The driver dropped them off in front of a multistory tan stucco building.

Betsy took hold of the handle of the smaller suitcase while Carol Ann struggled with the large one.

"We're on the fourteenth floor," said Betsy.

Carol Ann craned her neck, squinting against the brightness of the sun. Wrought-iron balconies marked the front of the building, their curved railings like question marks waiting for weather reports.

"This is so . . . so . . . different," Carol Ann exclaimed. The warm salty breeze rustled the fronds of the palm trees and wrapped itself around her like a hug.

"Let's go inside," said Betsy, smiling at her enthusiasm.

A doorman helped them into the building and over to the elevator. "Have a good day," he said, tipping his hat before hurrying across the marble lobby floor to his post.

Carol Ann tried her best to take all the fanciness in stride, but she was feeling more than a little overwhelmed and very much out of place.

"You get used to it," Betsy said, giving her a knowing look.

At the fourteenth floor, they got off and made their way down a narrow hallway to a corner apartment.

Betsy unlocked the door and swung it open. "Home sweet home."

Taking in every detail, Carol Ann stepped inside and gasped with approval. The condo was sleek, modern, and stunning, like those she'd seen in one of her favorite magazines. Glass tabletops sat on simple metal structures. Creamy white couches were offset by the pale blue fabric of the stuffed chairs. Soft blue accents in the cream-colored fabric edging the sliding glass doors matched the color on the chairs and kept the color scheme from being boring. Colorful pillows with a touch of orange and red reminded Carol Ann of pretty sunsets. Plants with bright-colored flowers softened the lines of the modern furniture and gave a tropical look to the rooms that Carol Ann admired.

"It's beautiful, Betsy," she exclaimed.

Betsy smiled. "We had a decorator do it. C'mon, I'll show you to your room."

She led Carol Ann to a good-sized bedroom. "This is where you'll stay. Leave your suitcases here and let me show you around."

The three-bedroom condo had a nice kitchen and eating area that opened onto the living room, making the space seem much larger than it was. The long balcony outside the apartment faced a grassy area and beyond it, a huge swimming pool and clubhouse.

Carol Ann clasped her hands together and grinned at Betsy. "Aren't you glad you moved here?"

Betsy returned her smile. "It's nice for a change, but I miss Williston." A shadow crossed her face. "Richie has promised to come see me, but he doesn't know if the children will be able to come."

"They'd love the swimming pool," Carol Ann said, hopefully.

Betsy shook her head sadly. "I can't talk about it. Let's get some lunch and then we can go down to the pool. I've rented one of the cabanas for the day."

As she followed Betsy into the kitchen, Carol Ann wondered what it would be like to live in such a place.

Later, lounging by the pool in the sun and reading a magazine, Carol Ann knew she'd love it.

CHAPTER TWENTY-SEVEN
SUKIE

After dropping Carol Ann off at the airport, Sukie drove to the Spring Hill Rehabilitation Center. One of the conditions of the program was the agreement from family members that they participate when asked. Though she and Ted were not together, Sukie was willing to do this for the sake of her children. One bright spot was that Elizabeth had flown into Atlanta the night before. Sukie could hardly wait to see her.

Walking into the brightly lit reception area of the center, Sukie immediately caught sight of her daughter. With her blonde hair and bubbly presence, Elizabeth was hard to miss.

"Mom!" Elizabeth cried, racing over to her.

Sukie wrapped her arms around the daughter she'd missed and held on tight to her. "It's so good to see you!"

"Yeah, me too." Elizabeth pulled back from hugging her and gave her a worried look. "I didn't think it would be for something like this, or have I missed something?"

Sukie led Elizabeth over to one of the serviceable gray couches and took a seat. Elizabeth sat down beside her. "As you've already been told, your father got a DUI. But it could've happened much before this.

Things have gone wrong with his relationship with Emmy Lou. His life at the moment is a big disappointment to him. In so many ways, he's out of control."

"So why do they want us here?" asked Elizabeth.

"I'm sure it's a matter of getting our support and understanding how to support him in the months ahead. As much as your father and I aren't together anymore, I hate seeing him get to this stage. We all need to be there for him."

As she said the words, Sukie realized how much she wanted Ted to be well. Her own happiness meant so much to her that she wanted others to be happy too.

Rob came into the lobby area and, seeing them, quickly walked over to where they sat.

Elizabeth jumped to her feet and gave her brother a warm hug. "How's that adorable little nephew of mine?" Her eyes sparkled. "I can't wait to see him and spend some time with Madeleine."

A smile spread across Rob's face. "They're both great." He turned to Sukie and embraced her. "Thanks for coming here, Mom. Dad wasn't sure you would."

"As I told Elizabeth, he'll need support in the months ahead—from all of us."

Rob shook his head. "He thinks there's a chance of getting you back, you know." There was a hopeful note in his voice.

Sukie knew that kids, no matter the age, often wished their parents would find some way to get back together. She studied Rob and Elizabeth. They were grown, but they'd always be her children. "You both should know that's never going to happen."

Elizabeth nodded. "I understand. I wish some man would look at me the way Cam looks at you."

Sukie smiled. "Cam's the most wonderful man I've ever known. I love him dearly."

A woman from the program entered the room, ending their conversation. "Are you the Skidmore family?"

Sukie nodded with her children, but her family had been broken apart by the man she once believed had loved her. And like a glass ornament, once shattered, it could never be the same again.

A couple of hours later, Sukie left the building with her children. She felt good about the meeting the center had overseen with her and Ted. When he'd started to rant at her for his downfall, calm voices quickly interceded, making Ted see the truth of what he'd set in motion and how his behavior was ruining his life. Vindicated, Sukie was able to tell Ted that while she cared about him, she was moving on with her life.

Outside, she hugged her children good-bye and let out a happy sigh. Ted had been made to understand so many things, among them that their life together was over. She felt freer now to be herself with a new man in her life. And it felt so very good.

CHAPTER TWENTY-EIGHT
CAROL ANN

The excitement at the cruise ship pier was something Carol Ann knew she'd never forget. Anticipation pulsed in the air like a heartbeat. Passengers milled about or stood in line with their luggage, waiting to walk up onto the ship's deck. She stood behind a family—husband, wife, and two teenagers who looked like they wanted to stand anywhere else but with their parents. Following them up the stairs, Carol Ann climbed up, up to the deck where the passengers were being received. She'd seen plenty of pictures of cruise ships, but the size of the ship she was going to sail on was still overwhelming.

Carol Ann studied the many windows lining the sides of the ship, wondering which one was hers. Karen had proudly told her she'd been upgraded to a small outside suite.

A uniformed officer greeted her and accepted the paperwork she handed him. "Ah, Ms. Mobley. You're a VIP guest, I see. Your luggage is on its way to your cabin. I'll have this steward behind me take you to it. You're on one of the nicest decks. Enjoy your cruise."

Feeling like royalty, Carol Ann beamed at him. She intended to have a most enjoyable stay, doing anything she felt like. She was tired of being a nobody in a small town in Georgia, a nobody who felt so alone.

Carol Ann's breath caught with pleasure when she stepped inside her cabin. She'd expected to see a small round porthole for a window. But a rectangular window at the far end of the living area gave her a clear view outside. A bedroom off the living area offered another smaller view outside. The bathroom was compact but very usable, with a shower, toilet, and sink set into what looked like a marble countertop.

"Is everything all right?" asked the ship's steward who'd accompanied her to her cabin.

She drew herself up as if she was used to making such judgments. "Yes, thank you. This is fine." The only thing missing from this setting was a man to share the bed with.

"Let me show you where the life vests are," said the steward. "Before we sail, you and everyone else are required to go through a lifeboat drill. Here's the map that shows where you'll meet. I'll see you there at four o'clock sharp."

A lifeboat drill? This was serious business. She brushed away thoughts of the *Titanic* and showed the steward out.

Eager to get settled, she opened her suitcase.

As she carefully unpacked her clothes, Carol Ann was very glad she'd splurged on her purchases. If the cost of them set her back a month or so on saving up her money for renting her own apartment, it now seemed worth it.

She held up the little black dress she intended to wear to dinner tomorrow night. It had a plunging neckline and spaghetti straps. She'd ordered it after seeing it online on a stunning model. It had looked so sexy, so playful almost, that Carol Ann knew she had to have it. She hung it up on a hanger, looking forward to the time when she could wear it. She'd purposely chosen a late dinner seating, figuring that would give her time to enjoy one of the bars beforehand.

With its turquoise background and tropical flowers, her new bikini was another purchase she especially loved. And it wasn't too daring. At least not to her. She knew her mother wouldn't agree, but Carol Ann didn't care. Betsy had told her it looked cute on her.

As soon as everything was settled in her cabin, Carol Ann put on her bikini, slid on sandals, grabbed her cover-up, suntan lotion, sunglasses, and hat and set off for the swimming pool.

The pool area was already filling up, but Carol Ann found an empty lounge chair and established her place. She applied suntan lotion, glancing around to see what the other women were wearing. Satisfied that she looked fine, she lay back against the cushions. Above her, puffy white marshmallow clouds floated in the blue sky. The sundeck was so high off the water, she felt as if she could magically reach up to touch one of them.

As her body warmed in the sun, Carol Ann sighed with pleasure. Later, feeling a little hungry, she went inside to the lido deck to experience the buffet line everyone had told her about.

The line in front of the buffet was crowded. Carol Ann stared at the variety of food—everything from salads to entrées to yummy desserts—and picked up a plate to sample as many things as she could. Just small tastes, she told herself, staring at the heaping platefuls some passengers were carrying.

After a quick, late lunch Carol Ann returned to her seat by the pool. She leaned back in the chair and closed her eyes. Life was so good.

Around four o'clock, she went to her cabin for her life vest and then found her assigned station for the lifeboat drill.

"Pretty exciting, huh?" said an older woman standing next to her.

Feeling award in the bulky vest, Carol Ann nodded. "It's my first cruise."

"I live in Florida and go cruising whenever I can. I never get tired of it." The woman smiled. "Have fun and don't forget to enjoy all the food. It's free, you know. Everything but alcoholic drinks."

Carol Ann returned the woman's smile. On her budget, free food sounded good.

After the drill, she went to the upper deck for the big send-off. The railings of the ship were crowded with travelers like her who wanted to share in the excitement of seeing the ship depart. People standing on the dock below them waved them off. Betsy and Karen, she knew, were not part of that crowd, but Carol Ann waved anyway, overcome with gratefulness to them for this trip.

A waiter came by, offering small paper cups of a tropical drink. Carol Ann took one and gulped it down, delighting in the exotic fruity flavor. As soon as the ship was well under way, she headed down to her cabin to change.

Walking along the passageway to her cabin, Carol Ann took in everything—the flocked wallpaper, the wall sconces, all the glitzy touches. They reminded her a little bit of the Glass Slipper. She thought of the women in the Fat Fridays group and felt a wide grin spread across her face.

I wish they could see me now!

CHAPTER TWENTY-NINE
TIFFANY

At Anthony's with her Fat Fridays friends, Tiffany wondered if she should say anything about her confusion over Beau's absence. Was he purposely waiting to serve her divorce papers, thinking they'd get together again? Or was he so busy with all his secrets he'd forgotten to do it?

"You okay?" Grace asked her.

Tiffany nodded and changed her mind about asking for their opinions.

"You're singing tomorrow night, right?" Lynetta said.

Tiffany smiled at her. "Yes. Are you coming to see me? Grace is going to babysit Vanna."

Lynetta's eyes gleamed. "I'd love to hear you sing. The boys' coach is having a party for the team and I'll be free to come." She looked around the table. "Would it be all right with y'all if I brought a date?"

Tiffany grinned. "That would be perfect. Sukie, why don't you bring Cam? With Carol Ann away that would fill a table."

Sukie nodded. "Okay. If we can get a sitter, we'll come."

"Great," said Tiffany. If they all came and the table was filled, then there'd be no room for Kevin to sit there, distracting her from her performance.

In her car seat, Vanna woke from her nap and let out a cry.

Tiffany took a last bite of pizza and laid her money on the table. "Guess I'd better go." She rose and blew each woman a kiss. "See you tomorrow night."

Outside, Tiffany hurried to her car, got Vanna settled in her seat, and quickly drove to her apartment. With the baby so young, Tiffany preferred to change her and feed her at home.

She'd just finished feeding Vanna when the phone rang.

Carrying Vanna in her arms, Tiffany went to her cell and picked it up.

"Okay, where is he?" came a voice Tiffany dreaded.

"Where is who?" Tiffany knew who Muffy meant, but she needed a few moments to pull herself together.

"You know very well who I'm talking about. Where is Beau? And what are you two up to?" Muffy's voice was strident, but Tiffany heard worry in it too.

"I don't know where he is, Muffy. I honestly don't."

"Do you know who does? I've tried and tried to get a hold of him, but he's never returned my calls. I know he's been angry with me, but this has been going on for weeks. Ever since Vanna was born. I'm his mother. I need to know he's all right."

Sympathy filled Tiffany. Of course a mother would worry. "All I know is he's out of the country. I have no idea where or when he's coming back."

"Surely, someone must know his whereabouts."

Tiffany hesitated. "Kevin Bascombe is someone I'm to contact in an emergency."

"Kevin Bascombe? Who is he?"

"Someone Beau knew at prep school, his dorm counselor his freshman year."

"Oh, yes," said Muffy in a tone that held no admiration. "That young man who was so rude to Beau and to us. Why in the world would Beau have anything to do with him?"

Tiffany grimaced at Muffy's dismissal of Kevin. It was so typical of her.

"I don't know what Beau was thinking, but those are the arrangements he made. Has Regard been able to talk to Beau?" Tiffany couldn't hide her curiosity. Beau's father had held such dominance over him.

"Neither of us have talked to him in weeks. It's so unlike Beau not to reach out to us. We're his parents, after all."

Tiffany had to bite her cheeks to keep from saying anything rude. There was so much she could say.

"Do you have a phone number for this Kevin?" Muffy asked in a strained voice.

"No, I don't," said Tiffany, realizing it was true.

"But how did Beau expect you to get in touch with Kevin?" Muffy asked.

Tiffany didn't dare expose Kevin to Muffy and Regard's constant interference. He'd never forgive her. "I . . . I'm not sure what he thought." Vanna's cries were a welcome relief. "Listen, I've got to go."

Tiffany hung up the phone. As she paced the room with Vanna on her shoulder, nagging thoughts did a little dance inside her head. What had Beau been thinking when he left the country? He'd trusted Kevin with more than keeping his destination secret. What else did Kevin know about what Beau was doing?

Settling Vanna in her crib, Tiffany understood Muffy's worries. In her place, she'd be worried sick. Fear crawled through her, a snake of concern that wouldn't go away. She'd been so willing to trust that things would eventually work out for Beau, now that he was receiving help. But suddenly she wasn't so sure.

That evening, when she heard sounds coming from the apartment next door, Tiffany gathered up Vanna and carried her to Kevin's door. At the voices she heard inside his apartment, she almost backed away. But thinking of Beau, she rang the bell.

A very attractive red-haired woman wearing shorts and a tank top opened the door. "Yes? Can we help you?" She gave Tiffany a confused stare.

"Oh, hi, Tiffany," said Kevin, coming up behind the woman. "What's going on?"

"I need your phone number. Beau's mother called me. She wants to talk to you. I'm sorry, but I had to give her your name."

"Okay. Let me get one of my business cards. That's the easiest way to handle this." He turned to the girl beside him. "Elise, this is the neighbor I was telling you about. Tiffany Wright."

He turned back to Tiffany. "This is my friend, Elise Thomason."

Tiffany exchanged a hello with Elise, curious about her. He'd never mentioned a girlfriend, but someone as nice and as attractive as Kevin would of course have one.

She left with his business card, feeling a little closer to Beau with the phone number in her hands.

◆ ◆ ◆

The next evening, Tiffany waited impatiently to go onstage at the Glass Slipper. Singing was one way for her to relieve tension, and ever since Muffy's phone call, she'd been wound as tight as a string around a yo-yo.

Sly Malone came up to her. "Hi, sassy girl. How're things going? That cute little baby of yours doin' okay?"

Tiffany nodded.

"Good, 'cause I'd like to hire you on a permanent basis here at the Glass Slipper." He gave her a hopeful look.

Tiffany shrugged. "I've got to see about going back to work at MacTel. Then I'll know if I can do this as well."

At his look of resignation, she hastened to say, "But Sly, I'll do my best to make it work. You know how I love singing here."

His face brightened. "Okay, then, we'll take it one Saturday at a time."

She gave him a quick hug. He really was a sweet guy. He'd come to her rescue when she needed help the most.

"Ready to go on?" he asked, still pink faced from her hug. With the ring of whitish hair forming a halo around his otherwise-bald head, she thought of him as a modern-day Santa.

"Sure, I'm set. Let's go."

Sly signaled to the musicians in the trio and the notes of the intro to "Only You" filled the air.

Tiffany stepped onto the stage, luxuriating in moments like this. She'd always called them Sassy Saturdays, but tonight she felt especially sassy. By the time she'd gone through a number of songs, the club felt alive. The music, the food, and the drinks combined to make it a special evening for the audience.

At intermission, Tiffany joined the Fat Fridays table. Lynetta was sitting beside a tan-skinned man who was strikingly handsome. Behind his glasses, his eyes were a warm brown. His smile was a little shy, which touched Tiffany.

Lynetta said, "I'd like you to meet James Mason, a friend of mine."

Tiffany shook hands with him. From the smile on both Lynetta's and James's face, she knew he was more than a so-called friend—or soon would be.

She turned to Sukie and Cam. "Glad you two could make it. Cam, I haven't seen you for a while."

He grinned. "Not since before Vanna was born."

Tiffany returned his smile. "Seems not long ago that my little girl arrived. You wouldn't recognize her, but then I suppose you know all about how fast little girls grow."

He nodded. "Yeah, I have a three-year-old going on twenty-three. Right, Sukie?"

Sukie laughed. "She's one to watch, all right, but we love her."

Sly signaled Tiffany to come. She got to her feet and turned to her friends. "Any requests?"

Lynetta stole a glance at James and smiled timidly at Tiffany. "How about 'My Love'?"

"You got it!" Tiffany hid a giggle at the way the two of them were casting adoring looks at each other. *Such a cute couple.*

As she took to the small stage again, she glanced around the audience. Her gaze rested on Kevin, who was sitting with Elise at the bar. Darn if the two of them didn't look good together. Her thoughts turned to Beau. Maybe when he got things squared away, they could give their marriage another try.

CHAPTER THIRTY
CAROL ANN

Sitting in the bar alone on a Saturday night, her second night on a cruise ship, felt so wrong to Carol Ann. She was dressed up as if she had the hottest date in the world, but nobody was paying attention to her. She fluffed her hair, pulled up the bar stool closer to the black marble counter, and ordered another blue martini. One more drink and she'd be ready to go into dinner. She'd signed up for a table of six so she wouldn't be the odd person out at a table for four or, heaven forbid, be forced to eat all alone at a table for two.

She wondered which songs of Tiffany's the ladies in the Fat Fridays group were listening to tonight. The music around her was loud and jarring, but she told herself it didn't matter. Listening to old-time love songs would only depress her more.

"Hello, pretty lady," said a voice behind her.

Carol Ann didn't turn around. The male voice obviously was talking to someone else. A movement at her side caught her attention. She turned and stared up into dark eyes that were deep pools of mystery. She blinked and pulled back from the face that was appearing a little too close to her.

"Didn't know I was talking to you?"

Startled, Carol Ann said, "Who are you?"

"Your date for the night, I hope," the gentleman said smiling. His teeth were white against his tanned skin.

Carol Ann straightened and smiled. This was more like it. The man's dark hair was thick and curly. His shoulders broad. Her gaze slid lower. The guy seemed fit.

Very fit.

"I've watched you here before, you know," the man said. "My name is Ramón. And yours?"

Flustered, Carol Ann stumbled. "C-Carol Ann Mobley."

He laughed. "Well, Ms. Mobley. What do you say? Can I buy you a drink?"

"Sure," she said, pushing away the drink she'd just ordered.

He noticed and pulled it toward her. "Finish that and I'll order the next one for you." Signaling the bartender, he said, "I'll have a Heineken and, later, give us a refill for my wife here."

As much as she liked the word *wife*, she was no fool. Carol Ann started to get to her feet. "Listen, I'm not your wife."

Ramón laughed. "I was just teasing. Being single I've learned it's the married dudes who seem to get better service. Haven't you noticed that? You are single, aren't you, because I'm not into hitting on married women."

Mollified, Carol Ann settled back onto the bar stool. She told herself she needed to relax. Isn't having a bit of fun what a cruise was all about?

Ramón was a good conversationalist. In no time, Carol Ann was telling him about Williston and the Fat Fridays group. In return, he told her of moving to Florida from Cuba as a kid, how his mother had raised him alone, and how they'd faced difficulties together.

His looks, his soft Spanish accent, and his interest in her made it easy to talk to him. She liked him and he seemed to really like her.

The time flew by.

When she thought of it, she checked her watch. "Oh, no! I've missed my dinner."

He waved away her concern. "No worry. We'll go to the buffet. Let's do that and then we'll go clubbing afterwards."

At the way he spoke of naturally being together, Carol Ann felt like swooning. It all sounded so wonderful, so sophisticated.

"You look lovely by the way," Ramón said. He took a moment to study her.

Nerves forced her to place her hand in front of the plunging neckline.

"Don't do that," he murmured. "You're a beautiful woman. That dress, that necklace . . ." he looked down at her strappy shoes. "Everything about you is perfect."

Carol Ann didn't know if it was the alcohol or the sexy look he gave her that sent the room spinning a bit. It didn't matter to her. She loved the feeling of being so admired.

He took her elbow, and they headed for the buffet.

Sitting with him at a table for two, it felt as elegant as the dining room, even with the noise and the sloppily dressed passengers around them.

Ramón eagerly dug into the assortment of food he'd selected.

Carol Ann poked at her salad and ate a few bites of roast beef, but she was too excited to eat much.

Ramón gave her an endearing look of concern. "Are you feeling okay?"

She nodded. "Guess I'm not all that hungry. I ate lunch here."

He nodded and finished the last of the pulled pork on his plate. "Good food," he murmured.

Standing, he helped her out of her chair. "Ready for some fun?"

Feeling as if she could soar with happiness, she smiled. "Sure."

The Bar Fly was a cute little nightclub not too unlike the Glass Slipper. Sliding onto a velvet-covered chair, Carol Ann took a seat at a table for two, feeling right at home. The featured singer was a young man named Dwayne Caruso. His voice was soft and seductive as he sang some of the same songs Tiffany liked to sing.

"Want to dance?" Ramón offered her his hand.

She rose and he led her onto a small wooden dance floor, where they mingled with other dancing couples and swayed to the music. Never, in her entire life, had Carol Ann felt so in sync with a man.

"You're such a wonderful dancer," she murmured.

"We were meant to be like this," he whispered. "Don't you feel it?"

Carol Ann nodded. "I really do. So when we get off the boat tomorrow, if you still want me to meet your mother, I will."

"Okay." He smiled. "She lives right here in Miami. She's been after me to find a nice young woman I wouldn't be ashamed to bring home."

Carol Ann nodded. If a man wanted you to meet his mother, he was sincere. "I've learned that I can't trust a man who doesn't have family. I got stung once; I don't want to get hurt again."

Ramón pulled her closer. "I wouldn't ever want to hurt you."

Carol Ann rested her head against his shoulder. After hearing stories about how he and his mother had survived in a strange country without knowing any English, she believed him. He was such a caring son, he'd surely be the same with a woman of his choice.

She inhaled the scent of his spicy lime aftershave and let out a sigh of contentment.

Moments later, she felt him gently shake her.

"Hey, you're falling asleep. Maybe I should walk you down to your cabin. What do you say?"

Carol Ann nodded sleepily. It sounded wonderful.

Later, she could hardly remember how she got to the cabin. She only knew it felt good to be wrapped in Ramón's strong arms.

At the cabin door, he asked for the keys and she handed them to him. Inside the cabin, it was dark. She'd forgotten to leave a light on.

Ramón turned on a light and then gave her a questioning look. "Should I stay?"

Barely awake, Carol Ann nodded. It was what she'd wanted all along.

On the way into the bedroom, she stumbled over her feet and laughed giddily. He joined in, and still laughing, she landed on top of the bed beside him.

When Ramón's lips came down on hers, Carol Ann felt her body go weak with desire. Only one other man had kissed her like this and he wasn't anyone she could marry—not when they worked together. Besides he wasn't handsome like Ramón.

Things happened fast. Before Carol Ann knew it, her dress was off and she was left wearing nothing but her panties. Ramón quickly removed them before taking off his own clothes.

As his hands explored her body, Ramón's kisses grew more intense. She was ready to explode with sensations when Ramón entered her. They began a dance that was so much better than the one in the club.

When it was over, Carol Ann let out a sigh of contentment and rolled over.

The next morning Carol Ann woke to a headache and an empty bed. Seeing her dress thrown onto the floor beside her panties, the scene with Ramón came back to her. She reached up to undo her pearl necklace. It had been an extravagant purchase but one she'd made thinking of the wedding she hoped to have one day. Her fingers found bare skin.

She frowned. Had she taken it off? She didn't remember doing so.

Suspicion roared through her, a waterfall of worry.

She hurried out of bed and checked the top of the bureau. It wasn't there. She opened the small purse she'd carried last night. The cash and her credit cards were gone.

Sick to her stomach, Carol Ann went into the small bathroom and threw up.

When she returned to the bedroom, she checked her purse again. As before, all her cash and credit cards were gone. Her driver's license and cell phone remained. A favor from Ramón, she supposed, feeling a rush of bile in her throat.

She checked both rooms for her necklace, but she soon realized it was a hopeless task. She collapsed in a chair in the living area. Ordinarily a theft would be reported to the crew of the ship. But the mere idea of having to explain what had happened kept Carol Ann's hands clasped in her lap, away from the phone. She'd die before being forced to confess what a pitiful person she was.

With a determination born of shame, she pulled herself up to her feet. Her necklace was gone, but she'd call the credit card companies and take care of everything she could on her own. Ramón, or whatever his name was, could go to hell!

Desperate to wash off any trace of the thief, Carol Ann climbed into the shower. Tears mingled with the stream of water splashing over her body. Her women friends had warned her about her vulnerability and her desire to make every wish come true. Why couldn't she have seen that Ramón was just using her for fun . . . for money . . . for sex.

She gagged and let out a sob.

Stepping out of the shower, she hastily dried herself off. The ship was due to dock in Miami at eight o'clock. All passengers had been instructed to leave their suitcases outside their cabins by six. She had only moments to spare.

She slipped on one of the sundresses she'd bought especially for the trip and studied herself in the mirror. She wasn't ugly. Not by any standards. But was she totally stupid? She sure felt like it.

Quickly packing, she decided she wouldn't say anything to the other women in the group about what had happened. They'd only shake their heads and give her knowing looks like they'd done when she was dating John.

She placed her suitcase outside the door and went back into her cabin. Aspirin. She needed at least three.

As she swallowed the medicine, Carol Ann tried to push aside the memory of making love with a man she now knew was an imposter.

When she lay down on the bed to ease her headache, she smelled his spicy lime aftershave on one of the pillows and groaned out loud. Last night was still fuzzy in her mind. Had he put on a condom? She was pretty sure he had. Even so, the thought of their intimacy sent a shudder of distaste rolling through her.

CHAPTER THIRTY-ONE

TIFFANY

Tiffany awoke with a start. Sunlight streamed through the window, beckoning to her to begin her day. She checked her bedside clock and sat up in alarm. Eight o'clock. Vanna never slept this late. Was something wrong?

In a panic, Tiffany jumped out of bed and ran into Vanna's room. All was quiet. Imagining the worst, she hurried over to the crib and peeked over the rail. Her little girl was sleeping peacefully, her body rising and falling in regular breaths.

Weak with relief, Tiffany sank into the rocking chair. Vanna had been asleep for six hours, the longest time ever. Tiffany's breasts swelled with milk, but there was no way she was about to wake her baby. Not when it might be the start of longer nights of sleeping.

Tiptoeing out of the room, Tiffany headed for the kitchen. A strong cup of coffee would help her face the day.

She started the coffee maker and, yawning, took a seat at the kitchen table. Her performance at the Glass Slipper had gone so well the audience hadn't wanted her to stop. After the show, an entertainment agent from Atlanta had asked to speak to her. She'd listened to his promises of bigger and better gigs and politely accepted his business card, but she had no intention of following through with him. With a baby to raise alone, she was content to do her singing in a smaller way among friends and supporters.

The coffee pot chirped and sighed as the last of the dark liquid brewed.

She got up and poured herself a cup. She was about to wander out onto the balcony when a tap sounded at the door. Puzzled, she went to answer it.

Cracking open the door, she was surprised to find Kevin standing there.

"Hi! Did you smell the coffee I just made," she teased, trying to get a smile out of him. "I'd be glad to give you a cup."

His expression remained solemn. "I need to talk to you, Tiffany. May I come in?"

"Sure." At the shakiness in his voice and his serious tone, a shiver crossed her shoulders.

She opened the door and he entered.

"Where can we sit?" he said. "I have something to tell you."

She felt the blood leave her face. "It's Beau, isn't it?" she said, pulling the words up from a stomach that had knotted with foreboding.

He took her hands. "Let's sit down."

Without knowing why, Tiffany began to cry.

Kevin led her to the couch and gently urged her stiffened body down on it.

Sitting and facing her, his brown eyes filled. "I'm sorry to be the bearer of such news, but there's been an accident."

"Oh my God! He's . . . he's dead?" She knew it in her gut.

Kevin nodded. "It apparently happened sometime yesterday. I got the news early this morning."

"What happened? Where is he?" Tiffany sobbed. "I don't even know where he went. It's all so crazy."

Kevin wrapped an arm around her. "Here's what I can tell you. He was on a hiking trip in Peru and apparently collapsed near the top of Machu Picchu. He died before they could get him to a hospital."

"Peru? Hiking trip? I don't think he's ever hiked in his life. Why would he do that?" Tiffany clapped her hands to her head, trying to take it all in.

Kevin drew in a deep breath and let it out in a shaky rumble. "Beau was working on a lot of issues, not just an addiction to drugs, but the reasons behind it. As part of a recovery program, he joined a gym and met up with a couple of guys who were going to hike Machu Picchu in Peru. They agreed to have him join them. He began conditioning for it several times a week to get ready. They left a few weeks ago, to travel to Europe for more training and then to go to Peru."

"But why did he want you here if he was going to take off to Peru? Aren't you supposed to be in business with him? Why . . ." she sobbed. "Why . . ." She couldn't finish. She'd hoped for Beau to stay in her life, for him to see their daughter grow, for him to still love her like he had in the beginning.

Kevin drew her against his chest and patted her back. "I'll be here to help you through it all. There's a lot of legal stuff involved. Muffy and Regard don't know the details of what Beau was working on, but you are very much a part of it."

Tiffany drew back. "I am? What are you talking about?"

"Beau has used all his inheritance from his grandfather to set up a trust, with you in charge. We'll talk about this later. First we'd better discuss what I can do to help you. There will be questions about a funeral for him."

"Me? Won't Muffy and Regard want to do that?"

"It's up to you, Tiffany, to make those arrangements. Not them. That's how he wanted it. There's a reason Beau never went ahead with the divorce. He loved you very much but he knew the only way to get you back was to tackle his issues, come to you as a new, better man."

The room around Tiffany began to spin. It all was too much, too painful for her to hold on to reality.

◆　◆　◆

Tiffany roused from her fainting spell to find Kevin's face above hers. He was saying something to her, but his words sounded as if he were speaking in a hollow tin can.

She blinked and struggled to sit up, then realized she was sprawled on her back on the couch. Looking down at herself, she saw that the front of her nightshirt was wet with her breast milk. She let out a groan and allowed Kevin to help her to a sitting position.

"Are you better now?" he asked gently. "Let me get you a glass of water."

She heard Vanna's cries and struggled to rise. "My baby. Beau's baby. I have to get her."

"Wait here," Kevin said. "I'll bring her to you."

Feeling as if she was in the midst of a nightmare, Tiffany sat back against the cushions in a daze.

Kevin returned to the living room with Vanna. Handing her to Tiffany, he said, "Sorry. I didn't know how to change her. She's wet."

Tiffany nodded. "Let's get her settled and then I'll change her." She unbuttoned her nightshirt, opened her nursing bra, and brought Vanna to her breast.

Wonder softened Kevin's troubled features as he looked on. He looked away and then back again. "Who can I call for you? Sukie? Or one of the other women in your group?"

"Sukie," Tiffany managed to say before she started to cry again.

Kevin placed a hand on her shoulder. "Okay. I'll call her. Then I'll call Muffy and Regard and let them know what has happened. I imagine they'll want to be in touch with you." He hesitated and then said, "I think it's best for you not to be alone with them, Tiffany. They don't know anything about what Beau's done. I suspect they won't be happy with his choices and I don't want them to turn on you or try to force you to make changes. Understand?"

Tiffany nodded numbly. She'd been blamed in the past for Beau's disagreements with their ideas.

She was still sitting on the couch when Sukie arrived. Vanna had finished nursing, but Tiffany had found it impossible to find the energy to get up and change her soaking wet diaper.

Sukie rushed over to her. "Oh, Tiffany! Kevin told me what happened to Beau. I'm so sorry." Her eyes overflowed as she gingerly wrapped her arms around Tiffany, careful not to hurt Vanna.

Hot tears burned a trail down Tiffany's cheeks and spilled onto her nightshirt.

With a tissue, Sukie wiped the wetness from Tiffany's face. "Sweetie," Sukie said in a soft, cajoling voice Tiffany thought she probably used on toddlers at the library, "look at you. You're soaked. I'll take the baby and change her. Let's have you take a shower and get cleaned up. People will be dropping by."

Sniffling, Tiffany handed Vanna over to Sukie and rose.

Sukie led her like a child to the bathroom and helped her get out of her wet, smelly nightshirt. "There. I'll be back to check on you."

Tiffany got the water running and stepped inside the shower. Standing under a stream of hot water, she felt as if her insides had frozen in a death of their own.

CHAPTER THIRTY-TWO
CAROL ANN

After her headache subsided, Carol Ann went up on deck to get some fresh air. A number of passengers were gathered in groups or stood alone at the railing staring down at the water or at the port in the near distance.

The sun was low in the sky but showing promise of a nice tropical day. Carol Ann breathed in the salty tang of air and steadied herself. She hated the idea of going back to Williston, but she couldn't afford to lose her job. Her phone pinged with a message. She checked her cell, and saw it was from Betsy: *Call when you get your luggage. K and I will pick you up at the spot where we dropped you off.*

It felt good to know she had friends waiting for her. She needed a friend or two to keep from feeling so alone, so vulnerable, so stupid.

The last time she'd been in a situation like this it'd been her boss, Ed Pritchard, who'd showed her how kind, how helpful, how sweet a man could be. He'd said it was better if they didn't date while they worked in the same office, but that was only after she'd told him she wasn't interested. Another stupid mistake? Maybe.

A waiter came around, offering small cups of Bloody Marys and screwdrivers. Carol Ann took the spiked orange juice, hoping her stomach would settle down. What was that saying? Something about the hair of a dog biting you? John had said it more than once.

The bustle of passengers getting off the ship was a letdown after the excitement of boarding the ship. Chaos reigned as passengers called out to one another, dragged suitcases around, and followed the instructions of people from the ship trying to control the situation.

As soon as she got her luggage, Carol Ann punched in the phone number for Betsy on her cell. It would feel great, she thought, to stretch out by Betsy's pool for a couple of hours before getting ready for her flight back to Atlanta.

Betsy picked up. "Hi, Carol Ann. All set for us to come and pick you up?"

"Yes. I'll be standing where you told me."

"Good. We'll be there," Betsy said and hung up.

Carol Ann stared at her cell phone, wondering what was going on. Betsy was usually chatty and upbeat. She'd sounded almost mad on the phone.

Shrugging, Carol Ann picked up the handle to her suitcase and began rolling it toward the pickup spot. Life was sure full of bumps and disappointments.

◆ ◆ ◆

Carol Ann stood at the curb, glancing around nervously. The last person she wanted to see now, or ever again, was that creep Ramón. The longer she waited for Betsy and Karen, the more worried she became that Ramón would show up. When she finally saw Karen's car pull up down the street, relief made her go weak. She drew a deep breath and grabbed hold of the handle of her large rolling suitcase. Struggling with the smaller carry-on, she hurried toward them. Betsy ran up to her. Her eyes were red-rimmed, her face puffy. "Hurry, hon! We've got to be on our way."

"Betsy! What's wrong?" Carol Ann said, alarmed by her appearance.

"It's Tiffany. Beau's dead. He collapsed on a hiking trip." She wrapped her arms around Carol Ann. "It's so awful. We all need to help. Karen and I are flying to Atlanta with you."

Carol Ann clasped a hand to her chest. All thoughts of Carol Ann's own troubles fled in a rush of sympathy. Her heart ached for Tiffany. She and the others knew how much Tiffany had hoped things would get better between them.

"I'm so, so sorry to hear this," Carol Ann said. "What can I do to help?"

"Just be there for her. We'll find out more about her plans when we get there," Betsy said, taking Carol Ann's small bag from her.

Carol Ann followed Betsy to Karen's car and lifted her suitcase into the trunk. Still in a state of shock, she slid onto the backseat and grabbed hold of the armrest as they entered traffic.

Karen smiled at her in the rearview mirror. "This is such a sad time for Tiffany, but we don't want to forget your exciting news. Did you have a nice cruise?"

"Oh, yes," Betsy said, turning around in the passenger seat and beaming at her. "Sorry I forgot to ask earlier. Was it fun?"

Carol Ann pasted a smile on her face. "It was wonderful," she lied. "Thank you both so much." She'd die before she ever let any of the other women know she'd made another dumb choice with a man.

Rather than going to their condo, Betsy and Karen took her to lunch at a small restaurant in South Beach, where they were seated at a table outside.

Betsy was unusually quiet. Numb herself from the news of Beau's death, Carol Ann hardly felt the breeze on her sunbaked skin.

She sipped her chilled wine carefully, still fighting the effects of too much booze the night before, and merely picked at the seafood salad Karen had recommended.

"You can't come to Miami without seeing this glitzy area," said Karen, making an obvious attempt to keep conversation going. "People watching is a sport here."

Carol Ann nodded, stunned by the number of beautiful young women she saw wearing casual, skimpy outfits that hid little of their thin, tan bodies.

Karen gave her a knowing smile. "A lot of these girls are models."

Watching a girl in a bikini Rollerblade down the street, casually dodging cars cruising along Ocean Drive, Carol Ann took it all in. It was so different from anything she'd known.

After lunch, they headed to the airport.

"I'd rather be too early than too late for our flight," Betsy announced. "Tiffany needs us."

Carol Ann nodded. "I'll do whatever I can to help. Anything at all."

She and Tiffany had had their disagreements in the past, but Carol Ann thought of her as the sister she should've had.

CHAPTER THIRTY-THREE

TIFFANY

Sukie handed Tiffany a sandwich and a diet soda. "Better get something to eat. Muffy and Regard will be here soon. They want to see you and the baby."

Tiffany let out a sigh. "I don't think I can choke anything down."

"I know, sweetheart, but I want you to try. For Vanna's sake." Sukie smoothed a lock of hair away from Tiffany's face.

Tiffany reached for Sukie's hand and held on. "I can't believe it really happened. It's all so unbelievable. I hoped . . . I hoped . . ." She couldn't finish. Now that Beau was gone she realized how much she'd counted on them being able to work things out.

In the beginning, their love had been so fresh, so beautiful. He'd meant everything to her. His parents had slowly changed that, changed him. She'd hated them for it, but she had never stopped loving the Beau she first met, the Beau who cared enough to try to change.

The doorbell rang. Sukie went to answer it.

Lynetta came inside carrying a casserole and a grocery bag. "I brought some food for everyone," she told Sukie as she went into the kitchen.

After leaving the food there, Lynetta hurried over to Tiffany and hugged her. "I'm so sorry, Tiffany. So very sorry to hear of this. God works in mysterious ways."

"Thank you," Tiffany murmured, not sure how she felt about the mysterious ways. It wasn't a mystery that she felt miserable.

"Grace said to tell you she's bringing food for tomorrow," Lynetta added. "She'll be here as soon as she can."

"Thanks," said Tiffany. "She called and I talked to her on the phone."

The doorbell rang again.

Tiffany whirled around, expecting to see Muffy and Regard. As Kevin had predicted, they'd called him back to say they were on their way, that they wanted their family to be together. She'd almost laughed at his words. Family? They'd never considered her the "right" person for the Wright family.

She was relieved when Kevin entered the apartment. "I figure Beau's parents will be here soon," he said. "I think I should be here too, in case any legal issues come up. Beau asked me to consult with him on the legality of those matters that might be of concern to his parents. You should also stay, Sukie. As a witness to what's being said."

"Sure. No problem," said Sukie. "I know how forceful his parents can be. I've made up sandwiches and have other snacks ready should you or they want them."

"I guess I'd better stay out of the way and get back to my boys," said Lynetta politely. She wrapped her arms around Tiffany. "Honey, call me any time of any day. Okay?"

Tiffany blinked back tears. "Thanks, Lynetta. I really appreciate it." She exchanged shaky smiles with her. "I'm glad you're part of the group."

"Me, too. I'll check up on you tomorrow," she said, waving goodbye to Sukie and leaving the apartment.

Not long afterwards, Muffy and Regard appeared.

Tiffany reluctantly rose from the couch and turned to face them, dreading the meeting with them.

Propped against Regard for strength, Muffy looked like a deflated blow-up doll. Gone was her usual haughty expression, her stiff-necked pose. She held out her arms to Tiffany.

Shocked by her mother-in-law's appearance, Tiffany moved forward to embrace her.

"He's gone! My baby's gone!" Muffy sobbed.

Tiffany wrapped her arms around this vulnerable stranger and let her own emotions out. She'd never questioned Muffy's love for her son, just the way she'd behaved toward him.

Regard came over to them and placed a hand on each of their shoulders. Glancing up at him, Tiffany saw pain etched on his face. He lowered his head and then his shoulders began to shake. He released deep, guttural sobs that tore at Tiffany's insides.

Tiffany reached for a tissue from the box on the coffee table and handed one to Muffy before wiping her own eyes. It was a wonder to her that her body could produce so many tears.

"Do you want to sit down?" Tiffany asked uncertainly, not knowing what else to say or do.

Muffy sniffled. "Can I see Savannah Grace? I need to hold on to something of Beau's."

With more sympathy than she'd once thought possible, Tiffany took her mother-in-law's hand and led her to Vanna's room. Regard's footsteps sounded behind them.

Inside the room, the three of them stood and stared down at the baby. Vanna was sleeping on her back, her face turned to one side.

"She's so beautiful," murmured Muffy. "Oh, my poor boy. He'll miss all of this."

Vanna stirred, and without asking, Muffy reached over the railing and picked her up.

The baby's eyes opened. She stared at Muffy, then the corners of her lips turned down. Flailing her arms, Vanna let out a howl.

"She's hungry. I'll take her and change her," offered Tiffany.

"No, I'll do it," announced Muffy, back to her former dominating self. "I want to be part of her life. I want her to come and stay with us, get to know us. She's a Wright, after all."

Wariness that Tiffany kept buried inside welled up, a deep force threatening to destroy her goodwill toward Muffy. Her "mother juices" flowing, she watched Muffy's every move as her mother-in-law carried Vanna over to the changing area.

"Here," said Tiffany, handing Muffy a jar of organic diaper cream. "Use this on her after you wipe her clean."

Muffy took it and opened the baby's dirty diaper. "Oh, my! It's been so long since I changed a baby." A sob escaped her. "I can't believe *my* baby is gone." When she turned to Tiffany, Muffy's expression changed from one of sorrow to anger. "Why was he in Peru? Why did you lie to me about what Beau was doing?"

Tiffany stiffened. "I didn't know . . ."

Regard placed a hand on Muffy's shoulder. "Remember, we're going to find out the facts, Muffy, not blame her for it."

Tiffany and Regard exchanged neutral glances, but that didn't stop a shiver from snaking down Tiffany's back.

Muffy completed putting a fresh diaper on Vanna and lifted her up.

The baby started to cry again.

"Guess I'd better feed her," Tiffany said, taking her from Muffy. "Why don't you go into the living room? Sukie has refreshments ready. And Kevin Bascombe is here. He might be able to tell you more about what happened."

"He's just the man I want to see," said Regard grimly.

From the nursery, Tiffany could hear the murmur of voices in the living room growing louder and louder. She tried to nurse the baby, but she felt sick to her stomach. Vanna got what she could of her milk, but Tiffany knew it wouldn't be enough. Carrying Vanna, she went to see what the trouble was.

Seated on the couch, Muffy was dabbing at her eyes with a tissue and quietly sobbing. As Kevin had instructed her, Sukie was sitting in the kitchen, where she could clearly hear everything being said. Kevin was standing toe-to-toe with Regard.

"What's going on?" Tiffany asked.

Regard gave her one of his penetrating icy-blue stares. "Kevin is trying to tell us you knew nothing about what Beau was doing with his inheritance. I find that hard to believe, Tiffany, what with you being placed in charge of it."

Frustration bubbled out of her. "What in hell are you talking about? Would the two of you explain to me what's going on?"

"Have a seat," said Kevin calmly. "There's a lot you don't know." He handed her a typed sheet of paper. A notary stamp was embossed at the bottom of it. "First of all, here are Beau's instructions for his funeral."

Tiffany could feel the blood drain from her face. She set down the paper. "Omigod! Did he know he was going to die?"

Kevin shook his head. "No, but he knew the trip could be dangerous. He drew up these plans, along with a detailed will, which I had executed and notarized by others."

"How dare he take all these steps without letting me know?" Regard snapped. His low angry growl startled Vanna. She began to cry.

Tiffany got up from the couch on shaky legs and took Vanna to Sukie in the kitchen. "Will you keep her here, please? She might be hungry. I'm so tense, I hardly had enough milk for the baby."

Sukie lifted Vanna and stroked her back. "She'll be fine. It's best for you to be able to concentrate on what's being said."

Tiffany returned to the couch and picked up the paper Kevin had handed her. Glancing at it, she said, "I'm too stressed out to read it. Just tell me what it says."

Kevin took the paper from her. "It basically says that he wants to be cremated and wants you to be in charge of his ashes. Furthermore, he wants you to scatter them in your special spot by the lake. It states you will know exactly where he wants those ashes to go."

Tiffany clapped a hand to her mouth, refusing to let out the scream of pain that tightened her throat.

He still loved her! He really did!

She hurried out of the room, sobbing.

CHAPTER THIRTY-FOUR
SUKIE

When Sukie got the call from Kevin, she'd raced to Tiffany's apartment. The sight of Tiffany sitting on the couch like a brokenhearted fourteen-year-old, a lost expression on her face, her nightshirt soaking wet from the baby's diapers, was something she'd never forget.

Now, she sat in the kitchen holding Vanna, as stunned as everyone else by Tiffany's reaction to Beau's funeral plans. Then she realized why it had happened. Beau had loved Tiffany enough to leave her in charge of things. More than that, he wanted his ashes in a place special to them both, which was as strong a declaration of love as there ever could be.

It pleased Sukie to know that Beau still loved Tiffany, but with that show of love came a challenge that not many people could handle—standing up to Muffy and Regard. Concern for Tiffany wrapped itself around Sukie like an itchy, wooly blanket. Tiffany would have to be strong, so strong.

Leaning forward to better see, she listened to the action in the living room.

"In a family as distinguished as ours, a proper funeral needs to take place," said Muffy, sounding very indignant. "Beau should have known that."

Kevin gave Muffy a steady look. "I believe he did know that, which is why he made sure *his* wishes would be carried out, not yours. He's left very specific instructions for Tiffany."

"Outrageous!" snorted Regard. "He's to be buried in the cemetery in the Wright plot."

"No," said Kevin. "He and I talked about it. He knew you'd be upset, so he said he didn't mind if you had a memorial service like you no doubt would want. But he was really firm about the rest of it."

"Why that ungrateful . . ." stormed Regard. "After all we've done for him, given him."

"What in the world happened to him?" asked Muffy, her voice taut with anger. "It was marrying that girl. I knew he never should have done it."

"That girl? Do you mean me?" asked Tiffany walking back into the room. Defiance radiated from her like steam from a pot of water boiling over. "We loved each other. You never understood that. And now I know he still loved me. And I will do whatever he's asked of me. Understand?"

Muffy clasped a hand to her forehead. "Oh, my! This has all been too much for me."

Regard reached for Muffy. "Lie down. You'll feel better. This has been a shock to all of us—Beau's death and now this idea of him defying our long-standing wishes."

Tiffany bypassed them and came over to Sukie. "Thank you so much for being here." She held out her arms for Vanna. The baby's eyelids were heavy with sleep. "Time for her to go down again."

As Tiffany walked by Regard, Sukie saw him stop her. "We have to deal with everything congenially, Tiffany. I'm sure there'll be difficult decisions to make in the time ahead. But we can make them together."

Tiffany gave him a noncommittal nod of her head and continued on her way.

In the silence that followed, Sukie rose and went to the kitchen doorway. "May I offer anyone tea or coffee?"

The two men shook their heads.

Muffy sat up. "Actually, a cup of tea sounds lovely." She got up and came into the kitchen.

"Have a seat," Sukie urged. "I'll get it for you. Would you like cream? Sugar? Lemon?"

"Just lemon, please," said Muffy. She gave Sukie a penetrating stare. "Edythe Aynsley is a friend of mine. She says you have great influence over your friends. Can you help me with Tiffany? She has no idea what it's like to be from a prestigious family. My son should have a proper funeral, be buried with his relatives."

Sukie bit her cheeks to keep from screaming at the woman. Muffy had just lost her son in a tragic accident, Tiffany had just lost the man she loved, and this is what Muffy was worrying about?

"Edythe Aynsley doesn't know me very well," Sukie said, fighting to control her temper. "As far as influencing Tiffany, I, like all her friends, will support whatever decision she makes. It's clear to me that Beau was counting on her to do the right thing for him."

Muffy straightened and let out a breath full of such outrage. Sukie stepped back before speaking again. "You've discounted Tiffany in so many ways, but I can tell you that she is an honest, caring and strong person."

She was about to say more when the doorbell rang, and Betsy, Karen, and Carol Ann walked into the apartment.

CHAPTER THIRTY-FIVE
BETSY

Betsy, with Carol Ann and Karen at her heels, walked into a space so filled with tension that she stepped back. Karen placed a protective hand on Betsy's shoulder.

After drawing a deep breath, Betsy announced to the stiff, angry-faced figures facing them, "We're here!" There was no use smiling at them.

Tiffany returned from the nursery and, upon seeing Betsy, ran over to her and threw her arms around her. "I'm so glad you're here."

"I'm so sorry, sweetie. So very sorry," Betsy murmured, holding Tiffany close.

Tiffany lifted a wet-cheeked face to her and whispered, "He still loved me. He really loved me."

"Yes," Betsy said, giving Tiffany an affectionate squeeze. "I've always thought so."

Carol Ann came over to them. "Tiffany, I'm so sorry. I truly am." Tears shimmered in her eyes.

Tiffany embraced Carol Ann, then she and Karen hugged. "Thank you all for coming. Things are in a mess right now, but come in and stay for awhile."

Regard Wright stared at them with a look of annoyance and then turned back to Kevin Bascombe. "Muffy and I will leave you now. We'll stay at Beau's house and see you in the morning. But let there be no mistake. You might think everything is settled, but it isn't. I will go through Beau's paperwork carefully to see what we can do to make things the way they should be."

Color crept into Kevin's face. "You're welcome to do so, sir. But we've done a good job of making sure Beau's wishes will be honored. I'd hoped you could find a way to understand what Beau wanted to do with his life going forward."

Finding herself in the midst of such arguing, Betsy wasn't sure where to go, what to do.

Sukie stuck her head out of the kitchen. "Come on into the kitchen. I have refreshments ready."

Betsy hastily headed for the kitchen, just as Muffy emerged from the room.

Muffy's lips tightened as she glared at Betsy and swung her gaze to Karen. Brushing by them, she said nothing. But her silence was filled with unspoken disdain.

Regard took Muffy's arm and turned back to Tiffany. "We'll see you tomorrow. Hopefully we'll have a better opportunity to privately discuss plans for Beau's funeral."

Tiffany shook her head. "I will follow Beau's wishes as he wanted," she said in a voice ringing with determination. "You and Muffy can plan a memorial service for him. That's all. Beau knew you would do that, regardless of how he felt about it."

Regard's cheeks flushed with anger. "There's no need to be disrespectful, young lady."

Tiffany held out her arms in supplication. "I'm just honoring Beau's wishes." Silvery wet tracks ran down her face.

Betsy flexed her fingers, so angry she couldn't help herself. "Why don't I show you out?"

Muffy turned to her. "I know what kind of person you are, Betsy Wilson. Everyone does." Her words were spiteful, mean.

In the beginning of her relationship with Karen, Betsy might have folded into a mass of shamed uncertainty. Now, though, she smiled. "My friends know me well and that's enough for me."

Funny thing, she meant it in a way she never had before.

CHAPTER THIRTY-SIX

TIFFANY

As the door closed behind Muffy and Regard, the tension that had all but crippled Tiffany left her body. Feeling weak, she collapsed on the couch.

Kevin came over to her and took hold of her hands. "I'll leave you with your friends for now. But before Muffy and Regard return tomorrow, you and I need to talk privately about all that's happened. They haven't heard all of it yet, Tiffany. You're now in charge of a small fortune."

"Me? Why would Beau do this?" Confusion enveloped Tiffany. So much was happening—and at such a fast, painful pace—that she didn't know what to think.

Kevin gave her a troubled, steady stare. "I think Beau wanted you to be free of them, like you once wished. He not only loved you, Tiffany. He respected you. And he thought you'd be strong enough to do what he wanted."

Tiffany wiped her eyes, unable to remember a time when she'd cried as much. "Beau and I had some really good times, sweet times, you know, before everything started to fall apart." She drew a shaky breath and straightened. "No matter what, I'll do what he wanted."

"That's good, Tiffany," said Kevin, giving her an encouraging smile. "We all will."

Tiffany walked him to the door and then joined her friends in the kitchen. Lowering herself onto a kitchen chair, she gazed at them with gratitude. The sympathy and kindness on their faces threatened more emotional outbursts, but she held them back.

"Thank you so much for being here," she said. "It means the world to me."

Sukie spoke up. "Tiffany, we've been talking. We don't think you should be alone with Muffy and Regard. They're bullies, and when they want something, they're determined to get it."

Tiffany nodded. "I know. That's why Kevin asked you to stay. Right, Sukie?"

"Yes," Sukie said and turned to the others. "He wanted a witness to hear anything spoken in case Regard challenged the will."

Tiffany thought once more about what enormous steps Beau had taken to break loose from his family and make his life worthwhile. He'd come a long way from the drug-addicted man who'd forced her to leave him. Knowing what courage he had to take such steps, she vowed to do what Beau had asked of her, the Wrights be damned.

"Can someone stay here with me tomorrow?" Tiffany asked. "I'll need someone to act as a witness, like Sukie did for me today. We'll tell Muffy and Regard that you're here to take care of Vanna."

They all began to talk at once.

"I'll be here," said Betsy grimly.

"And I'll be with her," Karen added.

"My afternoon is free so I can take over then," said Sukie.

"Grace, Lynetta, and I have to work, but I can stop by in the evening if you need me," Carol Ann said.

Touched by their quick responses, Tiffany smiled. "Okay, that's how we'll make sure I have someone on my side. Regard might think he has all the power to make things go his way, but he'll soon discover he can't match the power of the Fat Fridays women."

"Hear! Hear!" said Betsy. "The whole group will always stand beside you."

Her enthusiasm brought a weak smile to Tiffany's lips.

Betsy set aside her cup of tea. "Now that we've got that settled, how is that sweet little Vanna? I can't wait to see her."

Tiffany checked the clock on the microwave. "She should be getting up soon." She paused, asking herself if she was being overly dramatic, and then blurted out, "Muffy and Regard talk of Vanna coming to visit, but I don't want that to happen. I don't trust them."

Sukie patted Tiffany's shoulder. "There's no reason you should be forced to have Vanna visit them."

"Yes, if you're worried about it, don't do it," said Betsy. "A mother's instinct is always right. Be strong, Tiffany."

Tiffany let out a shaky breath. She hoped she'd have the strength everyone seemed to think she had.

◆ ◆ ◆

Later, after everyone had gone home, Tiffany lay in bed, staring up at the ceiling, her thoughts tangled into knots of uncertainty. Kevin hadn't given her all the details of Beau's will, but she was apparently now in charge of handling a lot of money. Beau had been terrible with money. They'd had fights about his spending habits—habits that came from having a lot of it. He'd accused her, someone who'd grown up without many extras, of being a cheapskate.

She clasped her cheeks in her hands. It was all such a crazy, crazy thing. "Beau," she whispered into the darkness. "What have you done to me?"

CHAPTER THIRTY-SEVEN

CAROL ANN

Carol Ann thanked Betsy and Karen for the ride home from Tiffany's apartment and climbed out of their rental car. It was a far different homecoming from her cruise than she'd ever expected.

"Sorry we didn't get much of a chance to talk about your cruise," said Betsy, getting out of the car to help Carol Ann with her suitcases.

Carol Ann smile was weak. "It's okay. Nothing exciting to report." She gave Betsy a hug and waved to Karen behind the wheel. "Thanks again for the trip and allowing me to stay at your condo. It was so sweet of you."

They drove off, leaving Carol Ann to face a reality she hated, a reality she'd hoped to change. But once again, she'd made a mess of things.

She straightened with determination. So she'd had a disappointing cruise. So she'd made a fool of herself over a man. So she'd learned a hard lesson. Nobody else needed to know anything about it.

Slinging her half-empty purse over her shoulder, Carol Ann managed to get her suitcases inside the house.

Her mother greeted her in the hallway. "So how was it? Are you going to be content to stay home now?"

Carol Ann shook her head. "No, Mama, I'm not. I'm still looking for an apartment. But I can't talk about that now. The most horrible thing has happened. My friend Tiffany's husband is dead. He died in Peru. Isn't that awful!" She still couldn't get over the horror of it.

Her mother frowned. "Peru? What was he doing in Peru?"

"He was climbing a mountain. Can you believe it?"

Carol Ann's mother shook her head. "Trouble. That's what he was asking for going on a trip like that. You young folks have to learn to stay home."

Anger flooded Carol Ann. She was well aware of the game she was being sucked into, but she couldn't help herself. "Well, I like being away from here!" she snapped.

Disgusted with herself for reacting to her mother's petty-mindedness, she rolled her suitcases into her room and closed the door.

Welcome home, she thought bitterly.

CHAPTER THIRTY-EIGHT
SUKIE

Sukie left Tiffany's apartment with a profound need to be with Cam. Having observed Tiffany's pain at the loss of Beau, she wondered what she herself would do if anything ever happened to Cam. In a short period of time, he'd become such a part of her she didn't know how she'd survive without him.

She pulled into his driveway and drew a deep breath to control her emotions.

The front door opened and Prince, Cam's golden retriever, trotted outside to greet her. Opening the car door, she climbed out and stood, taking a moment to rub the golden fur on the dog's head and ears. His tail wagged happily. When she stopped stroking him, he nudged her hand for more.

Cam hurried over to her. "Sukie, how are you? I've been thinking about you and Tiffany." He paused. "Hey, are you all right?"

Too emotional to speak, Sukie shook her head.

His face softened at the pain she couldn't hide.

"Come here." He enveloped her in a hug.

The feel of his arms around her, the aroma of his aftershave, so familiar, so comforting, brought relief to Sukie. She snuggled up against Cam's broad chest, grateful for how alive he felt. She let out a long sigh and wrapped her arms tighter around him.

Cam lifted her chin. "Hey! Want to tell me about it?"

"I'm so glad you're alive." The moisture in her eyes blurred her vision. "Poor Tiffany. Even though they were living apart, she never stopped loving him."

"I have plans to stick around for as long as I can. With you." He kissed her in a way that proved he meant what he said.

When they pulled apart, she said, "Maybe we shouldn't wait too long to get married."

He grinned. "Suits me. Chloe and I would love a wedding as soon as possible."

"Okay, then. How about a Christmas wedding?"

"With mistletoe and everything?" he teased.

She laughed. "With much, much more than that."

Holding hands, they walked toward the front porch, where Chloe was waiting for them. She was wearing the princess outfit Sukie had recently made for her.

Sukie wondered how Chloe would feel about being a real little princess in a wedding and smiled, well aware of the response she'd get.

◆ ◆ ◆

After Sukie and Cam got Chloe settled in her bed, they went downstairs. The evening had turned cool. Wrapping a blanket around her shoulders, Sukie took a seat on Cam's patio in a chair next to the open fire pit. The flames lit the area, giving it a golden glow in the growing dark. The stars would be out soon.

Cam came out of the kitchen and handed her a glass of red wine. She sipped it gratefully, delighting in this quiet time with him.

"I called Escapes, like you asked," Cam said. "The people at the restaurant said they're booked for events at Christmas." He smiled at her. "Why wait until then to have a wedding? Your house is bound to be sold soon. There's no other reason I can think of to hold off."

Sukie sat up. Cam was right. Why wait? "Okay, let's aim for the weekend before Thanksgiving. That would make us official for all the holidays."

"You're beautiful when you smile like that, Sukie." He stood up and ambled over to her. Bending down, he lowered his lips to hers. After a thoroughly satisfying kiss, he pulled back and gave her a look that spelled trouble. "Tonight we'd better practice for our honeymoon."

She laughed. She had every intention of doing just that.

"Where do you want to go on a honeymoon?" Cam asked, turning serious.

"I don't know. We can talk about that later." Sukie, practical as always, began drawing up a mental list of the things she'd have to arrange for the wedding. "Hold on! I'll be right back."

She went into the kitchen, grabbed a calendar and a piece of paper and a pen, and hurried back outside.

Taking a seat in her chair, she looked at Cam. "Ready?"

"For what?" He gave her a puzzled look.

"For a wedding."

Seeing a smile spread across Cam's face, Sukie's heart filled with joy.

CHAPTER THIRTY-NINE
TIFFANY

At the sound of Vanna crying, Tiffany dragged herself from a sleep that had held no real rest for her. Images of Beau calling to her from an impossibly high mountaintop had dominated her half-dreaming state, making her feel helpless and so very, very sad.

As she made her way into Vanna's room, Tiffany's thoughts turned to the little girl who was all she had left of Beau. Such a precious, precious gift she was. Now more than ever.

Crooning softly to her, Tiffany picked up Vanna and hugged her close.

She changed her and took a seat in the rocking chair with her baby. The movement of the chair back and forth eased her racing thoughts. Though the future was frightening, she liked the idea of being able to follow through on Beau's wishes. His trust of her spoke of so many things—their love, his appreciation for all she'd tried to do for him, the fact that he was willing to break away from a destructive situation. If only he'd lived . . .

When Vanna had had enough and been burped, Tiffany put her in an infant seat and carried her into the kitchen. She started the coffee machine and turned on the television for the morning news.

As she was pouring herself a cup of coffee, she heard the announcement of Beau's death come through the airwaves. Stunned, she turned around to face the television screen. A picture of Beau, looking so handsome, so alive, shot a streak of pain through her. The pain was quickly followed by anger. Muffy and Regard must have worked quickly to get all the information to a local station in time for the early news report.

She sank down on a kitchen chair. Beau would've hated this publicity. Tiffany let out a long sigh. The fight to honor Beau's wishes wouldn't be easy. She glanced over at Vanna sitting in her infant seat, studying the lights in the ceiling, and fresh determination filled her. She'd do what she had to in order to keep Vanna safe from the manipulation of Beau's parents.

The doorbell sounded.

Tiffany checked her clock. It was too early for Beau's parents. Muffy was a late sleeper.

She went to the door and opened it.

"I've brought a nice hot breakfast for you," Betsy announced, hurrying by her with a casserole in her hands.

Karen followed, carrying a bag of groceries.

Tiffany shut the door behind them and hurried into the kitchen. Betsy had already exchanged the casserole for Vanna. The baby lay contentedly in Betsy's arms, waving her own little arms with excitement, as if she knew what kind of silly quotes Betsy liked to say.

Tiffany smiled at the scene.

"We've brought other things too. Should I put them in the refrigerator for you?" said Karen politely.

Pleased, Tiffany nodded. Leave it up to the women in her group to take care of her. Faced with eating a warm, cheesy egg dish, she discovered she was hungry after all. Hoping it would help her produce milk, she ate it all. With all the turmoil in her life, her limited milk supply seemed to be dwindling, something she couldn't afford to have happen.

"Have you heard from Regard today?" Betsy asked.

Tiffany shook her head. "No, but did you see Channel Two? Beau's story is all over the news. It's awful."

Betsy nodded. "I wondered how you'd feel about it."

"Beau left strict instructions on how he wanted things handled."

"You won't be able to stop Muffy and Regard from doing things their own way," Karen warned her.

"I know," said Tiffany, "but at least his ashes will be in my control." She dropped her face into her hands and let out a trembling sigh. "I never would have imagined such a scene—me scattering Beau's ashes." When she lifted her face, she exclaimed, "Beau was much too young to die. And he was getting his life in order. It's so not fair!"

"Oh, hon, life isn't fair," said Betsy kindly. "It's one of the hardest things to accept."

Tiffany was glad Betsy didn't add one of her silly sayings to that simple statement. Overcome with sudden, unexpected anger, Tiffany rose to her feet, determined not to take it out on her friends. She needed a good, hot shower. Maybe then she could wash away the fury she felt building inside her.

"Kevin said he'd come over if he saw any sign of Regard. I'm going to take a shower," Tiffany announced.

"Sure, go ahead, hon," said Betsy, giving her a look of concern. "That's one of the reasons we're here. To help you by watching the baby. Take your time. We've got things under control."

The tired, haggard-looking woman reflected in the mirror looked back at Tiffany with eyes drowning in misery. She couldn't stop thinking of Beau and all he'd done to break free from parents who even now resented the idea of him making his own decisions. She and Beau were alike in many ways. Both were products of parents who cared more about image than about hugging their children, or even being kind to them. Remembering the talks she'd shared with Beau about it, she vowed to do a better job of parenting with Vanna. She never wanted her daughter to know the kinds of abuse either of her parents had suffered through. She'd do everything she could to protect her.

After a shower, Tiffany entered the living room to find Kevin was sitting on the couch. "How are you today?" he asked her, rising to his feet.

She shrugged. "Trying to deal with everything. Did you see the morning news?"

He nodded. "That's why I wanted to talk to you. Regard called me to say that he was going to fight us on everything. I knew, and Beau knew, that would happen, which is why we prepared some extra paperwork. I need to tell you what's in the will. Do you want to come over to my place? We can talk privately there."

"Sure. That might be best." She needed time alone to digest what the will might reveal.

She said good-bye to Betsy and Karen and followed Kevin to his apartment.

His living room was filled with what Tiffany thought of as guy furniture—leather couch, a comfy recliner in front of a huge flat screen, a lamp and coffee table, and very little else.

"Haven't really had time to do much with the space," Kevin said. "But take a seat anywhere. I'll get my notes."

Tiffany took a seat on the couch, feeling as if she was a child sitting in the principal's office. No matter what Kevin told her, it wouldn't be all good.

He returned with a leather-bound notebook and a sheaf of papers. Taking a seat at the far end of the couch, he leafed through the papers. Removing one, he faced her.

"We've already talked about Beau's funeral wishes. Here are some things you need to know. Beau's body might not be returned to us for a week. The bureaucracy in Peru is the same as anywhere else— outrageous. In the meantime, we need to pick a crematorium so we can have the body delivered there."

Faced with the reality of what Beau wanted her to do, a deep-seated shiver traveled through Tiffany. Beau, the man she loved, the man who'd given her Vanna, would become ashes.

"Did he choose to do this to get back at his parents?" she asked. Kevin's answer was important to her. It would tell her so much about Beau's state of mind.

Kevin shook his head. "No, he thought of it as a very spiritual thing. Dust to dust and all that."

Tiffany nodded with satisfaction.

"When we get the death certificate and all the required paperwork we need, we'll enter the will into probate court. It can take weeks, even months, for everything to be settled. In the meantime, you should know that you are the sole beneficiary of his will. The house, the car, the furnishings—everything becomes yours. And with his insurance, investments and all, some of which are already in your name, you probably won't have to work for the rest of your life, with one exception. You now are the head of WCFI, the Wright Children's Fund International."

Overwhelmed by all she'd been told, Tiffany folded herself against the cushions of the couch. She'd been poor most of her life. Now she was wealthy? Beau's parents had thought she was after his money, but that had never been true. And even so, she had no idea he had money like this. His parents would be furious when they found out it was now hers.

"It's a lot to take in," Kevin said sympathetically. "But it needn't be a burden. Beau put you in charge because he knew you well. He talked about you all the time, you know."

She shook her head and let out a trembling sigh. If only she had known, maybe things would be different.

Kevin reached over and took hold of her hand. "That's why we're going to make sure his parents don't change his wishes."

Tiffany drew a deep breath. "What can they do?"

"Like I mentioned earlier, Regard has already told me he'll fight me on this. He doesn't know, though, that Beau and I set this up very carefully. Beau insisted on it."

"So what do you want me to do about all this?" The thought of facing an angry Regard Wright made her stomach knot.

"I want you to be aware of what's been done and to be willing to let me handle Regard. Beau was well aware of Regard's lack of respect for women."

"He was?" Surprise heightened the tone of Tiffany's voice.

Kevin nodded. "Regard isn't the courtly Southern gentleman he'd have everyone believe."

With new insight, Tiffany wondered if that was why Muffy was so difficult.

CHAPTER FORTY
BETSY

Betsy left Tiffany's apartment with a sense of urgency. She had to see her son. She'd called Richie at his office and was told he was in a meeting. She wasn't sure if he was avoiding her or if he really had a meeting, but she was about to find out.

After dropping Karen off at a friend's house, she drove into Alpharetta, a northern suburb of Atlanta. She entered a business park, found the building, and parked the car in the parking lot.

Outside in the sunshine, she stood a moment, gathering her thoughts before walking into the building that housed CRC, a consumer research business where Richie worked.

The receptionist, an older woman, smiled with recognition when Betsy approached. "Hi, Betsy! Here to see Richie?"

Betsy smiled. "Yes. How are you, Sylvia?" Betsy had always made it a mission of hers to remember people's kindness to her.

Sylvia smiled. "I'm fine. Just waiting for retirement. Here, let me ring Richie for you."

Her nerves on high alert, Betsy stood by the receptionist's desk. She'd hate to admit it to anyone else but her fingers were cold with apprehension. What if he refused to see her? Maybe Sarah had told him he could never see her, just like she'd told him their children could never be with Betsy because of her relationship with Karen.

Sylvia smiled at her. "He said to go on in. You know where his office is."

Letting out a sigh of relief, Betsy nodded. "Thanks. I'll find my way there."

Walking down the carpeted hallway to Richie's office, she thought how proud her husband Rich would've been to know of their son's financial success. Lord knew it was a good thing. Richie's Sarah loved to spend money.

Richie's wasn't a corner office, but it overlooked the small park on the property.

From behind his desk, Richie stood when he saw her at the doorway. "Hi, Mom! This is a nice surprise. What are you doing here?" He walked over and embraced her.

Betsy told him about Beau Wright's accident.

He nodded. "I saw it on the morning news. I forgot that his wife is one of your Fat Fridays friends."

"When we heard, Karen and I flew up here from Miami. Tiffany, the poor girl, is devastated by Beau's death, and with that new little baby of hers needing attention, we're all pitching in to help."

Richie showed her to one of the sleek leather chairs in his office. "Have a seat."

Betsy lowered herself carefully into the chair and stared thoughtfully at her son. What she was about to say could set off another disagreement between them. But Beau's death had reminded her that none of them could plan on how long they'd be around.

"Richie," she said calmly, "I want to see my grandchildren. I know Sarah thinks she's in the right for keeping me away from them, but I'm your mother. You know I would never harm your children. They are of my blood—your father's and mine. I adore them."

"I know." He got up out of his chair and closed the door to his office. Turning to her, he let out a long sigh. "I'm thinking of leaving Sarah. I know that goes against all I've been taught—faithfulness and all that. But she's unwilling to compromise on anything. Aside from that, she's put me so far into debt I don't know how I'll ever get out of it. Even the counselor I've gone to has said she doesn't think there's much hope in saving the marriage. Sarah has turned into a very angry, selfish person. The children are affected by it. Garrett has started to wet his bed again. Nothing anybody says makes any difference to her. I'm done with it all."

Listening to her son's litany of problems with his wife, Betsy's heart ached. He was such a good guy.

"Well, what do you think?" he asked her.

Betsy's first thought was that she hadn't heard such good news in a long time. Holding back her enthusiasm, she said carefully, "It's a big decision to make, but I understand how frustrated you must be."

"She hurt you, Mom. I'm sorry I didn't fight her harder on you not seeing the kids, but I was already working with a marriage counselor and felt like I couldn't rock the boat too hard."

After struggling to rise to her feet from the modern chair, Betsy walked over to Richie. She wrapped her arms around him and drew him close, as if he were her little boy, not the six-foot man he'd become. "Thank you for saying that, Richie. She couldn't have hurt me more, especially after all the babysitting I did for you both."

"Would you like to see them today?" His face brightened. "I'll call the school. We can go together."

Happiness engulfed her. She clapped her hands. "Could we?"

Richie gave her a firm nod. "I'll call now."

Betsy stood aside while he made the phone call. Staring at a family portrait atop his desk, she wondered what had happened to the woman she hadn't wanted Richie to marry. Sarah had never been a warm and happy person, but Betsy had hoped Richie's good nature, his kind soul, would temper hers. Apparently, it hadn't.

Richie hung up the phone. "We're set. But let's get there before Sarah is due to arrive. Once we're there, I'll call and explain to her there's no need for her to pick them up."

He smiled at Betsy in a boyish way that warmed her heart.

◆ ◆ ◆

Betsy waited in Richie's car while he went inside to get the kids. Her heart pounded in excited beats when she saw Garrett emerge from the school. He was holding onto his father's hand and skipping at Richie's side. Caitlin walked behind them, very subdued, like an imperious princess.

Stepping out of the car, Betsy stood and held out her arms.

"Grammy!" Garrett shouted. Letting go of his father's hand, he sprinted to her.

Betsy threw her arms around him and rocked him back and forth, the way he used to like her to do.

He looked up at her. "I missed you so much!"

"Not as much as I missed you," she said, blinking back tears of joy.

Richie and Caitlin joined them.

"We're not supposed to see you," said Caitlin in a haughty tone like her mother's.

"Well, that is no longer true," said Richie. "Your mother was wrong to say such a thing. Grammy loves you. We all should be thankful she even wants to see us."

Betsy smiled at Caitlin. "Come here, beautiful girl, your Grammy needs one of your special hugs."

Caitlin looked up at Richie. "Can I, Daddy? Can I?"

Richie smiled and nodded. "Of course. She's your Grammy. And she always will be."

A smile crossed Caitlin's face. She ran into Betsy's arms.

"I missed you, too," Caitlin said, giving her a big hug.

She stepped back and looked up at her father. "Will Mommy be mad at me?"

Richie shook his head. "No. Mommy and I will talk so she understands that you'll always be able to see Grammy, that we love her."

A look of satisfaction filled Caitlin's face. "Good."

"It's true, Grammy loves you," said Betsy in a familiar singsong way the kids loved. It was a saying she'd used often in the past.

She drew her beloved grandchildren closer and shared a happy smile with her son.

CHAPTER FORTY-ONE
TIFFANY

Tiffany woke from her nap feeling as if she'd run a hundred yards in quicksand. Earlier, in Kevin's apartment, she'd listened to Kevin's end of a conversation with Regard and had become as terrified as if she herself were arguing with him. After arriving home and feeding Vanna, she'd given in to Betsy's suggestion to try to nap.

Beneath the blanket Betsy had placed over her, Tiffany let her mind wander back to her first days with Beau in Savannah. She hadn't gone to bed with him the first time he'd asked. As drawn as she was to him emotionally, she wasn't used to giving in to guys like that. In fact, for an attractive college student she was quite innocent.

The first night in Savannah, Beau bunked with her and her friend. After the St. Patrick's Day celebration, he managed to find a hotel room of his own. When he asked Tiffany to stay on for a couple of days after her friend left, it didn't take long for Tiffany to say yes. She moved in with him, and they had a wonderful four days together—four days in which to talk and have the best sex she could've imagined.

His tenderness with her, his worry about hurting her during their lovemaking, had touched her heart. She sensed how vulnerable he was, how in need of love. His openness reached deep inside her, made her want to please him, to show him how love between two people who'd been hurt in the past could bring them together in a healing way. Their lovemaking was so much more than selfish sex. It was all about pleasing the other. Thinking back to those times, the center of her core tightened with longing.

She rolled over and studied the ceiling. That is what she'd remember about their times together. Not the fights at the end, but the beginning of what could've been—what should've been—their lives together. Beau had fought for her, had insisted they marry over his parents' objections.

Now, she'd fight them for him.

Feeling stronger, she rose and went into the living room to find Betsy.

Sukie smiled at her. "Well, hello. Betsy had to leave, so I'm filling in for her."

"Oh how nice! Thanks for coming. I really appreciate it."

"Sure," said Sukie. "We're all here for you and the baby. What's going on?"

Tiffany took a seat on a chair opposite the couch. "Kevin and Regard have talked. Beau's parents are going to fight his will, but Kevin assures me they won't win, that the will is airtight."

"Have they come to see you again?"

Tiffany shook her head. "No. When they do, Kevin wants to be present. He's sent a copy of the will to Regard." She faced Sukie, unable to hide the awe in her voice. "I'm going to be a wealthy woman, Sukie, and it scares me to death."

"Scares you? Why?"

"I'll be in charge of a lot of money. Beau set up a foundation for kids."

"That's wonderful," Sukie said and then frowned. "Is being in charge of that bothering you? If so, I'm sure you'll do a good job. And Kevin will be there to help you, right?"

Tiffany nodded. She didn't know what she'd do without him.

"I want to do the right thing, to be grateful and all of that. But I don't want the house that's now mine or some of the other stuff."

"So sell the house," Sukie said matter-of-factly.

A new sense of wonder filled Tiffany. With money, she could make some things happen.

The doorbell rang, ending their conversation.

Sukie sprang to her feet. "I'll get it, sweetheart."

Tiffany wandered into the kitchen for a drink of water and decided to have a cup of coffee instead. She stopped what she was doing when she heard Muffy's voice.

"I have to see her." There was a painful plea in her mother-in-law's words that Tiffany recognized.

Tiffany went to the front door. "Hello, Muffy. What do you want?" she said as gently as possible. She looked awful.

"I want to see Vanna." Muffy's eyes filled. "She's all I have left of Beau."

"Does Regard know you're here?" Tiffany said, checking for signs of him.

"No, no. He doesn't want me near you because of the will." The panic in Muffy's voice told Tiffany it was true.

Tiffany opened the door. "Come in."

"Thank you, thank you," Muffy said. "You understand what I'm saying about needing to see Vanna?"

Tiffany nodded. "Have a seat. I'll bring her to you."

Muffy dutifully headed for the couch.

Tiffany checked the clock. It was time for Vanna's feeding.

With a change of heart, Tiffany motioned to Muffy. "Come on. You can help me."

Like a puppy following its mother, Muffy trailed behind Tiffany as they headed toward the nursery.

Tiffany tiptoed over to the crib and motioned Muffy forward.

Vanna lay on her back. Seeing them, her lips curved.

"Oh," gasped Muffy. "She's smiling at you."

Tiffany's heart warmed. "She started this a couple of days ago. I think she's going to be advanced for her age."

"Of course," snapped Muffy. "She's a Wright."

Tiffany's goodwill wavered. "She's a combination of Beau and me."

"Oh, yes, you're right," Muffy quickly agreed. "May I hold her?"

Tiffany hesitated, then handed Vanna over. "Go ahead and change her if you want."

Muffy smiled. "Thanks. I can't feed her, but I can do that."

Tiffany stood by while Muffy carefully changed Vanna's diaper. After doing so, Muffy held the baby in front of her and gave her a kiss on the cheek.

Vanna stared at Muffy and then another smile crossed her face.

"Oh, my!" gushed Muffy. "Such a beautiful, bright baby."

Vanna kicked her feet and waved her arms.

Tiffany took her. "I'll feed her in the living room so you can be with her."

Muffy's eyes welled up. "Why are you being so kind to me?"

"Because you loved Beau," Tiffany said simply.

Muffy's face crumpled and a pitiful wail left her lips.

With a promise to keep their meeting a secret, Tiffany closed the door behind Muffy. *Let the lawyers sort out the legal stuff*, she thought. She and Muffy were working to sort out their relationship.

"You were so nice to her," Sukie commented, rocking the baby in her arms." I think she really appreciated it."

"That feeling probably won't last long," said Tiffany. "I've decided to sell the house, along with Beau's BMW and a pile of other things."

"Where will you live?" said Sukie.

Tiffany grinned. "Actually, I was thinking of buying your house. I've always loved it. Would you consider selling it to me? I'll be able to pay for it after I get the insurance money and other funds that are already in my name."

"Really? You want my house? You could buy something bigger, something on the lake." Sukie chuckled. "My real estate agent wouldn't like to hear me say that, but it's true."

"Your neighborhood is perfect for children," Tiffany said, becoming more and more excited by the idea. "And I want Vanna to have lots of friends and to live in a house that's comfortable for everyone. Not some big, empty house full of things no child would be allowed to touch."

Sukie's eyes brightened, lighting her face. "I'll set up a meeting with my real estate agent. If you feel the same way after seeing the house, we'll work something out."

"Deal," said Tiffany.

Considering the circumstances, the afternoon had gone better than she'd thought.

But Tiffany knew trouble lay ahead.

CHAPTER FORTY-TWO
CAROL ANN

Carol Ann left work early to take care of Vanna. Ever since her return from the cruise, Carol Ann had been distracted—unsure of herself and her plans for the future. So she'd been pleased to get the phone call from Tiffany asking for her help.

Standing outside the door to Tiffany's apartment, she heard the sound of a baby crying and hesitated. Babies were a challenge to her. It seemed all they did was cry, drool all over everyone, and poop in their diaper. She'd found her three nephews terrifying with their appearance one after the other.

Taking a deep breath, she rang the bell. For Tiffany, she'd do her best.

Holding Vanna in her arms, Tiffany opened the door. "Thank God you're here. I'm late to meet Kevin. We're going to a special funeral home in Atlanta to decide what we're going to do about getting Beau's body here."

Tiffany handed the crying baby to her.

Carol Ann stared down at Vanna, who was red-faced and screaming. "What should I do with her?"

Tiffany gave her an apologetic look. "My milk supply isn't what it used to be, which was never that good. So I've fixed a supplemental bottle of formula for her. It's in the refrigerator."

"Me? Give her a bottle?" Carol Ann couldn't hide her dismay. When she agreed to watch Vanna, she'd thought the baby would be asleep.

"Hold on. I'll get it ready." Tiffany hurried into the kitchen and emerged a couple of minutes later. "Here, I've heated it for you. I've gotta go."

Tiffany left as Carol Ann was juggling the baby and the bottle. Carol Ann stood in a cloud of uncertainty. "Okay, baby, let's try this."

She sat on the couch with Vanna and offered her the bottle.

The baby sucked a time or two, turned her face away, and screamed with fury.

Carol Ann looked down at her breasts. They weren't nearly the size of Tiffany's, but maybe she could make something work. Drawing the baby closer to her, Carol Ann manipulated the bottle so it seemed as if the milk were coming from her.

Vanna calmed for a minute or so, then started fussing again.

So much for that.

Carol Ann carried Vanna into the nursery and sat in the rocking chair with her. Offering her the bottle again, Carol Ann started to sing one of her favorite songs, a song about seeing the moon, a song she knew as a kid.

Vanna stopped fussing and stared at Carol Ann with round, blue eyes. The look of surprise on the baby's face caused laughter to bubble out of Carol Ann.

"I know I'm not as good as Mommy, but I'll do anything to keep you from screaming," Carol Ann said in a soft, lilting voice. She began singing the moon song again.

The chair's movement, Carol Ann's calming voice, and the little bit of milk Vanna desperately took did the trick. Soon Vanna was asleep.

As she rocked in the chair with the sleeping baby against her chest, Carol Ann felt a sweet love for this little girl. She wondered if she'd ever know what it was like to be rocking a baby of her own. She'd never been wise about men, but maybe it was time to try the dating service again. She'd had a couple of dates that weren't that bad.

Carol Ann rose, placed Vanna in her crib, and then went into the living room and out onto the balcony. Staring out at the woodsy area beyond the lush green lawn, she sighed.

"Will I ever find true love?" she whispered.

A bird chirped, a butterfly flew past, but her question hung in the air, unanswered.

CHAPTER FORTY-THREE

SUKIE

Sukie entered Anthony's and searched for her group. From a back booth, Betsy waved to her.

Inhaling the tantalizing aroma of tomato and garlic, Sukie hurried through the noisy, crowded tables.

"So good to see you here like old times," Sukie said. She wrapped her arms around Betsy and gave her an enthusiastic hug.

Unable to reach her, Sukie blew a kiss to Karen sitting on the far side of Betsy. "I'm so glad you're still here. When do you go back to Miami?"

"Actually, we're leaving tomorrow," Karen said. "But we'll be back whenever Tiffany needs us."

"Where are the others?" Sukie asked. "Lynetta and Carol Ann were ahead of me at the traffic light." She turned around. "Oh, here they are now. Is Grace coming?"

"Yes," said Betsy. "But she told me she'd be a couple of minutes late. Tiffany, of course, won't be here."

Sukie slid onto the red plastic-covered bench alongside the booth and scooted over to make room for Lynetta and Carol Ann.

Grace quickly joined them.

"Nice big group today," Sukie said, glancing around.

"Fat Fridays forever!" Betsy said, pumping her fist in the air.

Amid the sounds of approval, Grace checked her watch. "What does everyone want? Shall we order a couple of pizzas?" She shook her head. "Y'all tend to talk so much you forget how little time we have for these lunches."

"Pizza sounds good," said Karen. An impish grin flashed across her face. "I sometimes think I should diet, and then I think of pizza."

"Yes, but remember, these lunches are called Fat Fridays for a reason. Right, girls?" Betsy said. "No calories counted."

Sukie laughed with the others, pleased Betsy was the one who'd come up with the idea. But the idea of letting go for one meal was something they all enjoyed.

After the pizza and drinks were ordered, Sukie said, "What's new, everyone?" She loved these times of getting together, being part of a group of women who unconditionally accepted her. After being the center of malicious gossip, it made her feel safe.

Betsy grinned at them. "You won't believe it! Richie took me to see the kids. He got them out of school early so we could spend some time together." She clapped a hand to her heart. "It was wonderful. We went to the park, and then before Richie had to take them home, we got ice-cream cones."

"Wow! What did Sarah say about this?" asked Sukie. She, like the others, knew all about the ongoing fight between Betsy and her daughter-in-law.

Betsy drew a deep breath. "I'm not saying much about it to anyone else, but Richie is going to get a divorce. Among other things, Sarah has put him into deep debt. He can't save the marriage, but he's hoping to save what he can of his assets."

A murmur went around the table.

"Does that mean you'll get to see the kids again?" Grace asked.

Betsy smiled. "Whenever Richie has them. I was so proud of him when he told the kids that it was okay to be with me. Bless their hearts, they both hugged me and said they'd missed me." She pulled a tissue out of a pocket and dabbed at her eyes.

Sukie reached across the table and patted Betsy's hand. "I'm happy for you. I've known Richie since he was a young boy. I'm glad he finally stood up to Sarah."

"He didn't speak up before because he was trying to save his marriage. He'd hoped to work it out with Sarah," Karen explained, giving Betsy an affectionate smile. "He loves his mother."

Watching their interaction, Sukie was reminded how important love was to everyone. Her glance rested on Carol Ann. She seemed subdued.

"How is your search for an apartment going?" Sukie asked her.

Carol Ann shrugged. "I'm still looking, but I haven't found anything I can afford. All the good ones are taken."

"Give it time. Something will come up," Sukie said. She knew how desperate Carol Ann was to be on her own, but it wasn't her place to say anything about Tiffany possibly moving out of her apartment.

The pizza arrived. Sukie sat back and listened to the conversation going on around her regarding happenings on the exec floor of MacTel. Carol Ann, Grace, and Lynetta filled Betsy in on some of the projects they were working on in Betsy's place.

Later, turning to Lynetta, Sukie said, "I have a favor to ask. Is your son Jackson willing to help out at the library? I could use him for a short while this Saturday evening."

"What would he have to do?" said Lynetta.

Sukie told her about the group of toddlers at her Nighty Night series.

Lynetta's face brightened. "He needs to find something to keep him busy on the weekends when he isn't playing football. A group of kids at the apartment complex keep after him to party with them. I've already grounded him for going to their parties."

"It's an experiment. So, we'll see how it goes. If he likes it, there are lots of things he can do both with the kids and for the library."

"Just might be the thing he needs." Lynetta grinned. "Don't worry. I'll see that he's there."

◆ ◆ ◆

Sukie left the luncheon feeling as if her soul was as nourished as her body. She loved the diversity of the women in the group and the way they all supported one another.

Instead of going back to the library, she headed home. She'd agreed to meet her real estate agent there. It had surprised Sukie that Tiffany thought she might like to move into her house. But after thinking about it, Sukie understood how perfect her comfortable home would be for her. The upscale neighborhood was full of young mothers and children. She'd always been grateful to be able to raise her own children there.

After a brief meeting with the real estate agent, Sukie walked through the house alone. Sweet memories filled her mind, but she'd be happy to leave the house behind and begin to make different memories in Cam's house. Happier ones.

She made a mental note as to what furniture she'd keep. Even though he hadn't wanted any furniture from the house earlier, she'd make Ted another offer to take what he wanted and give the rest to the children and charity.

On an impulse she decided to drive into Atlanta to visit Ted. The suspicion that Emmy Lou's baby might be Jordan's weighed heavily on her mind. By talking to Ted, she might find a kind way to tell him. His dalliance with Emmy Lou had made a fool of her and a mockery of their marriage, but she didn't want him to be humiliated in the same way, especially while he was trying to put his life in order. Gossip in a small town could be cruel. How well she knew.

The Spring Hill Rehabilitation Center was a long, one-story brick building that covered a majority of the acreage in a parklike setting. She parked and got out of her car. The bright sun cast a ray of hope around the building and its surroundings. A few people were strolling the grounds outside.

As she approached the main building, one of the figures outside waved to her. She stopped and, recognizing Ted, waited for him to cross the lawn to her.

"Hey, what are you doing here?" Ted said, giving her a smile that lit his eyes.

She studied him. The tension lines that had creased his face in past weeks were now gone. Color filled his cheeks in a healthy way that had been missing for some time.

"I thought I'd say hello. There are some things we need to talk about." She looked around. "Shall we go sit on one of the park benches?"

He shrugged. "Sure. It's a nice day, and I like taking breaks outside." He checked his watch. "I don't have another session for twenty minutes."

They sat on a wrought-iron bench beneath a wide shade tree.

"You look great," Sukie said. "How are you doing?"

Ted let out a sigh. "It's not easy, but I'm willing to try my best. Among other things, I want to return to my job at the bank. They've been holding it for me."

"Elizabeth called me," said Sukie, moving into one of the reasons she was here. "She said you weren't sure you could pay the tuition. What's up? That money was all set aside for her."

She gazed steadily at him, waiting for him to tell her the truth. No more crap from him about this.

He looked at her and then away. When he finally turned back to her, his face was a mask of pain. "Everything with Emmy Lou is fucked up. She doesn't want to get married, but she thinks she and the baby should stay in the condo on the lake."

"How do you feel about that?" Sukie was careful not to say too much, though her fingers had knotted into fists. She wanted to scream at him for even considering to allow Emmy Lou to interfere with their daughter's plans.

Ted shook his head. "I'm not sure the baby is even mine any more. But if he is, I am morally obligated to take care of him."

"And what about your other two children?" Though she kept her voice low, the mama bear feelings inside her roared. "It's important to protect their interests."

"Yes, but they're grown. They don't need as much from me."

"Elizabeth needs her tuition paid, Ted." Sukie's voice was firm. She hesitated then blurted out, "I've got something to tell you."

He raised his eyebrows and gave her a questioning look. "Sounds serious."

She nodded. "It is. While Cam and I were at Escapes, the new gourmet restaurant in Millville, Emmy Lou came in with Jordan Smith. She dated him before he left town. Then she dated you . . ." She let her voice trail off, hoping he'd see the connection.

He frowned. "So what are you saying?"

Sukie took a deep breath. "They were definitely together as a couple. Like they used to be. As I recall, she told you she was pregnant soon after you two got together . . ." Again she let her voice trail off, waiting for him to connect the dots.

"So you think Jordan Smith is the father?" Ted gave her a steady look.

"I'm just saying he could be."

Ted's lips thinned. "That bitch! That's why she kept pushing me to buy her all these things. Do you know she even wanted me to buy a house on the lake?"

"Oh, yes. I know all about it. Think of all the things you've given her, Ted." Emmy Lou had a new Mercedes SUV, access to the country club, and everything else she'd told the women in her Pilates class she wanted someday.

With a stunned expression, Ted sat back against the bench. "My God!" His shoulders slumped. "I've been such a fool about so many things."

Sukie's voice was gentle as she said, "The baby might be yours, Ted."

He straightened. "Right, because we always . . ." His cheeks brightened with color. "Sorry, Sukie."

Sukie shook her head. Ted was healthier, but he'd always had a problem with his ego. And that wasn't something that could be fixed without a lot more work.

"Rob and Madeleine brought Jonathan to see me," Ted said, changing the subject. "He's real cute, huh?"

Sukie held back a snort of disgust. When he'd learned they were about to become grandparents, Ted had gone into a tailspin. He'd taken up with Emmy Lou, dyed his hair, and generally acted like an ass.

"Yeah, he's cute." She got to her feet. "Look, I've got to go. Shall I tell Elizabeth not to worry about her tuition, that the money is safe after all?"

He stood beside her. "Yes. There won't be any need for me to move out of the condo. I'm staying right there." A look of shame crossed his face. "Alone, no doubt."

"I'm sorry, Ted," said Sukie. "Keep up the good work here. Simon Prescott and others at the bank and in town are rooting for you."

"Thanks." Ted gave her a little salute and walked away.

Sukie hurried to her car, anxious to get home to Cam. He was thrilled with the idea that her house might soon be sold and they could get on with their lives together.

CHAPTER FORTY-FOUR

TIFFANY

Tiffany sat in the passenger's seat of Kevin's car, clasping her hands with nervousness. The thought of Beau's body being transported by plane to Atlanta in a small box made her stomach do a jerky tango inside her.

"You okay?" Kevin asked her.

She swallowed hard. "How does this work, getting Beau back here?"

"I'm staying in touch with the US embassy in Peru as to the paperwork. So is the funeral home I've contacted, which is designated as an acceptable business for the transportation and receipt of bodies. We'll have to decide how you want to proceed and then make payment for any services. Beau and I set up a small checking account with both our names on it, to be used in emergency circumstances such as this."

Tiffany's breath came out in a puff of worry. "It sometimes seems to me as if Beau knew he was going to die. Do you think he did?"

"No, but he was aware the trip could be a dangerous journey and wanted to cover any contingencies. I've discovered he didn't get the right travel insurance though. If he had, it would've made some of this easier."

Tiffany remained silent. She finally said, "Couldn't you make these decisions alone?"

Kevin shook his head. "I want Regard to know you're aware and involved in following Beau's requests. I'm sorry, but I think it's important."

"Okay. I understand." She knew he was right. Regard would think of it as a sign of weakness if she didn't participate. Then he'd try to take over.

They entered a white clapboard building that resembled a classic Southern plantation home. A man in a dark suit greeted them at the door and said in a soft modulated voice, "Welcome. You are the Beau Wright party?"

Kevin held out his hand. "Kevin Bascombe." He turned to her. "And this is Tiffany Wright, Beau's wife."

The man clutched Tiffany's hand and gave her a look of regret. "I'm Jeremy Pratt, owner of the Pratt Funeral Home. We are so sorry for your loss. We'll do everything we can to make this process as easy for you as possible."

He took her elbow. "Please, come this way. We can talk in my office."

The depressing smell of the floral arrangements that filled every room nauseated Tiffany as she walked to a tastefully furnished office in the back of the building.

"Please have a seat." Jeremy indicated chairs for them. "Would you like anything to drink? Water? Coffee? Coke?"

"No, thanks." Tiffany sat down in a chair alongside Kevin's. Images of Beau, so alive, so happy, filled her mind.

"We've been in contact with the embassy in Peru," explained Jeremy. "Nothing's been done to prepare the body for return as of yet." He turned to Tiffany. "One thing you might want to consider is cremation. It will make it much easier for you to get his remains home. The easiest way, of course, is to have someone carry them back on a flight. But they can be shipped as well."

Tiffany looked at Kevin. "I think Beau would be very pleased if you went to Peru and brought him home." She'd go if she could, but with the baby it was impossible.

Kevin gave her a penetrating look. "If you want me to do it, I will, Tiffany. For Beau and for you."

"Will Regard be upset if you do it?" She couldn't hide the worry in her voice.

"I don't see how. Beau wanted to be cremated anyway. Maybe this will forestall any continuing argument from Muffy and Regard concerning burial. Of course, it won't stop them from having the memorial service they want."

Kevin turned to Jeremy. "Okay, then, let's make sure all the paperwork is in order. As we discussed earlier, as a designated funeral home for transporting bodies, you can help us at both ends. Right?"

"Of course," said Jeremy. "You'd be surprised how many times we're called upon to do this sort of thing. With people traveling all over the world encountering accidents and natural endings, it's become a needed service."

Tiffany half listened to the details of the arrangements being made to take care of Beau's remains. She told herself his body was now an empty shell, but that didn't stop the ache in her heart.

When the discussion ended, she stood with Kevin. Swaying on her feet, she tried to steady herself. Kevin's strong arm came around her. He said good-bye to Jeremy for both of them and they left the building.

Outside in the fresh air, Tiffany took deep breaths and tried not to think of Beau's body being reduced to ashes.

Tiffany arrived home to find Carol Ann marching around the living room with Vanna. The baby was wailing, her cries rising above the song Carol Ann was singing slightly off-key.

She rushed forward to take the baby from Carol Ann. "Oh my goodness! Has she been crying the whole time I was gone?"

"She took a little nap and awoke around fifteen minutes ago." Carol Ann's voice was high with tension as she handed Vanna to her. "I tried everything I could think of to get her to take a bottle, but she kept pushing it away."

Tiffany looked down at Vanna's red, tear-streaked face. "Poor baby girl. Okay, I'll feed you," she crooned. "Carol Ann, want to stay a bit? Maybe have a cup of coffee or tea?"

"A cup of coffee sounds great. I'll get it for myself. Would you like one too?"

Tiffany smiled. "That would be nice. I need something to keep me going." She undid her blouse and lowered herself onto the couch with the baby.

Carol Ann brought a cup of coffee to Tiffany and sat in a nearby chair. "You're such a good mother," she murmured. "I don't know if I could ever handle it." She let out a snort. "First, though, I have to find a man. I'm thinking of signing up for the dating service again. What do you think?"

Tiffany gave Carol Ann a steady look. "Do you really want to go through all that again?"

"How else am I going to find anyone in this town?"

Tiffany couldn't think of another good way to meet men in their small town. It was more of a family-type community. "Maybe online dating would work this time," she said, seeing how upset Carol Ann was. "How are you doing in your search for an apartment?"

Carol Ann let out a sigh. "I haven't been able to find anything decent. I even looked in Lynetta's complex, which is farther out than I wanted. But they're all rented at the moment."

Tiffany couldn't hide a grin. "How about this apartment?"

"What do you mean? I couldn't afford to live here." Carol Ann indicated the room with a wave of her hand. "This must cost a bundle."

"Actually, it doesn't," said Tiffany. "I rent it from Karen. I'm sure she'd give you the same break she gave me."

Eyes aglow, Carol Ann clasped her hands together. "Really? Do you think she would?" She stopped. "But wait a minute! Where are you going to live?"

"I'm going to buy Sukie's house. Wouldn't that be cool?"

Carol Ann's head bobbed enthusiastically. "I love her house. I always have." A look of wonder filled her face. "If this works out, it would be fantastic! You have no idea what it would mean to me."

Tiffany smiled. She, like everyone else in the group, knew very well how miserable Carol Ann was living at home. They'd been talking to her about it for what seemed like forever.

"I don't know when the purchase will take place." Tiffany's breath caught. "I have a lot to take care of before I can think about moving."

Suddenly it was all too much. "I'm sorry," Tiffany murmured and burst into sobs.

Her life had turned into a carousel of emotions that spun her round and round. She couldn't imagine being able to deal with all that lay ahead, not without the hope of being with Beau again.

CHAPTER FORTY-FIVE
SUKIE

Saturday evening, Sukie met Lynetta and her son outside the library. She smiled inwardly at the teen, who towered above his mother. He was wearing a frown that told Sukie that Lynetta was in charge.

"Sukie, I'd like you to meet Jackson," Lynetta said and turned to him. "And this is Ms. Sukie Skidmore."

He politely held out his hand and, giving her a steady look, nodded. A handsome boy, Sukie thought. No wonder the girls in that apartment complex were interested in him.

"Come on inside, Jackson. I'll show you where the story hour takes place."

"I'll see you later. I'm going to stop by Tiffany's place," said Lynetta. "I'll be back to pick you up, Jackson."

He gave a small wave and followed Sukie inside.

She turned to him. "Having a teenager read to the little kids is an experiment. If this goes well, we'll find other teens to do the same thing. It's really important to me and the library that this works well."

His face brightened. "How many kids?"

"Anywhere from eight to twenty," Sukie said, remembering how the innovative program had started with six and had grown under her direction. Everyone but Edythe Aynsley had been a big supporter—she'd objected to kids wearing their pajamas to the library. Edythe had declared it unseemly. Even now, thinking of it, Sukie was annoyed.

Jackson picked out two books to read, leaving two for Sukie.

"Do you like to read?" Sukie asked.

He shrugged. "Not stuff like this. I read all the Harry Potter books, though. And Rick Riordan's stuff is pretty cool."

"Good," said Sukie, hiding another smile. She'd bet anything he was one of those kids who became involved in anything he read. She hoped so, because she wanted to start a reading group for teens.

"Hello, there."

Sukie turned to see Cam walking toward her with Chloe.

Dressed in pink pajamas and wearing her favorite pink ballet slippers, Chloe all but danced across the room to Sukie. "I'm here!" She threw her arms around Sukie's legs and gazed up at her with a huge smile. "And I brought Sally." She held up the doll whose hair had seen too many combings.

"That's nice." Sukie lifted Chloe and hugged her. Turning to Jackson she said, "Chloe is about to become my stepdaughter. And this is Cameron Taylor, my fiancé. Cam, Jackson Greene."

"Cool," Jackson said, accepting Cam's extended hand.

"Who's he?" Chloe said, pointing to Jackson. She wiggled to get down from Sukie's arms.

"That's Jackson. He's my helper this evening."

Chloe looked up at Jackson with round blue eyes. "Are you gonna read to me?"

Jackson nodded. "Yes."

"Can I sit in your lap?"

Jackson shot Sukie an uncertain glance.

"He'll be busy reading, but you can sit right next to him. How about that, Chloe?"

"Okay." She grinned and took hold of his hand.

He walked Chloe over to the circle of chairs and pillows and they sat down.

"Bless his heart," Sukie murmured. As Cam left, she went to greet the other children entering the room.

Later, listening to Jackson reading aloud to the children, Sukie couldn't hide her satisfaction. Her new fall program was working. The kids loved Jackson and he'd come alive with the telling of it, even adding a few gestures to the story.

By the time Sukie read the last book, children's heads were nodding. Two of the children were already asleep, curled up on the carpeted floor like kittens.

After all the children were escorted outside with their parents, Sukie locked up the library behind her and waited with Jackson and Chloe for Lynetta to show up.

In no time, Lynetta pulled into the lot. As soon as the headlights blinked off, she emerged from her car and walked over to greet them.

"How'd it go?" She gave Sukie a quizzical look then turned to Jackson.

Jackson shrugged. "Okay, I guess."

"He was wonderful," gushed Sukie, meaning every word of it. "I told him he'd make a wonderful teacher someday."

Lynetta's eyes glistened. "Like James."

Jackson let out a snort of disgust and started to walk away.

Sukie held him back. "I mean it, Jackson. You have a way with kids that not many do."

"Can he teach me?" said Chloe, standing at Sukie's side.

Sukie and Lynetta looked at each other and laughed.

"Maybe someday Jackson will be a teacher. We'll have to wait and see." Sukie exchanged a smile with him.

Sukie waved them off, thinking no one, not even Edythe Aynsley, could object to what she'd done to make the program even better.

CHAPTER FORTY-SIX
TIFFANY

Tiffany sat with her friends at a table in Bea's Kitchen, waiting for the waitress to bring their orders for the Fat Fridays luncheon. Vanna lay in her car seat, staring around the noisy room with interest. It seemed strange to Tiffany to be here without Betsy and Karen, but she was pleased to see the others. She felt so trapped in that apartment with no one else to talk to that she sometimes cried.

Sukie patted her hand. "Are you all right?"

Tiffany let out a sigh and looked around the table. "I'm thinking about switching Vanna to a bottle. I need to be able to have others feed her. I'll be very busy with Beau's charity and I can't always have her with me. If I don't continue nursing Vanna, will that make me a bad mother?"

"No," said Grace firmly. Lynetta and Sukie quickly agreed.

"You're a good mother," said Carol Ann. "I don't know how you do it. I don't think I could."

"Thanks. I want to be the best mother I can, but I don't think I can handle nursing anymore. The physician's assistant at the pediatrician's office told me to keep on with it. I tried to explain everything to her, but she wouldn't listen."

"You've given Vanna a good, healthy start," said Sukie. "Don't let anyone tell you what to do. You know your body and your life best."

Grateful these women weren't as quick to judge, Tiffany smiled. "Thanks." She'd been feeling so inadequate lately, and their opinions mattered.

"So what else is new, everybody?" Sukie asked the group.

Tiffany and Carol Ann exchanged secret smiles but said nothing about the apartment. Not all the arrangements had been made.

"I've got news," Lynetta said. A smile lit her face and spread to her dark eyes.

Tiffany leaned forward with the others.

"James and I had a date. Sort of," said Lynetta.

"And?" Carol Ann said.

"And it was wonderful. He came to my apartment and we watched a movie—one of those spooky ones he likes."

"And?" Tiffany said, laughing at the heightened color in Lynetta's cheeks.

"And after the movie and with the boys asleep, we had some time alone and decided to see each other exclusively." She gave them a shy grin. "Not that anyone else is interested in me."

"Is he . . . you know, is he, well, hot?" Carol Ann said, bringing leers and laughter to the other women.

"Gawd," Carol Ann complained. "Y'all know what I mean."

"That we do," said Grace, shaking her head. "You and men!"

At the hurt expression that crossed Carol Ann's face, Tiffany rose to her defense. "She just cares. That's all."

"Well," said Lynetta, playing along, "I can honestly tell you he's smokin' hot."

Carol Ann clasped her hands together. "I knew it!"

"I'm happy for you," said Sukie, smiling. "We all need someone like that."

Tiffany's heart ached. In the beginning, she and Beau had been smoking hot together.

They finished lunch, and after the MacTel women left to return to the office, Tiffany put Vanna in the car and drove to Sukie's house.

Sukie was already there when Tiffany pulled into the driveway. Tiffany took a moment to take a fresh look at the house she hoped to buy. The large brick home, with its gables and peaks, sat atop a small knoll like a well-respected Southern lady. The white trim was spotless, the black front door a glossy background for the fall wreath that hung there. The lush landscaping added a softness to the building that was pleasing.

As Tiffany slid out of the car, Sukie greeted her. "Come on in."

She held the car door open while Tiffany unhooked Vanna's car seat and gingerly lifted the seat out of the car, careful not to wake her baby.

Inside the front entrance of the house, Tiffany felt a sense of peace wrap itself around her. She'd always loved this house. Even now, it produced a dichotomy of reactions from her—it was stately; it was warm. It was large; it was comfy. It was classic; it was homey from all the added touches Sukie had made to it over the years. In truth, it wasn't that much smaller than the house Muffy and Regard had given her and Beau. But it didn't have an air of pretension about it. And to Tiffany, that made all the difference.

Sukie checked her watch. "My real estate agent will be here soon. I thought it best if you and she talked about the house without my presence."

"Thanks." She couldn't be foolish about making a big decision like this. No matter what she did, it would piss off Regard.

"All my furniture will be removed," said Sukie. "I'm sure you'll want your own."

They walked into the kitchen. Gray granite countertops and pale yellow walls gave a nice setting to the space. The French doors leading to the patio and garden outside lent an openness to the eating area. Tiffany could already envision a playground swing set beyond the large flagstone patio.

At the sound of the doorbell, Sukie left her to greet her real estate agent. She returned a moment later and introduced Tiffany to Cherie Dickerson.

"Good-bye. See you later." Sukie gave Tiffany a hug. "Good luck."

Tiffany watched her go, wondering if she could make this house as welcoming as Sukie had.

By the time she had toured the house and talked to Cherie about the neighborhood, Tiffany felt a new kind of excitement. It would be a wonderful home for Vanna and her. She could hear the sounds of older kids playing outside, and through the windows she saw other mothers walking babies in strollers. Best of all, Sukie would be living close to her. After feeling so alone, so lost, it seemed the perfect choice.

CHAPTER FORTY-SEVEN
CAROL ANN

At the thought of a means of escape sometime soon, Carol Ann found it almost impossible to be at home. One more paycheck and she'd have enough for first and last month's rent, plus extra for all the little things she'd need to set up housekeeping in Tiffany's apartment. If, and it was a big if, Karen would agree to the price. She'd have to add furniture in bits and pieces.

Carol Ann stretched across her bed and leafed through one of her favorite magazines. With Tiffany unable to sing, there was no group gathering at the Glass Slipper on this Saturday night. Sukie was at the library doing her Nighty Night thing, Lynetta was visiting Tiffany, and Grace, she knew, was attending the single parent's support group she'd recently joined.

Bored, Carol Ann put aside the magazine and got to her feet. Bending over, she pulled out the large storage box she kept under her bed. For years, she'd picked up housekeeping items on sale—anything from towels to kitchenware to sheets—for the day when she could own a house of her own. It was a sad situation for someone who hadn't been able to find a man to share those things with her. Now, she was thankful to hopefully rent a place. After being swindled by John, her online boyfriend, that was the sorry state of her affairs.

Carol Ann opened the box and lifted out the white terry robe she'd bought on the cruise—the one that said Ocean Sea Lines. She'd thought it so classy the first night aboard the ship. But after using it to cover her nakedness following her night of sex with Ramón, she'd almost left it behind.

At the thought of him and what she'd done, a sick feeling rolled through her. How could she have been so dumb? She let out a very unladylike burp and decided that once she moved out, she'd never have the frozen pizza her family had for dinner. Every. Damn. Saturday. Night.

She pulled out one of the cookbooks she'd purchased a few months ago. Inside were scrumptious-looking recipes for healthy, low-cal meals. Leafing through it, Carol Ann thought about how much fun it would be to cook for someone. Here at home, her mother criticized everything she did in the kitchen. And the few times she'd attempted to make something her mother would call fancy, the woman had fussed about the mess in the kitchen.

Carol Ann sat back on her heels. It amazed her sometimes to think she'd come from this family. She'd never related well to her sister or her parents. They'd never wanted to try anything new. Lord help her if she urged them to do things differently.

Carefully folding the robe, she gently placed it and the cookbook back in the box and then slid it under her bed, where her mother wouldn't see it. She rose, went over to the small desk she'd purchased at a garage sale, and took out her checkbook. The figures wavered before her. As soon as she could, she'd move into Tiffany's apartment and live in a style more suitable to her. Then her sister could do their parents' bidding, for a change.

As if her sister had read her mind, Becky called. "Got your message. Sorry I wasn't home when you called. What's the big news you wanted to tell me about?"

"I might be able to move out sooner than I thought." Carol Ann shivered with joy. "I just wanted to give you a heads-up."

"You know it's not fair to dump Mama and Daddy on me, Carol Ann."

She ignored the whine in her sister's voice. "For years, while you've been living your life, I've been Mama's slave."

"What's gotten into you, Carol Ann?" snapped Becky. "You used to be so sweet."

Carol Ann knew the game Becky was playing, and this time she wasn't going to join in. "It's time I lived on my own, Becky," she said, working hard to control her voice. "It's my turn to have some freedom."

"It's those friends of yours, the ones Mama told me about. They've changed you."

"I hope so," said Carol Ann, loving them.

She intended to live life well, maybe date, maybe travel. Maybe she'd find a man she could bring back to the apartment if she wished—or not. The choice, for once, would be hers.

Before things could break down into a sister spat that went nowhere but down, Carol Ann said, "Gotta go. Talk to you later."

As she hung up the call, Carol Ann felt a sense of satisfaction. It hadn't been too long ago that she'd quietly done what her family expected of her. No more.

CHAPTER FORTY-EIGHT
SUKIE

Now that the sale of the house was imminent, Sukie began packing in earnest. Sitting on the floor beside her were three empty boxes—one for Rob and Madeleine, one for Elizabeth, and one for Ted. What she didn't want for herself, she'd pack up for the others.

She was sorting through kitchen drawers when the chirp of her cell phone made her pause. She checked caller ID. Ted.

Smiling, she picked up. "I was just thinking of you. I'm packing up the kitchen and setting aside some things I thought you might be able to use in the condo."

"Thanks, but I'm calling to tell you that I'm not coming back to town. I've met someone in the program and I'm moving to North Carolina."

Sukie was so surprised she couldn't speak for a minute.

"Well, aren't you excited for me?" Ted asked.

"Who is she? What are you going to do in North Carolina? And won't you miss the kids?" North Carolina wasn't that far away, but he'd miss so much of little Jonathan's growth.

"It's not a her and it's not like that. I'm going to be president of a new small bank outside of Raleigh." Ted's voice rang with his old self-importance, and for once Sukie was glad to hear it. "It turns out that the guy I met here knows Simon Prescott. We got to talking and when he told me about this opportunity, I called Simon. We all agreed to make it work."

"I'm really happy for you," Sukie said sincerely. "What about your condo?"

"I've decided to gift it to Rob and Madeleine." The excitement in his voice filled Sukie with tenderness. "What with paying all the tuition for Elizabeth's law degree, I owe them something, too. We'll have to work out all the tax issues, of course, but they are totally thrilled. I asked them not to say anything about it until I'd talked to you. What do you think?"

"I think you've become the man I first married. I'm really proud of you."

"Thanks. Emmy Lou and I have parted ways for good. When I threatened to take away the Mercedes if she didn't tell me the truth, she admitted the baby is Jordan's. She gets the SUV and nothing else. As it is, she's damn lucky to get it. I just want her out of my life, out of yours."

The husband who'd deceived her had disappeared in a cloud of goodwill. It was a very nice feeling. "Maybe I can help you. The house has a contract on it, and I'm packing up everything. You didn't want anything from the house before, but do you want some of it now?"

"Yeah. I'm going to get a condo when I move and I might be able to use some of the furniture. You're the one with the good taste. Can you help me decide what to take with me?"

"Sure," Sukie said, liking Ted more than she had in many years.

They talked about timing and then it was time for Ted to go.

As soon as she disconnected the call, Sukie phoned Madeleine.

"Hi, I just got a call from Ted . . ."

"Can you believe it?" said Madeleine before Sukie could finish. "The condo is so beautiful and it's going to be ours." She sounded close to crying. "Ted is giving us a good deal on it or we'd never be able to buy it. Rob is working out those details with Ted, but it's going to happen."

Sukie frowned. "Ted told me he's *giving* it to you, not selling it to you."

"Uh, not exactly," said Madeleine. "But like I said, it's enough of a good deal for us that we can swing it."

Sukie decided to let the matter drop but inside she was annoyed. Maybe Ted hadn't changed all that much. She wondered if he'd misspoken about other things. "Is Emmy Lou still living in the condo?"

"She left this morning. She took the car, and when we checked, all her personal belongings were gone. Everything else is still there and in good shape." Madeleine lowered her voice. "I'm surprised she didn't try to steal some things."

"After stealing my husband? Maybe taking him taught her a lesson," Sukie said wryly.

Sukie and Madeleine laughed together. Until Ted went into rehab, he'd been a gigantic pain in the ass.

They chatted about the logistics of making the move to the condo on the lake.

"I've agreed to help Ted select furniture for a new place in North Carolina. He can have whatever furniture he wants from the house."

"And he can take whatever he wants from the condo," said Madeleine. "Let's meet and walk through the condo together to see what he might like to take from there."

"Sounds good."

As Sukie was ready to hang up, Madeleine said, "Hold on, Rob just walked through the door."

"You heard?" said Rob to her as soon as she said hello. "Can you believe it?"

"It's wonderful," said Sukie, delighted for him. "Your father hasn't been known to be too generous in the past. I'm glad to see him change, and I'm happy that you and Madeleine are the recipients of this big-hearted gesture."

After chatting a little longer, Sukie hung up smiling. Some days were filled with little miracles.

CHAPTER FORTY-NINE
TIFFANY

Kevin phoned Tiffany from the airport in Atlanta to say he was on his way home. The trip to Peru and back had taken longer than either Kevin or Tiffany had thought, but it somehow felt right to her that one of the two people Beau trusted most was bringing him home.

After disconnecting the call, Tiffany wandered out to the balcony of her apartment. She inhaled the air, cooler now with the appearance of fall. The trees were beginning to show touches of oranges and reds, a precursor to the winter ahead. It was her favorite time of year.

At the sound of her cell phone ringing, Tiffany hurried inside to answer it. She'd just put Vanna down for a nap and needed a break from her endless routines with the baby.

Checking caller ID, Tiffany froze. It was Regard.

"Hello?"

"Tiffany, Regard here. We just wanted to make sure you and the baby will be attending the memorial service we've gone ahead and planned for Beau. We expect you to be here."

As much as she hated the idea, Tiffany said, "We'll be there for the service and leave for home directly afterwards. That'll make it easier for everyone." Muffy had suffered a total collapse and was only now resurfacing.

"Yes, I think that will be best," Regard said regretfully, and Tiffany's heart squeezed at the pain she heard in his voice.

"You're welcome here whenever Muffy is feeling up to it," she said sympathetically. Tiffany preferred to have them come to Williston, where she could more safely meet them on her own turf.

"You know, Tiffany, that apartment isn't really suitable for our Vanna," said Regard. "You'd better move back into Beau's house."

Tiffany drew a deep breath and willed herself to be strong. "Actually, I plan on selling it and buying another house, one in a neighborhood I know and like. There are plenty of children living there and lots of people my age."

"Sell it?" Regard's voice rose dangerously. "Do you know how much I paid for that house? You'll never get our money out of it. I can't allow you to do it. I wanted it in Beau's name only for this very reason, but I was overruled."

"I've been assured the house is mine to do with as I wish." Tiffany's knees shook almost as much as her voice.

"This whole business is crazy," snapped Regard. "And I'm pretty sure this Kevin Bascombe is a big part in all this. I'm having him investigated. Do you know where he is? I've been trying to get hold of him."

"I believe he's on his way back here from the airport. He went to Peru to get Beau's ashes."

"Ashes? What in hell and damnation are you talking about?"

At the fury she heard in Regard's words, Tiffany's hands turned so cold she almost dropped the phone.

"Well, young lady. Are you going to answer me or not? Do I have to come down there this instant?"

Tiffany swallowed hard. "Beau requested to be cremated, so we followed his wishes. You knew we would. We told you so."

"His wishes be damned! He's a Wright and needs to be treated as such."

His words stung Tiffany. "He was my husband and I loved him. I wanted him to be well and happy and see our daughter grow. Now he never will! But I can do my best to follow his wishes. Don't you get it?"

"What I get, young lady, is a plot against Muffy and me, his parents."

At the sound of a knock at the door, Tiffany wanted to weep with relief. "There's someone at the door. I've got to go. But Regard, this isn't about you and Muffy and a plot. Beau just wanted things his way for once. Why don't you understand?"

Regard was still shouting when Tiffany clicked off the call with shaking fingers.

She hurried to the door, opened it, and all but flew into Lynetta's arms.

"What's going on?" Lynetta asked, wrapping her arms around Tiffany. She stepped back and gave Tiffany a worried look. "You all right?"

Tiffany shook her head. "Beau's father called. He gets so angry that he sometimes scares me."

"Well, now, he's not here and I am. So let's go inside and calm down."

Lynetta's words were like velvet caressing Tiffany's skin. She drew a deep breath and steadied herself. "You're right. I shouldn't let him upset me so. And Kevin said he'd be at any meeting I had with Muffy and Regard."

"Such a nice man," Lynetta said. "One of Beau's best friends, I understand."

"His only real friend, I think," Tiffany said, and realized it was true. She hadn't heard from any of his so-called buddies—the guys, no doubt, who used to do drugs with him.

"Come on inside," Tiffany said. "It's a little chilly. How about a cup of hot coffee or tea?"

"Sounds good, hon," said Lynetta, following her into the kitchen.

Sitting at the kitchen table, sipping coffee with Lynetta, Tiffany felt her fear ebb away. As scared as she'd been, it'd felt good to stand up to Regard. She wished she'd done more of it when Beau was alive.

Vanna woke up with a cry.

"Can I help?" Lynetta said, her eyes alight.

Tiffany smiled at her eagerness. "If you'd give her a bottle, that would be perfect. Kevin is on his way here from the airport, and I'd like to go outside to meet him." She checked the clock on the microwave. "He should be here any moment."

Tiffany accompanied Lynetta into Vanna's room. They tiptoed over to the crib and peered down at the baby.

Vanna stopped making noises and stared up at them, her blue eyes wide. Then a smile crossed her pink face.

A surge of love filled Tiffany. For a moment Vanna had looked so much like Beau that it hurt, but it pleased her to see a part of him so alive.

"Such a beautiful little girl," crooned Lynetta, picking Vanna up.

Tiffany laid out a change of clothes for her baby. "I'll leave you to this and go outside."

"Go ahead. I've got her," said Lynetta. A smile spread across her face. "So nice to hold a baby again."

◆ ◆ ◆

On the lawn outside the apartment building, Tiffany looked up at the bright blue sky and wondered about Beau's spirit. Certainly a part of it would live on in their daughter. And she'd keep his memory alive in her heart forever. He'd been her first real adult love.

Puffy white clouds drifted by, turning the sky into an easel of possibilities. Staring at the shapes of the clouds, Tiffany imagined she saw Beau's familiar face and let out a sigh at all that might've been.

Kevin's car drew into the parking lot, catching her attention.

She walked over and stood by as he parked his car and got out.

Studying him, Tiffany realized how tired he was. She gave him a quick hug. "Thank you for making the trip, Kevin."

His smile was tender. "I'm glad I did. There were a lot more details to work out than I thought."

Tiffany gazed at the car. "Is he . . . inside?"

Kevin nodded. "I've got the remains. Hold on. I'll get them for you." He reached into the backseat of his SUV. Turning, he handed her a small canvas bag.

With trembling hands, she accepted the bag and looked inside. A very plain-looking square box sat inside.

"The container had to be lead-free and simple so it could go through security. I picked out a more permanent container in case you want to keep a few of the ashes around. I think Beau would like that. Don't you?"

A shudder crossed Tiffany's shoulder. "I don't want them, but maybe it would help Muffy to have them. She's devastated by the death of her son."

Kevin nodded. "Okay. We'll work that out. How are you doing?"

"I just had a call from Regard. He's furious about everything. And Kevin, he's having you investigated."

Kevin made a face. "That bastard. He won't find anything to worry about, but still, it's damn degrading."

"I'm going to ask the women in the group to go with me to scatter all but those few of Beau's ashes. Would you like to come?"

"Yes. Thanks for asking. I also made promises to Beau. Promises I intend to keep."

As they walked together to the apartment building, Tiffany wondered how she could manage the next few days when her spirits were so low.

CHAPTER FIFTY
SUKIE

Sukie was helping Chloe out of the good dress she'd worn to church when her cell phone rang. She checked caller ID and clicked on the call.

"Hi, Tiffany! How are you?"

"Okay, I guess. I need to ask a favor of you. Can you come to my apartment? Kevin has brought back Beau's remains. It's such a beautiful fall day I've decided to go ahead and scatter his ashes this afternoon. I want everyone in the Fat Fridays group to be there. Will you come?"

"Of course," Sukie said simply, touched by the invitation. It proved to her how valuable their friendship was.

Downstairs, she explained to Cam what was going on. "Sorry I won't be able to help you with the project in the garage." They'd decided to make part of the three-car garage a storage area for things Sukie would bring from her house.

"No problem. I'll continue by myself."

Sukie hugged him hard. "Anyone ever tell you how wonderful you are?"

"A few women here and there," he said grinning, "but none in the same way as you."

She laughed. "Guess I'll have to keep showing you, huh?"

Smiling, he lowered his lips to hers.

His kiss sent pleasure singing through Sukie's body in delicious notes. She leaned into him, loving the feel of his body pressed against hers. Their curves fit so nicely, soft against strong.

When he pulled his face away, the smile that had coated his features was replaced by a look of concern. "Give Tiffany my regards. I'll be here for you when you return."

She hugged him even harder, grateful for his support. "I know. Thanks."

◆　◆　◆

Sukie pulled into the parking lot of the Glenview Apartments. Grace and Carol Ann were heading up the walkway to Tiffany's apartment building.

She scrambled out of her car.

"Wait for me!" she cried and hurried to catch up to them.

"Glad you're here," said Grace. "It's such a sorrowful time we all need to stick together. I promised Tiffany I'd take pictures for Betsy and Karen." She flexed her fingers. Her cast had been removed, but physical therapy was still very much a part of Grace's recovery from the gunshot wound.

"I'm so glad you'll do that." Sukie patted Grace on the back. "Betsy will be disappointed she wasn't able to be here, but she'll understand. It's such a difficult situation and Tiffany wanted it over."

They entered Tiffany's apartment to find Lynetta holding Vanna. The baby was dressed in blue overalls, pink socks, a pink shirt, and a blue sweater.

"Can I hold her?" Grace said.

"Sure. Here you go," Lynetta said, handing the baby over to her. "Tiffany's getting ready."

"How is she?" Sukie asked quietly.

Lynetta shook her head. "It's a tough time. She and Kevin saved some of the ashes for Muffy." She indicated the fireplace mantle with a nod of her head. "They're stored in that beautiful box."

Sukie turned her gaze to the brass box sitting there. "I'm sure Muffy will appreciate it. It's a lovely gesture on Tiffany's part."

Tiffany appeared, her eyes red and swollen. Seeing them, her lips curved into a quivering smile. "Thank you for coming. I knew you'd all be there for me. I talked to Betsy and Karen. They said they'd be with us in spirit."

"So where is this place you want us to go?" said Grace. "Someplace on the lake you said?"

Tiffany nodded. "I'll take a few of you in my car. Maybe, Sukie, you can follow me and take the rest of the group in yours. Kevin will ride with me."

"I'll be glad to," said Sukie.

A somber group, they left the apartment.

In the parking lot, Kevin was standing next to Tiffany's SUV. He acknowledged them with a nod and waited for Grace to get in before sliding onto the passenger's seat in front.

Lynetta and Carol Ann followed Sukie to her car, and they headed out.

Willis Lake was touted as the finest feature of Williston. Shallow along the edges, it quickly sloped to a greater depth in the center. Roughly thirty square miles, it was the site of an expensive condominium complex and a number of upscale homes. Sukie had always loved the area, which was why it had irked her to have Ted buy there after he left her.

"Where is she leading us?" asked Carol Ann as they bypassed the condos, the small marina, and a number of houses. "We've been driving forever."

"I know nothing about the spot," said Sukie. "Just that it was a special place for her and Beau."

Sukie drove past even more houses and then followed Tiffany onto a dirt road. The dusty drive led into a wooded area that had remained undeveloped. She pulled up beside Tiffany's car and lowered her window. "Is this it?"

From inside Tiffany's car, Kevin nodded and opened his car door.

Sukie parked the car, unbuckled her seat belt, and climbed out, glancing around with interest.

The clean smell of pine met her nose in delightful waves. The only sounds she heard were the whispers of the trees as the wind gently caressed their swaying green branches.

"It's beautiful," said Carol Ann softly.

They gathered in a group, and Tiffany, holding Vanna, approached them. "Follow me down the path. There's a perfect spot that overlooks the water. Beau and I used to come here before we were married." She sniffed. "It's where he proposed to me."

Silently, filled with the importance of the moment, Sukie followed the others. Their steps were cushioned by the pine needles spread on the ground. At this uninhabited end of the lake closer to the water, the calls of birds and waterfowl broke the silence, adding a solemn note.

Tiffany led them to an opening among the pine trees. Below them, at the bottom of a gentle slope, the water met the shore in rippling waves. Above them, the sun shone through the trees, forming shadows on the ground around them.

Tiffany handed Vanna to Kevin and held out her hands. Sukie grabbed hold of one of them, Lynetta the other. Grace and Carol Ann joined in, forming a circle.

They stood in silence.

Sukie couldn't help but remember the time they'd formed a circle around Grace, willing her to live. She felt that same tenderness for Tiffany and the others who'd banded together for this occasion. She searched for words to comfort Tiffany.

"May I speak?" Sukie asked her.

"Please. It would mean so much to me."

"To quote Kahlil Gibran, one of my favorites—'Life without love is like a tree without blossoms or fruit.' Tiffany, I'm so glad you knew love with Beau. I know things weren't always easy for either of you, but to have shared that love is something special. And now you have a precious reminder of him and your love."

"Yes," said Grace. "We love you too. In a different way, of course, but deeply, my dear."

Lynetta nodded earnestly.

"Truly," said Carol Ann quietly.

"Thank you all for coming," said Tiffany, her voice trembling. "It is through your friendship that I was able to leave Beau in order for him to get help. He got that help and was getting his life back on track so that maybe someday we could get back together. I have to remember that." Tears streamed down her face. "And now with you, dear friends, I'm able to say good-bye to him."

She lifted her face and began singing "Only You" in a clear soprano voice that sent shivers darting down Sukie's back. When Tiffany finished singing, Sukie's cheeks weren't the only ones wet from weeping.

Tiffany dropped her hands and turned to Kevin.

Kevin handed Vanna to Sukie and left the group with Tiffany, carrying a simple square box.

From a distance, Sukie watched Tiffany and Kevin walk up to the water's edge. Opening the lid of the box, together they tossed the ashes up in the air. The breezes caught them and sent them flying in a cloud over the water. In moments, they were gone.

To give Tiffany and Kevin privacy, she turned with the others and walked away.

Life was so fragile, she thought, and determined to make the most of hers.

CHAPTER FIFTY-ONE

TIFFANY

Of all the things Tiffany was being asked to do for Beau, attending a memorial service he would've hated was her least favorite. Even though they both knew Regard might consider it an act of defiance, Kevin had agreed to accompany her. He'd previously warned Kevin to stay out of his family's business—a warning counter to his son's requests.

Sitting in Kevin's car, Tiffany stared out the window at the scenery going by like a fast-forward tape of a travel film. They'd agreed to leave before dawn so Tiffany wouldn't be required to spend the night before with Muffy and Regard. They'd also agreed to leave as soon as they tactfully could after the service and reception.

Betsy and Karen had called Tiffany to say they'd ordered flowers to be sent to the church. Tiffany had told the others in the group that they needn't take the time off from work to attend the service, but they'd all agreed to be there to support her. Now she was glad they'd insisted. Just knowing they would be nearby helped with the jitters that were already racking her body.

Kevin turned to her. "We'll be there shortly. Do you want to stop before we get there?"

"Yes, there's a very nice rest area up ahead. I'll change Vanna there." In honor of Beau, she'd make both the baby and herself as presentable as possible.

◆ ◆ ◆

Driving into Charleston, myriad feelings embraced Tiffany. Charleston was full of such history, such elegance, such beauty. As always, it made her feel insignificant.

Kevin drove up to the historical home that had housed the Wright family seemingly forever. As soon as he pulled to a stop in the driveway, Regard came out of the house to greet them.

"Glad you're here. Muffy's been worried sick you wouldn't show up," he said to Tiffany. A frown formed on his face at the sight of Kevin getting out of the car, but he said nothing more, simply standing by while Tiffany climbed out of the car.

She reached into the backseat to get Vanna.

Lifting the car seat out, Tiffany faced Regard. "How's Muffy? I have something for her, for both of you actually."

"She's about the same," said Regard. "She's inside. Come with me."

Regard led them inside the house, into the drawing room. Sitting on a sofa, wearing a black suit, looking half her normal size, Muffy held a Bible in her hands. When she looked up at Tiffany, her eyes filled. "Thank you for coming."

Muffy's gaze shifted to Vanna. She reached for the baby.

Glad she'd changed Vanna into a dress Muffy had given her, Tiffany handed the little girl over to her grandmother.

"Sweet, precious baby," murmured Muffy, nuzzling Vanna's cheek. Vanna waved her arms and kicked in protest.

"It's almost time for her bottle. Would you like to give it to her?" asked Tiffany, startled to see how frail Muffy had become.

Muffy's face brightened. "Could I?"

"Yes," Tiffany said. "I think she'd like that." She turned to Kevin, who'd been quietly standing by with Regard.

Wordlessly, Kevin handed Tiffany the small canvas bag he'd brought inside.

With trembling fingers, Tiffany lifted out a brass box containing a portion of Beau's ashes. She handed it to Regard. "I thought you'd like to have this. After following his wishes, it's all we have left of Beau."

Regard's eyes widened. His cheeks grew flushed. A number of emotions crossed his face and then he glared at her.

Tiffany braced herself for a scolding.

A sound, like the howl of a wolf, reverberated in the room, sending chills down Tiffany's spine.

Vanna let out a wail.

"Ohhh!" cried Muffy.

"I'm sorry," Tiffany said, stepping closer to Kevin. He placed a protective arm around her.

Regard rushed from the room.

Tiffany turned to Muffy. Tears were streaming down her cheeks. "Oh, Tiffany," she said. "You don't know what that means to Regard and me."

"But what about Regard? I thought . . ." she couldn't finish. She was so confused by Regard's actions and the emotions she'd seen on his face.

"You don't understand," said Muffy. "Regard's not angry with you. He's touched by your gift, but he didn't want to break down in front of you. He wants to be tough like all the Wright men are supposed to be."

Beau had had to fight against this type of thing all his life, Tiffany thought. It was such a shame—for Beau, for Regard, for everyone. A shiver crossed her shoulders. She'd never forget Regard's wail of pain.

Tiffany lowered herself onto the couch next to Muffy and rubbed Vanna's back until she'd quieted.

Muffy took hold of Tiffany's hand. "Thank you for your gift. I will always keep it with me."

"You're welcome," said Tiffany, forcing words out through a throat tightened with emotion.

◆　◆　◆

Sitting inside St. Michael's Church, Tiffany hardly saw the beauty throughout the historical building. True to form, Muffy had designed a memorial service for all of Charleston's society. And the family that was being described for all to hear wasn't the family Tiffany knew.

Aware of how much Beau would have hated such a showy splash and hollow words, Tiffany bowed her head, concentrating on the baby who'd fallen asleep in her lap.

Kevin's presence beside her was comforting. On the other side of her, Muffy wept into a lace handkerchief. Beyond Muffy, Regard sat tall, stoic and untouchable. Tiffany felt the supporting presence of Carol Ann, Grace, Lynetta, and Sukie sitting in the pew behind her and silently blessed them.

At the end of the service, guests were invited to a nearby restaurant for a reception to celebrate Beau's life.

In a cloud of memories, Tiffany walked with Muffy and Regard to the restaurant, not far away. There, in a large room reserved for the group, Tiffany was swept up into a crowd of people she didn't really know—friends of Muffy's and Regard's. She remembered a few of them from the fancy, extravagant wedding Muffy and Regard had put on for Beau and her—a wedding neither she nor Beau had wanted. But these people meant little to her. They'd never done more than socialize with her on a large scale she'd always found superficial.

Tiffany glanced at the buffet table. A ham sat at one end of the table, a roast beef at the other. In between were a variety of salads and heavy hors d'oeuvres. A bar had been set up at both ends of the room and seemed to be the busiest areas of activity.

Muffy carried Vanna among her friends, showing off the baby she insisted on calling Savannah Grace. Unable to think of eating or drinking while her stomach was knotted like a braid of bread, Tiffany waited for the moment she and Kevin could head back home.

She went to join her friends of the Fat Fridays group. Though they'd stayed close, Tiffany was happy to see that they were intermingling with others at the buffet table.

Sukie smiled at her. "We're going to head home. If we're lucky, we can get to Atlanta before the traffic becomes unbearable."

Tiffany threw her arms around her. "Thanks so much for coming. I really appreciate it. It's a lot of driving to do in one day."

"We were happy to make the trip for you."

The other women joined them. Grateful for their support, Tiffany hugged each woman so dear to her.

Kevin approached. "I think we should head out too."

Tiffany nodded. "Okay. I'll tell Muffy."

For once, Muffy didn't put up an argument about it, and Tiffany once more was reminded of how fragile Muffy had become.

Regard and Muffy walked Tiffany and Vanna out to the front of the restaurant, where Kevin was waiting for them with his car.

"Thanks," Muffy whispered as she gave Tiffany a hug.

Regard briefly embraced Tiffany. "I'll be in touch. There's still a lot to settle."

Tiffany knew enough about both of Beau's parents to understand they would persist until they got what they wanted. But this time, she had Beau on her side in a way that had never happened before. This time, she, not they, would win.

CHAPTER FIFTY-TWO
CAROL ANN

Overwhelmed by all she'd seen and heard, Carol Ann followed the others out of the church. St. Michael's, with its history and beauty, was awe-inspiring. And the people, with all their wealth, were like another species to her.

The soft slow cadence of Southern language floated around her as Carol Ann studied the stylish clothes the women wore and admired the wink of diamonds on their ears, fingers, and throats. The thought of moving out of her parent's humble home and making a new life for herself was like the taste of sugar on her tongue.

"Ready? Let's go to the reception," Sukie said, hurrying her along.

"I didn't get breakfast so I'm ready for a bite to eat," said Grace, following behind with Lynetta.

Carol Ann became part of the crowd walking down the street to the restaurant, a place called Belle's.

Inside the restaurant, Carol Ann was once again struck by the elegance around her. Pale coral velvet draperies hung at the windows, picking up those same hues in the light-blue patterned rug. Crisp linens topped the tables. Crystal sconces on the walls sparkled as sunlight poured through tall windows, forming beams of light that danced in the air.

Carol Ann trailed her friends to the buffet table, but the sight of food made her stomach turn. How, she wondered, could anyone think of eating after knowing what Tiffany was going through? She'd always admired Tiffany, had often been jealous of her, but of all the women in Fat Fridays, Tiffany was the least judgmental toward her. Maybe because they were closest in age.

Seeing Tiffany's pain, Carol Ann's heart had twisted in sympathy. Tiffany would never see Beau again. He'd never see their baby grow. Theirs had been a romance novel in the making, but with Beau's death, Carol Ann didn't know how it could ever have a happy ending.

"You're not having anything to eat?" Grace said to her.

Carol Ann shook her head. "I'll just have some water. The service upset me."

Grace patted her back. "It sure is a sad thing. Beau was turning his life around." She nodded in Vanna's direction. "That little one won't know her father." Regret entered Grace's voice.

Carol Ann knew Grace was thinking of her own daughter. "Heard from Misty yet?"

"Not yet, but at least she hasn't returned my letters. That's a move in the right direction. At least that's what my support group says."

"I hope to meet her one day," Carol Ann said, hoping to give Grace a note of encouragement.

Grace smiled. "I hope you meet her too."

Carol Ann left her to sit down at one of the empty tables. Carrying a plate of food, Lynetta joined her.

"Everything looks wonderful," Lynetta said. "You'd better get something to eat. We're heading back home soon."

Carol Ann sighed. Maybe she could choke something down. She got up and stood in line at the buffet table. Seeing all that food reminded her of the buffet lines aboard the ship. Her stomach took a dive. She closed her eyes until she grew steady and left the buffet table to find some ginger ale.

Sipping the bubbly beverage a few minutes later, Carol Ann vowed that when she got her own apartment, she'd have nothing but wholesome food for breakfast, not the frozen waffles her mother liked to keep in the house. That morning she'd rushed through two of them and now her stomach was rebelling.

Sukie motioned to Carol Ann. "Come here. We're getting ready to say good-bye."

Carol Ann joined the group forming around Tiffany.

"Thanks for coming," Tiffany said, giving Sukie a hug and then hugging each of them.

When it was Carol Ann's turn, she hugged Tiffany as hard as she could.

CHAPTER FIFTY-THREE
TIFFANY

Lying in bed, the empty space beside Tiffany seemed enormous. On the ride home from Beau's memorial service, she and Kevin had talked about what lay ahead for her. The Wright Children's Fund International would be in her hands. Tiffany had never felt so alone, so unsure. Not even striking out on her own at eighteen to attend college had seemed so scary.

Kevin had explained that while the legal paperwork setting up the charity was complete, the real guidance behind it would be up to her. In addition to being trustee of the estate, he was listed as CFO of the foundation. He went on to further explain that if she chose, she had the right and the ability to fire him and get someone else to take over the financial aspects of the charity.

At that possibility, she'd shrunk inside. "You'll stay, won't you?"

He gave her a solemn look. "As long as you want me to. Beau thought you and I would be able to work well together. He was going to bring you into the charity when he got back from Peru."

That surprised her as much as anything else. He'd always pooh-poohed her job at MacTel.

Now, thinking of all Kevin had told her, an eerie feeling came over Tiffany. It was all so neat and tidy, as if Beau knew something would happen to him and he'd chosen Kevin to take his place.

Exhausted, emotionally drained, she rolled over and hugged a pillow, wishing she could go back to an earlier, simple time when she and Beau had been happy.

◆ ◆ ◆

Tiffany awoke to Vanna's cries. After a restless night and time spent thinking about her situation, Tiffany decided to go ahead and call her boss, Glenn Mitchum, at MacTel as soon as she could. She'd once liked the thought of going back to work there, but her whole life had changed.

She entered Vanna's room and called softly to her daughter. Vanna's crying stopped. When Tiffany bent over the crib railing to pick her up, Vanna's face lit with pleasure. Tiffany smiled. "That's my baby girl. Come on. We've got a new day to face."

Tiffany quickly changed Vanna's diaper and then carried her into the kitchen. Resting the baby on her hip, she prepared a bottle for her.

Vanna kicked her feet and waved her arms with eagerness.

Tiffany took her and the bottle into the living room and took a seat on the couch. While Vanna was eating, Tiffany thought of the day ahead. She and Kevin were going to meet the lawyer handling Beau's will. He, too, was someone Beau had known from prep school days. It was interesting to her how Beau had chosen both old schoolmates to help him make the biggest decisions of his life.

Later that morning, while Carol Ann watched the baby, Tiffany and Kevin headed into Atlanta.

"Tell me about George Walker," Tiffany said. "You told me he also was a classmate of Beau's. I wonder why Beau never mentioned him or you to me."

Kevin stared straight ahead and then turned to her with a look of chagrin. "Probably because at one time he hated our guts for calling him out whenever he was being a total asshole."

"Oh." Tiffany hadn't seen the bad side of Beau until his parents had entered the picture.

"Beauregard Wright III was a spoiled little brat who lorded it over those of us who didn't come from backgrounds like his," Kevin continued. "His parents taught him his name would give him a lot of power and gain him whatever he wanted. Trouble was, he wasn't as good or as bright as he thought. Beau tried everything he could to take over for George Walker, the school's quarterback and football star. It got pretty ugly. Me? I wouldn't give in to his pleading to eliminate any black marks against him for bad conduct. George and I were among the few who stood up to Beau and his bullshit."

"So George is a lawyer now?" She couldn't wait to meet the guy who'd tackled Beau's parent-driven ego.

Kevin grinned. "In addition to being a great athlete, George has a brilliant mind. He got a full scholarship to Duke's law school. And when you meet him, you'll see that he's a true gentleman. The guy could run for public office, but he's way too smart and honest to do that."

Tiffany's curiosity grew.

Later, walking into the law office of White, Scoville, and Pemberton, she was struck by its quiet elegance. As she waited for Kevin to introduce himself to the receptionist, Tiffany glanced around the reception area. Massive glass windows filled the outside wall and displayed the heart of Atlanta. Oriental rugs covered the dark wooden floors like collections of colorful butterflies resting on wide tree branches. Plush chairs in muted tones offered places to sit down. Even the soft, modulated voices she heard around her added to the office's respectability.

The receptionist, an attractive middle-aged woman dressed in a gray suit, rose from behind her impressive desk and stood at the entrance to a long hallway.

She waved them forward. "Please come this way. George is expecting you."

Tiffany followed her down the hallway to its end and into a small conference room, where she and Kevin took seats at an oblong, highly polished mahogany table.

"Good morning," said a deep voice behind Tiffany.

She turned around to face a tall, broad-shouldered man whose brown eyes sparkled in a face of deep brown. His lips curved as his gaze settled on her. "You must be Beau's wife, Tiffany." He held out a large hand to her. "George Walker. I'm pleased to meet you, though I wish the circumstances were different."

Awestruck by his large presence and the way his personality dominated the room, she could barely speak. "Thank you. Kevin has told me a lot about you."

Kevin came over to George and they shook hands.

"Good to see you again, man," George told him. "We've got a lot to talk about. Have a seat."

George sat in a chair at the end of the table and faced them. "I got a call from Regard Wright this morning. He threatened to have his lawyer friends rip Beau's will apart. I told him in unequivocal terms the outcome would not be good, that it would cost him money and hurt his son's reputation."

"And what was his response?" Kevin said tersely.

"Surprisingly, he backed down. He did say, however, that he doesn't think the two of you should be the ones running the charity. He said a real Wright needs to be in charge."

Kevin laughed. "Beau knew his father would say this, which is why he even set up a board of directors that not only includes you, George, but a family friend he trusts."

George turned to Tiffany. "Regard mentioned that you're a nice girl, but that you should be staying home with the baby, not working on something like this."

Tiffany felt a flush of anger creep to her cheeks. "He's never liked the fact I worked, even when the money I brought in was very crucial to Beau and me when we tried to be independent. If Beau trusted me to run the charity, I'll do it. For him, for me, and for our daughter." The words came out with more force than she'd intended, but Tiffany was not about to soften what she'd said.

George and Kevin looked at each other and smiled.

"Good for you," George said. "I needed to know how determined you are to follow his wishes. Over the next weeks and months, we'll work to put WCFI into play with you on board." His features softened. "Beau told me his daughter was beautiful."

Smiling, Tiffany took out her cell phone and showed him a picture of Vanna.

"Yeah, she's gorgeous, all right. I see a bit of her father in her." He shook his head. "It still amazes me that Beau showed up here with Kevin, asking for my help. Over the last few years, I lost track of him. He and I were always at cross purposes."

"Kevin filled me in on it." Tears stung her eyes. "It's so heart-wrenching that with all the changes for good that Beau made recently, we won't ever get to work together on this. It's such a wonderful idea to use money to help children everywhere."

"He turned into a good man. That's something to remember," George said, giving her an understanding smile.

Later, leaving the office, Tiffany's mind whirled with facts and figures. Her life would be very busy with all she'd been given.

On the way home, she talked to Kevin about her plans.

"With the insurance money and other funds that are in your name, you'll have no problem purchasing Sukie's house," he told her. "If you'd like, I'll help you with the offer. We want the best price we can get. Right?"

Tiffany nodded, though to tell the truth, buying Sukie's house was another way to help Sukie and Carol Ann, and she'd do anything for the women who continued to stand by her.

CHAPTER FIFTY-FOUR
SUKIE

Sukie signed the purchase and sale agreement for her house with a happy sigh. This part of her life was over. Now she could concentrate on building her new life with Cam. He was a miracle, a second chance at love she'd never expected. She intended to enjoy every minute with him. Though she was glad to be moving on, she hoped Tiffany would fill the house with love of her own. It was a nice house, a good house.

After delivering the paperwork to her realtor, Sukie drove to Millville to talk to the people at Escapes about her wedding reception. The small wedding itself would take place in the little chapel at the Congregational church downtown.

Sukie drew up to the restaurant and got out of the car, full of excitement. In a short period of time, she'd be Cam's wife.

Inside Escapes, she saw the restaurant in a different light. Here she and her friends would celebrate one of the most important days of her life. Once more, she admired the finishing touches the owners had added to make their restaurant special.

"Hello, Ms. Skidmore?"

Sukie turned to face a small, thin woman with striking features. Dark hair was pulled away from a face lit by a beaming smile. "Hi, I'm Estelle, Glenn's wife."

Sukie introduced herself and explained why she was there.

Estelle gave her a thoughtful look. "Ah, yes. I remember our conversation. I think the Paris room will do very well. We can reserve it for a group of your size and work together to come up with a suitable menu and accompaniments." She urged Sukie forward. "Come. We'll take a look."

Standing in the room with pale yellow walls. Sukie admired the Monet paintings and other artistic touches that gave the room its name.

"This will be perfect," Sukie said, imagining the joy of celebrating here with Cam as Mrs. Cameron Taylor. Yes, Sukie Taylor was a fine name.

"How about music?" Sukie asked. "Could we have someone playing a piano or keyboard in here?"

Estelle frowned, then nodded. "As long as it's soft and tasteful, so to speak. We wouldn't want the other diners to be disturbed."

"Of course," said Sukie.

They left the room and went into the office, where Sukie signed some papers and made a deposit.

As she left the restaurant, Sukie felt like leaping for joy. It was all coming true. She and Cam would officially be together, living and loving and parenting one of the sweetest little girls in the world.

She checked her watch and climbed into her car. She'd have just enough time to call Cam before heading to the Fat Fridays lunch.

He answered her call right away. "Hello, gorgeous," he chirped. Ever since they'd set a date for the wedding, he'd become more and more pleased about their plans.

"How would you like to go to France for our reception?" she said.

He laughed. "You got the room?"

"Yes, and it's going to be lovely. We can even have our own music."

"Are you going to ask Tiffany to sing?"

"That's my plan," said Sukie, "but I want her to enjoy the reception too. So we'll have a keyboard player making soft background music for most of the evening." She couldn't keep the excitement out of her voice. "I'm so pleased!"

"Yeah, me too. Sorry, I gotta go, but I'll see you tonight and then we'll have the whole weekend to talk about it and get in some more practice for the honeymoon."

She laughed. "You're incorrigible!" But the idea of that kind of practice, as he called it, made her body heat up with anticipation.

On her way back to Williston, Sukie thought of Grace. It had been Grace's hope to have her daughter come for a visit at Thanksgiving and perhaps attend the wedding, but that wasn't going to happen. Now Misty was telling Grace she'd come at Christmas when she had more time. Sukie couldn't help wondering if that would turn out to be another broken promise. She hoped not. But only time would tell.

Life with the women in the Fat Fridays group was one surprise after another.

CHAPTER FIFTY-FIVE
CAROL ANN

Carol Ann sat at her desk on the exec floor of MacTel and stared with dismay at her credit card bill. It was a couple of hundred dollars more than she'd thought. Studying the figures, she realized the evening spent with Ramón in the bar on the cruise had been paid for by her, not him. He'd apparently offered her drinks and then had had the gall to have them billed to her tab. She'd missed it because they'd both had a lot to drink. And when she'd called the credit card company, she hadn't thought about fraud before that morning.

As the consequence of it struck her, Carol Ann's breath left her in a rush. She'd needed all the money she could get for a move to the apartment. Now, she'd have to wait a while longer. The memory of him in bed with her, telling her lies, satisfying himself, washed over her in sickening waves of humiliation.

She tossed the bill on her desk and raced into the ladies' room. Gagging, she barely made it to a toilet before getting sick.

Rising to her feet, her eyes filled. On wobbly legs, she went to the sink to rinse her mouth. She dabbed a cold, wet paper towel against her cheeks and wondered not for the first time how she could've been so foolish. A handsome man, a yearning for love, had made a fool of her yet again.

"Are you all right, Carol Ann?" said Lynetta, coming into the bathroom. She gave Carol Ann a worried look. "I saw you hurry inside."

Determined not to spill her pitiful story, Carol Ann nodded. "I just had some disappointing news, that's all." Lynetta didn't know the whole story about John cheating her out of money, and Carol Ann wasn't about to tell her or any of the other women what really happened on her cruise. They'd be as disgusted with her as she was with herself.

"I'm sorry about the bad news. When you feel like it why don't you come on out? The rest of us on the floor are talking about the need to find someone to permanently take Tiffany's place. Her boss got a call from her this morning. She's not coming back."

"I'm not surprised," said Carol Ann, pulling herself together. "And truthfully, it'll be a relief not to have to cover for her."

"Yes, indeed," agreed Lynetta. "Do you know of anyone who wants to come up here?"

Carol Ann shook her head. The exec floor was fast-paced and sometimes difficult for those dealing with the demanding top people of the company. Carol Ann managed it by having the best boss in the world.

"I guess they'll post the opening soon," said Lynetta. "We can talk more about it at lunch."

The morning flew by with one after another project being tossed her way. Having someone pick up Tiffany's share of the work would be welcomed by all, Carol Ann grumbled. But she wouldn't complain about it to the others. She needed this job more than ever if she was going to be able to move out of her parent's house.

Carol Ann was silent as she rode with Lynetta and Grace to Bea's Kitchen for the Fat Fridays luncheon. She couldn't stop thinking how she'd been cheated again. She shook her head. She was as stupid as her mother sometimes made her feel.

Sukie was already sitting at a table with Tiffany when Carol Ann joined the others inside the restaurant. She hurried over to them and took a seat. Vanna sat in her car seat beside Carol Ann, already a real part of the group.

Carol Ann smiled at the baby and shook her little hand, bringing a bright look to Vanna's face.

Once they were all seated, the waitress hurried over to take their orders. "What are all y'all having today?"

They placed their orders and then Sukie said, "I've got some good news. The wedding reception is going to take place at Escapes, the new restaurant in Millville. Naturally, you all are invited. Formal invitations should be coming out soon. Be sure and save the date—the Saturday before Thanksgiving."

Carol Ann halfheartedly joined in the jabber of congratulations. She'd probably never have such happy news.

Tiffany smiled at her. "It's official. I've bought Sukie's house. And Carol Ann, I heard from Karen. She'll honor the same low rent for her apartment."

Carol Ann clapped a hand to her mouth. "You mean it?" she said, and surprised herself by bursting into tears.

"Oh, hon," said Sukie. "Are you all right?"

"Sorry to be so emotional, but I can't tell you what this means to me." She swiped at her eyes. "So when are you moving, Tiffany?"

"Three weeks. Right after Thanksgiving. I want to be moved in for the Christmas holidays. I'm having the house repainted inside and new carpeting put down."

Carol Ann smiled. Three weeks. Two more paychecks. "Great. I can't believe I'll have my own place in time for Christmas."

The waitress brought their food, momentarily ending the conversation.

Carol Ann gazed down at the fried chicken plate. It was normally a favorite of hers. Growing woozy, she grabbed hold of the table's edge.

"What's wrong?" Grace said. "Are you sick?"

Carol Ann shook her head. "No, why?" She didn't want to tell them about Ramón and the sick feeling it gave her to think of what he'd done.

Grace gave her a steady look but said nothing more.

Carol Ann took a bite of chicken and swallowed hard. Instead of going down, the chicken gave her the weird sensation of rising in her throat. She jumped to her feet and dashed into the ladies' room.

When she emerged, her stomach empty, the other four women wore identical expressions of suspicion.

"What?" she said, easing herself down onto her chair.

"I know the signs. You're pregnant, aren't you?" said Tiffany.

"Me?" Carol Ann was barely able to control a high-pitched shriek. "How can I be pregnant? I don't even have a boyfriend!"

"What about the cruise?" asked Lynetta kindly. "You haven't told us much about it."

The blood left Carol Ann's face so rapidly, she felt faint.

"Put your head down between your knees," said Sukie gently. "Now take deep breaths."

Carol Ann sucked in air and let it out in nervous gasps. Thinking of the recent changes in her body, the nausea she'd been fighting for a number of weeks, she felt like throwing up all over again.

When she lifted her head, she was blinded by the moisture in her eyes.

"Do you want to tell us what happened?" Sukie asked, her voice soft with concern.

"I might as well," said Carol Ann, sniffling. "It was on the cruise, like Lynetta said. I met this guy, Ramón." Her voice trembled. "I don't even know his last name."

"And?" prompted Grace, reaching across the table and taking hold of one of Carol Ann's hands.

"And he asked if he could buy me a drink." She let out a snort of self-hatred. "Only it turns out I was buying the drinks, not him.

Anyway, one thing led to another and we ended up in my cabin." A shiver crossed her shoulders. She stopped.

"Take your time, hon," said Sukie.

Carol Ann drew a deep breath and began again. "When I woke up, he was gone and so were all my credit cards and my money." She couldn't hold back the tears that were flowing from her eyes in a steady stream. "It was just like John all over again."

"With one difference," murmured Grace.

Carol Ann lowered her head. She couldn't face these women. Not after she'd been so stupid.

Sukie rose and put an arm around her. "Listen, Carol Ann. You're not alone. We've all been fooled by other people. The whole town knows how I was fooled. We're here to help you, hon. No matter what you choose."

"Yes," said Tiffany. "We'll help you get through this." She gave Carol Ann an encouraging smile. "Maybe it will be a girl, and we can share Vanna's clothes."

The thought of having a real baby, taking care of someone so helpless, so small, sent terror racing through Carol Ann's body like a rabbit on the run. She clutched the edge of the table.

"I don't think I can do this."

"Let's take one thing at a time," coached Sukie.

Carol Ann listened, but she had no idea what she'd do. The thought of her mother finding out sent her into an emotional tailspin. Her mother would become even more impossible to live with. Maybe three weeks would be too long to wait for Tiffany's apartment. But where else would she go?

Carol Ann held her head in her hands and sobbed.

CHAPTER FIFTY-SIX
TIFFANY

Tiffany left the luncheon as shocked as everyone else by Carol Ann's pregnancy. As many times as they'd all previously warned her to be careful with her overly romanticized ideas about meeting a man, no one in the group had said one derogatory thing to Carol Ann about her being pregnant—she was obviously shattered.

Tiffany knew how that felt.

Looking down at her baby, she wondered how she could ever have thought about not having her.

She decided to give Carol Ann all the furniture and most of the other items in the apartment. It was a mixture of gifts from the other women in the group as well as a few purchases she'd been able to make on her own. She'd even include the furniture in Vanna's nursery. It was suitable for either a boy or a girl. She smiled at the thought of surprising Carol Ann. Just as Karen and the other women had helped her, she'd help Carol Ann.

After settling Vanna in the car, Tiffany drove to the house she and Beau had shared. Pulling up to it, she stared at the large brick home with wide columns lining the porch. It had never been a real home. It had always seemed too grand, too pretentious, to suit her. Beau had never really liked it either. All the decorating inside had been done by Muffy. She no doubt had thought Tiffany wouldn't do a suitable job of it.

Initially, Tiffany had thought she'd sell the house completely furnished. But now she wanted to take a second look at the furniture inside, use what she could and let the women in the Fat Fridays group choose what they wanted before she sold the rest.

"Okay, baby girl," Tiffany said, lifting the car seat out of the back of her car. "This is where Mommy used to live with Daddy. Let's go inside."

Vanna's face wrinkled into a scowl Tiffany recognized as her own. "I know," Tiffany said sympathetically. "I don't like this place either. This is where everything fell apart."

With Vanna in her seat, Tiffany went to the massive front door and inserted the key into the lock. She swallowed the feeling of gloom that suddenly washed over her, turned the key, and waited until the door unlocked with a click.

She drew a deep breath and stepped inside the entrance. In the eerie emptiness, pain hit her like a blow to the gut. She gasped and set the car seat down. The last time she'd been in the house, Beau had chased Sukie and her out of it, screaming obscenities at them.

"I can do this," Tiffany said to the empty space. She lifted the car seat with fresh resolve.

Walking into the living room, she forced away bad memories and recalled the good times in this very room. She and Beau had once made love on the rug in front of the fireplace. She felt her lips curve. The beginning of their marriage had been so wonderful. Even now she could clearly recall what it'd felt like for him to make love to her.

She studied the furniture with a critical eye and imagined what each piece might look like in her new, more relaxed home. Pleased with her inspection, she moved on.

In the dining room, Tiffany had to admit, Muffy had done another nice job. The dining room table, chairs, and sideboard would all be wonderful in the new house.

A quick glance at the kitchen made it easy for Tiffany to decide to take everything from there. The bar stools, table, and chairs would be perfect. More than that, the kitchen was equipped beautifully, with gadgets and tools that had encouraged Tiffany to try her hand at cooking.

Upstairs she toured each room, making decisions.

She saved the nursery until last. The last time she'd seen it, graffiti had marred the pale pink walls. Back then, Beau had fought against the idea of a baby girl because his parents had insisted the baby be a boy.

With trepidation, she opened the door and let out a sigh of relief. The walls were now clean. Tiffany caressed the blonde velvety locks of hair on Vanna's head and reminded herself Beau had come full circle. He'd told both Kevin and George his daughter was beautiful. He was getting his life in order.

Tiffany closed the door behind her with a vow to make a new life for Vanna and herself. A happy life. A good life. A loving life.

CHAPTER FIFTY-SEVEN
CAROL ANN

"Carol Ann? You gonna get up?"

Carol Ann groaned and rolled over. Why, just once, couldn't she sleep in on a Saturday morning? She rubbed her swollen, red eyes, wishing she'd magically disappear through the floor of her room. Her life was a mess and it was all her fault.

Willing herself not to be sick, she stumbled out of bed. More aware of her body, she touched her tender breasts. Would they one day nourish a baby like Tiffany had fed Vanna? The harsh reality of her situation brought another groan out of her. This was one time she couldn't dream away her troubles.

She made her way to the bathroom and stepped into the shower. Looking down at her flat stomach she wondered how she'd feel when it bulged as if a watermelon were inside. There was no question about her keeping the baby. She'd already decided to go through with the pregnancy and birth and to raise the child alone. If Tiffany could do it, so could she.

The hot water sluiced the soap off her body, but it couldn't erase the shame she felt.

Thinking of what she'd done with a total stranger, she felt her stomach heave. Dripping wet, she raced to the toilet.

A knock sounded at the door. "You all right, Carol Ann?"

Carol Ann wiped her mouth. "Yes, Mama. Just a touch of the flu." She dried herself off and wrapped the towel around her, then opened the door to go to her bedroom.

Her mother stood in the hallway, staring at her. "Wanna tell me what's goin' on?"

Carol Ann's pulse sprinted with alarm. "What do you mean?"

"I've been watchin' you. You've been acting real sneaky. Are you dating that nice boss of yours?"

Carol Ann was so surprised she couldn't answer. Struggling for a response, she finally said, "Why would I do that? He and I work in the same department. It's not allowed."

Her mother shook her head. "Something's goin' on. You've changed. Better not be any news I'd be ashamed of. That's all I can say."

Carol Ann opened her mouth to answer and let out a rumbling burp. When she clapped a hand over her mouth, the towel slipped.

Her mother's eyes widened. "Oh my gawd! You're pregnant!"

"No, I . . . how did you know?" Carol Ann's stomach lurched. She bolted inside the bathroom and slammed the door behind her.

Her mother opened the door and waited until Carol Ann had finished and was dabbing her face with a cold washcloth.

"Like I told your sister when she was dating, if it ever happened to her, she'd better start planning a wedding. I'm not having a pregnant girl living here at home. Understand?"

"But, Mama . . ."

"No buts, Carol Ann. I mean what I say. We're a God-fearin' family. I'll not have you living sinful-like here."

Too dizzy to answer, Carol Ann simply nodded.

CHAPTER FIFTY-EIGHT
TIFFANY

Tiffany's heart squeezed with sympathy as Carol Ann sat on her couch, sobbing hopelessly. She understood Carol Ann's pain. Her own mother had always been a trial to her.

"I can't stay there a minute more," said Carol Ann. "I swear I hate that woman. What am I going to do?"

Tiffany brought a glass of water and a tissue from the kitchen and handed them to Carol Ann. "Don't worry. I have an idea." She forced a smile. "This is a time for the Fat Fridays ladies to take action. Stay right there while I make a few phone calls."

She went into her bedroom, where she could talk in private.

After she'd placed calls to Sukie, Grace, and Lynetta, Tiffany returned to the living room to find it empty.

"Carol Ann?"

She checked the kitchen. Finding it empty too, she went to Vanna's room.

Peering inside, Tiffany paused.

Carol Ann was sitting in the rocking chair with Vanna, singing a song. The singing was horrible, but the tenderness in the words touched

Tiffany. Carol Ann might not know it, might not want to even think about it, but she was going to make a wonderful mother.

Noticing Tiffany, Carol Ann smiled. "I heard Vanna making noises and thought I'd come get her." She gave the baby a hug. "She's so beautiful."

Tiffany nodded. "Thanks. I think so too."

"What's up?" Carol Ann asked.

"Everyone is meeting here after lunch. We're going to help you move out of the house. Lynetta is bringing James and her boys; Sukie is bringing Cam and a truck. Grace is going to babysit Vanna."

A wide smile spread across Carol Ann's face. She clapped a hand to her chest. "Really? You'd do that for me?" Frowning, she shook her head. "But wait! Where am I going to stay? Where am I going to put my things?"

"I've got it all worked out. You're going to store your things here in the apartment and stay with Grace. I'll move out of here as fast as I can. I've placed a call to the painters to see if they can finish their work early."

Carol Ann collapsed against the back of the rocker, setting it into motion. "What would I do without you and the other women?" Her voice wavered. "If I moved out of the house without my furniture, I'm sure my mother would claim it as hers."

"She's not going to be able to do that," said Tiffany. "And don't worry about what you don't have. I'm leaving all the furniture and everything else here for you."

"Do you mean it?" Carol Ann's voice wobbled. "Wow! I can't even think of how to thank you."

"Just enjoy it," said Tiffany. "We'll all be so happy to have you here."

Vanna let out a cry and kicked her legs, drawing their attention.

"She's hungry." Carol Ann stood and handed the baby to Tiffany. Placing an arm around Tiffany's shoulder, she said, "You're the best, Tiff. The best."

"Every woman in the group is the best," Tiffany replied with conviction. Not one woman had said no to her sudden plan.

Carol Ann left to go back home to organize things for the surprise move.

After feeding Vanna, Tiffany went to work packing up some of her clothes to make room in the closet for Carol Ann. As people were helping Carol Ann remove her things from her parents' house, Tiffany would take as much as she could of her clothing and personal items to her new house.

◆　◆　◆

At the appointed time, the whole group showed up. Tiffany greeted the women with hugs and thanked the boys, Cam, and James for coming.

Grace stayed inside with Chloe and the baby, as the others in the group helped Tiffany load her things into her SUV. Then, with a promise to her to return shortly, they left to go to Carol Ann's house.

Driving into the driveway that used to be Sukie's and now was hers, Tiffany filled with happiness. The house already had the feel of home to her. She opened the garage door and was about to enter it when she noticed a black BMW pulling in behind her.

Smiling, she parked the car and got out. "Kevin! You're just in time to help me carry in some things."

He grinned. "Actually, that's why I'm here. Grace told me you might need some help. What's going on?"

She filled him in on the situation.

It took a number of trips, but they got Tiffany's clothes and several boxes of various items inside and stored into closets, safe from the painters.

"C'mon, I'll show you around," Tiffany said.

Walking through the house, seeing it as it would be with fresh paint and carpets and with her own furniture, Tiffany was struck by how lucky she was. For the first time in her life she would have a home of her own that would be filled with unconditional love.

"This is really nice. I like it a lot better than the house you and Beau had," said Kevin, looking out to the backyard through the glass of the French doors in the kitchen.

"Me too," said Tiffany, smiling up at him.

His features grew soft. A wistfulness filled his eyes, turning the brown in them darker.

Tiffany reached out and took hold of his hand. "Thanks for everything, Kevin. I don't know what I'd have done without you helping me."

"Beau set it up that way, remember?" Kevin's voice had an edge to it that confused Tiffany.

She withdrew her hand. "Guess he knew how good you'd be at it."

"Happy to help," he said and abruptly turned away, leaving her even more puzzled.. *What just happened? I thought we were such good friends.*

◆ ◆ ◆

When she returned to the apartment, Tiffany found pieces of a bed, a mattress, and a box spring sitting on the lawn outside the entrance to the building. Several boxes were stacked alongside them. Cam, James, and Lynetta's two boys were standing nearby.

"Where's the storage area?" Cam said, approaching her. "We didn't want to take this stuff upstairs if we didn't need to."

"No, of course not," she said. "The storage area is in the basement. I've got the key right here. I'll open it for you."

"Hey, Martin!" Cam called. "You and your brother want to give James and me a hand?"

Lynetta's boys hurried over to him. Jackson and Cam held up one end of the mattress, James and Martin the other. Struggling, they managed to get the mattress through the basement door.

She raced ahead of them, over to the metal storage cage for her apartment. She unlocked it and held the door open for them. With collective sighs, the guys set the mattress on its side on the floor.

Tiffany handed Cam the key. "I'd better go see what's happening upstairs."

As she drew near to her apartment, Tiffany heard laughter.

She opened the door. Lynetta was wearing a lampshade on her head and dancing to the beat of tinkling music coming from a stuffed dog in Chloe's hands.

"Lookin' good, Lady Lynetta," Tiffany teased, laughing with the other women.

Lynetta grinned. "I couldn't resist." She pulled the lampshade off her curls and placed it on Tiffany's head.

"Dance, Tiff'ny," said Chloe, her blue eyes alight with excitement.

Tiffany grabbed Chloe's hands. They wiggled back and forth in a dance of their own.

After the music stopped, Tiffany handed Sukie the lampshade. "So how did the move go at Carol Ann's house?"

Sukie's expression sobered. "We left Carol Ann at her house so she could say good-bye in private. I have to say, that mother of hers is the most unpleasant person I've met in a long time."

"She sure didn't like us showing up like that. She threatened never to speak to Carol Ann again." Lynetta shook her head. "Poor Carol Ann! No wonder she's always looking for love."

Sukie nodded. "It's a terrible situation. Especially now when Carol Ann is going through a hard time."

Tiffany thought of Sukie's words on the day she'd scattered Beau's ashes. For a period of time, she and Beau had found a special love. Maybe the day would come when Carol Ann would find love too.

CHAPTER FIFTY-NINE
SUKIE

Sukie awoke early and gazed out the window. The sun had not yet risen but the weatherman had predicted a nice sunny November day for her wedding.

Lying in bed, Sukie thought back to her first wedding, hastily arranged because of Rob's forthcoming birth. Even so she'd gone through the motions of a normal wedding—white gown, veil, ugly bridesmaid dresses, chaos, panic, and all. She vowed this wedding would be different.

Beside her, Cam stirred and reached for her. She moved back against his solid body, loving the feel of his arms around her.

As she often did, Sukie wondered how she could've landed the hottest man in town, almost eight years younger. Most guys kept going for far-younger women.

"Excited?" murmured Cam.

Sukie rolled over and faced him. Cupping his cheeks in her hands, she kissed him—long and slow and sweet. "I can't wait to make this official."

"Me, either. I've never gone through this before. Am I supposed to be doing anything? You've made all the arrangements."

She smiled. "Just show up."

He drew her closer. "I could show up right now."

She pushed at him playfully. "Down, boy! We have a lot to get through today. It may be a small wedding, but I want it to be perfect."

"Okay, you take care of the wedding, I'll take care of the honeymoon. Are you sure this is what you want, a couple of nights on Sea Island until we can take a real honeymoon in Europe?"

"Yes. I don't want to leave Chloe until she's comfortable with all the changes. Besides, the weather in Europe is so cold at this time of year."

"April won't be hot, but it'll be better than now." In the growing light, she could see a smile spread across his face. "Besides, we'll have put in a lot of practice by then."

She laughed.

"Daddy? Sukie?"

Sukie turned in time to help Chloe climb up into bed with them. Holding her doll Sally, Chloe settled between them. "Is this the day I get to call Sukie 'Mommy'?"

"Yes," said Cam. "Today she becomes your true mommy."

Smiling, Chloe turned to Sukie. "And this is the day I wear my true princess dress?"

"Yes," said Sukie. "After your nap, we'll both get dressed up for the wedding. Until then you can wear your everyday clothes."

"Can I carry my flowers?"

"Not until it's time to walk down the aisle," said Sukie. "But I have a surprise for you. You're invited to a special breakfast this morning."

Chloe's eyes lit with excitement. "Can Sally come too?"

Sukie brushed back a blonde curl from Chloe's forehead and gave her a quick kiss. "I'm sure the ladies in the group won't mind one bit."

"While you women are having your breakfast, the guys and I are going to get in a round of golf," said Cam. "I want my friend Bob to meet Rob. And Lynetta's boyfriend James has finally agreed to join us.

He said he doesn't play very well, but when I asked Lynetta about it, she told me he's pretty good at everything he does."

Sukie laughed. "The two of them are a hoot together."

"He's a good guy, quiet but capable."

"How about me? Am I capebull?" asked Chloe.

Sukie and Cam looked at each and laughed. "This girl doesn't miss a thing," said Cam proudly.

"I know. We have to be careful what we say."

Cam nodded. "I hear you. That's one reason I try not to say *damn* or *hell* or worse."

Chloe drew herself up with indignation. "Daddy, you said a swear."

Sukie elbowed him. "Better stop teasing. Little pitchers have big ears."

"I'm not a picture," said Chloe, making Sukie and Cam laugh even harder.

"Come on, little girl," said Sukie. "Let's get ready for our breakfast."

Sukie and Chloe arrived at Sally Jean's Breakfast Buffet in Millville at the same time as Betsy and Karen. Sukie helped Chloe out of the car and turned to them with a smile.

"So glad you're back home!" said Sukie. "And thanks for arranging this breakfast. It's such a sweet thought."

She gave Betsy a warm hug.

Betsy drew back and studied Sukie. "You look wonderful! I swear you look younger every day."

"It must be Cam," said Karen, giving Sukie a hug. "I'm so happy for you."

Inside the restaurant a special room had been set aside for the party. Carol Ann, Grace, and Tiffany and Vanna sat at a long pine table. Calico curtains lined the windows and woven rag rugs sat on the floor, giving the room a country feel.

"Where are the others?" Sukie asked.

"Elizabeth and Madeleine are on their way with your friend, Mary Anderson," said Grace. "And here's Lynetta now."

Sukie brought a booster seat over to a chair, settled Chloe in it, and took a seat beside her.

Elizabeth and Madeleine arrived with Mary.

"Sorry, we're late," murmured Madeleine, taking a seat.

Sukie hugged her and rose to greet Mary. Her husband Bob was Cam's best man. "I'm so happy you and Bob are part of our day. You were the first couple to know Cam and I were dating."

"Yes, and I was the first to know you really loved him." Mary's eyes twinkled.

Sukie smiled at the memory of their dinner together in Atlanta. And when Sukie had thought the relationship with Cam was over, it was Mary who'd tried to convince her that Cam really was interested in her. Grateful for the way things had turned out, Sukie gave Mary another squeeze and turned to her daughter.

"Dad said he hopes you and Cam will be happy." Elizabeth whispered in Sukie's ear as she gave her a hug.

Sukie smiled. Amazing what becoming sober had done to Ted.

"'Lizbeth and me are a princess," said Chloe giving Elizabeth a look of adoration.

Elizabeth took a seat next to her and ruffled Chloe's curls. "Not exactly princesses. We're maids of honor."

A look of distress crossed Chloe's face.

Sukie quickly said, "You still get to wear your princess dress."

The smile that filled Chloe's face was repeated by everyone else at the table. A maid of honor was not the same as a princess.

"This is quite a day for you, Sukie," said Betsy, beaming at her. "A big day for all of us, really, to see you happily married. I'm so glad you decided to join the Fat Fridays group."

At the chorus of agreement, Sukie smiled with affection. She'd been so low, so embarrassed, so insecure when they'd all taken her under their wings.

After a waitress had taken their orders, Tiffany placed a gaily wrapped package in front of Sukie. "A little something for you to wear on Sea Island."

Chloe clapped her hands. "Can I open it?"

"You can help," said Sukie, suspicious of the looks of amusement on the faces of her friends.

Sukie and Chloe unwrapped the present, and then Sukie lifted a short red filmy gown out of the box. The skimpy top consisted of see-through fabric with two round holes in it.

"Actually the gift is for Cam," said Tiffany, giving Sukie a wily grin.

"What is it?" said Chloe.

"A nightgown," Sukie responded, forcing herself to keep a straight face. It wasn't like any nightgown she'd ever worn, but like Tiffany said, Cam would love it. She put it back in the box, feeling her cheeks grow hot as she imagined Cam's response to it.

"A happy marriage is a long conversation that doesn't end," said Mary shyly.

Betsy grinned at Sukie. "Marriage is a relationship where one is always right and the other is the husband." Everyone laughed.

Elizabeth lifted her Bloody Mary. "Here's to second chances." She smiled at Sukie. "I'm so glad you got one, Mom."

"Here! Here!" said Madeleine, giving Sukie a loving hug.

Sukie, Chloe, Madeleine, and Elizabeth left the breakfast and went to Henri's Hair Designs. Bless Henri's heart, he'd told Sukie he'd set aside the whole late morning for them to get their hair done.

Sitting in her chair at the beauty salon, waiting for the streaks of color in her hair to come to life, Sukie reveled in this girl time together. She'd missed her daughter, and though she saw Madeleine from time to time, Madeleine was busy with her baby and with the new condo.

Chloe stuck to Elizabeth's side, peppering her with questions which Elizabeth answered patiently until Sukie, with sympathy, pulled out a couple of books and read quietly to her.

When Sukie and Chloe arrived home, Cam was waiting for them. "Hi, gorgeous and gorgeous!"

"Mommy got a present! It's a red nightie. But Tiff'ny says it's for you," Chloe proudly announced.

"For me?" Cam wiggled his eyebrows playfully.

Sukie laughed. "You can't see it until tomorrow night at the resort."

"That's fine with me," said Cam. "Tonight I have a different plan."

Chloe studied her father, a serious expression on her face.

Sukie gave Cam a stern look. "Don't say another word."

At his naughty grin, heat crept into Sukie's cheeks.

She knew exactly what he had in mind.

CHAPTER SIXTY
BETSY

Betsy sat in a pew next to Karen in the front of the small chapel attached to the Congregational church. The Fat Fridays group, Mary Anderson, and Madeleine, holding her son Jonathan, sat close by.

For Betsy, this was a very fulfilling moment. A little over a year ago Sukie had been a defeated woman. After joining her group of friends, Sukie had become, in many respects, their leader. It was very satisfying to her that Sukie was about to marry Cam after suffering through years of coping with a husband whose ego trumped kindness.

The chapel was lovely in its simplicity—white pews with green cushions, a mellow-colored pine pulpit, and a simple gold cross on display. Soft organ music played in the background.

Tiffany stood in front of the small gathering and began to sing. Accompanied by piano music, her sweet voice rose on the notes of "Ave Maria," adding a touch of solemnity to the happy occasion.

At the end of the song, Tiffany sat down.

The music changed to the familiar "Bridal Chorus" by Wagner.

Cam and Bob Anderson stepped through a side door and stood in front of the altar with the minister.

With anticipation building, Betsy rose with the others and turned to watch the procession.

Elizabeth and Chloe came down the aisle hand in hand, two blonde visions of loveliness. Elizabeth's simple sheath in a rich plum set off the light color of her hair and the sleek shape of her body. *Perfect for this small private wedding,* thought Betsy with silent approval. She smiled as Chloe, wearing a long, flowing dress in a complementary softer purple, tugged on Elizabeth's hand, urging her to go faster. Each girl held a small bouquet of orchids, whose purple accents offset the colors in their dresses.

Karen nudged her. "Here comes Sukie."

Betsy's breath left her in a gasp of admiration.

On Rob's arm, Sukie made her way toward them. The champagne-colored silk suit she wore was stunning in its simplicity, so much more elegant than a fancy dress.

Sukie's gaze swept the people in the audience and rested on Betsy for a moment, acknowledging their special friendship.

When Sukie lifted her eyes to Cam, her cheeks flushed a pretty pink and her face lit with love.

Cam stared at Sukie as if she were an angel from heaven.

Betsy and Karen looked at each other and smiled.

"They make such an adorable couple," murmured Betsy, reaching into her purse for a tissue.

Sukie and Cam each read words they'd written for each other—tender words full of love and promise.

Vows were exchanged and then the minister said, "You may now kiss the bride."

Betsy's heart melted at the lingering kiss Cam gave Sukie.

When they pulled apart, the minister announced, "I now present Mr. and Mrs. Cameron Taylor."

"And me," said Chloe.

Amid laughter and applause, Sukie and Cam moved down the aisle and outside to where a number of limos were waiting.

Betsy and Karen joined Lynetta, James, and her two boys in one limo. The others piled in the other cars.

Later, walking into the restaurant, Betsy became fascinated by the idea of different rooms representing different countries. She entered the French room and let out a sigh of admiration. With its pale yellow walls and paintings, it was lovely, like everything Sukie had planned for her special day.

CHAPTER SIXTY-ONE
TIFFANY

Tiffany ate the last bite of her slice of wedding cake and got to her feet. Lifting Vanna out of her infant seat, she handed her to Elizabeth. Singing at the wedding and reception was a very small way for her to show her appreciation for the many times Sukie had helped her.

A little stage had been set up along one wall of the room. Tiffany walked over to it.

The man playing soft background music on a keyboard nodded and gave her a smile. They'd worked together at the Glass Slipper. He continued playing, waiting for her to give him a signal to wrap up his song.

Holding a small mic, she stepped up onto the stage. From this vantage point, she took a moment to look out at the group gathered together for this joyous occasion.

Elizabeth, holding Vanna, was smiling and talking to Chloe. The new sisters looked adorable together. Chloe was enamored of Elizabeth's very high heels and dangling earrings. She'd announced to all who would listen that she was going to have shoes and earrings just like 'Lizbeth when she got a little bigger.

In a little white dress and matching tights, Vanna, sitting on Elizabeth's lap, looked like a little cherub. She was staring up at Elizabeth as if she, like Chloe, couldn't wait to wear such sparkling things on her ears.

Tiffany's gaze turned to Madeleine and Rob. They were holding hands and smiling at their son, Jonathan, sitting in a high chair between them. The loving look in their eyes as they turned to each other gave Tiffany the feeling that before long Jonathan would have a sibling.

Carol Ann, sitting beside Grace, stirred restlessly in her seat, looking uncomfortable. Grace patted Carol Ann's hand with sympathy. Tiffany knew how unpleasant pregnancy could sometimes be. Maybe by Christmas, Carol Ann would feel better, and maybe by then, Grace would be able to spend some time with her daughter.

At the next table, Lynetta sat with her two boys and James. Throughout the wedding and the reception, the boys had been very polite, but Tiffany could tell from the way they tugged at their shirt collars that they'd be happier playing video games at home. Lynetta's eyes sparkled as she smiled at James in a way Tiffany understood.

Betsy and Karen sat at a table with Sukie and Cam. Observing the love that emanated from the four of them, Tiffany let out a sigh.

She watched Cam discreetly place a hand on Sukie's thigh. Sukie looked over at Cam and gave him a dazzling smile. Tiffany sighed again. This wedding was so perfect.

Her gaze settled at the table she'd just left. Sitting next to Bob and Mary Anderson, Kevin smiled up at her. Sukie had insisted that he be invited. Tiffany was happy to have him here. He'd become such an important person in her life.

"Well? Are you going to sing?" said Grace in her usual brisk manner.

Laughter filled the room.

Smiling, Tiffany lifted the microphone in her hand and nodded to her friend on the keyboard. This wasn't her usual Sassy Saturday, but so much more.

She took a shaky breath and began singing "Only You." The song held so many meanings for each one of them.

Putting her heart and soul into the music, she gazed at each of the women in the Fat Fridays group. They were so different, with individual challenges, but together their love and support of one another made them strong. She let her love for them pour into her song, telling them in her own way how much they meant to her.

AUTHOR'S NOTE

I hope you've enjoyed reading more about the women in the Fat Fridays group. If you have, please help other readers discover them by leaving a review on Amazon, Goodreads, or your favorite site. It's the best way to say thank you!

LUNCH AT THE BEACH HOUSE HOTEL

Please enjoy an excerpt from my next book *Lunch at the Beach House Hotel*. Readers asked for more stories about Ann and Rhonda's adventures running a small boutique hotel in Florida. I listened. It is coming soon! Stay tuned . . .

CHAPTER ONE

I'd just stepped out of the shower when my business partner Rhonda—Rhonda DelMonte Grayson, as she proudly called herself—phoned in a tizzy.

"Annie, you've got to get over here right away. Something's come up."

She hung up before I could ask her about it, but I knew I'd better get moving. In the hotel business there were a lot of "somethings"—some good, some bad.

My mind whirled with possibilities as I quickly dried off and dressed. After brushing my hair and dabbing on some lipstick, I took a moment to put on the chain and pendant Vaughn Sanders had given me. He wouldn't return from filming for another six weeks, and I missed him like crazy. The gold pendant spoke of so many things. His initial *V* formed one side of my *A*. Across the middle of it was a bar with five diamonds—a symbol of us, our collective three children, and the hope that we'd all share a life together.

I left my house on the hotel property and headed toward the hotel. Warm air wrapped around me, caressing my skin in silky strokes, and I joyfully inhaled the tang of salty air. After living most of my life in Boston, I relished the tropical setting along the Gulf Coast of southwest Florida.

As I approached the front of the Beach House Hotel, I paused to stare at the beachside estate Rhonda and I had turned into a small, upscale hotel. The pale-pink stucco, two-story building spread before me at the water's edge like a palace, regal and splendid. Wide steps led to carved wooden double doors that invited guests inside. Potted palms sat on either side of the doorway, adding a tropical elegance to the entry. Along the front of the hotel, brilliant pink hibiscus blossoms vied for attention with bougainvillea and other colorful plantings and softened the lines of the building.

Gratitude filled me.

In the troubling days following my ex's dumping me for his receptionist—Kandie with a *K*, as she called herself—I never would've imagined being part owner of such a beautiful place. We'd started out better than expected, but the fear of failing kept me working day and night to make sure the hotel succeeded. So many didn't. And though I loved Rhonda, it was sometimes frustrating to be left with most of the detailed, follow-up work she disliked. Doing it as cheerfully as I could while she stayed busy doing the stuff that was more fun was a way to pay her back for all she'd done to help me.

Rhonda appeared at the top of the stairway. Dressed in one of the lightweight, colorful caftans she loved to wear, she urged me forward, flapping the green sleeves of her dress like a tropical bird about to take flight. *Or more like the early bird who got the worm,* I thought wryly, as I got a closer look at the grin on her face.

She placed her hands on her ample hips and shook her head at me. "Annie Rutherford, how can you look so freakin' beautiful and put together at this early hour? I swear, if you weren't my best friend, I'd hate your guts."

I laughed. Rhonda was known for speaking her mind. It was amazing we even got along—we were as different as two people could be. My strict grandmother, who'd raised me after my parents died, would shiver in her blue-blooded Boston grave at the language Rhonda used. I'd gotten used to it, which was a good thing, because Rhonda didn't even notice it. She'd come from a loud Italian family in New Jersey.

"What's up?" I asked. "It better be good. I haven't even had my coffee yet."

"Oh, it's good all right. We have a decision to make—an important one that can't wait."

"And?" I prompted, giving Rhonda a dubious look.

"And I promised Valentina Marquis's agent we'd call her right back. She's at LAX, ready to put Valentina on a private jet to us."

"Oh, no!" My heart thudded with dismay. "Are you talking about the same Valentina Marquis who costarred with Vaughn in that awful short film, the one he tried to get out of several times?"

Rhonda nodded. "The very same one. But Annie, this could mean a lot of business for us."

As usual, talk of new business stopped me cold. I was consumed by overseeing the finances of the hotel. At best, the hotel business was a series of ups and downs, fluctuating as bookings rose and fell. At worst, I had invested every cent of mine into my share of the business. Weather, holiday dates, and fierce competition affected bookings for room reservations, which created a lot of uncertainty.

"Okay, you'd better tell me about it. Why does she want Valentina to come here?"

An even bigger grin spread across Rhonda's face. Beneath her bleached blonde hair, her dark eyes sparkled with mischief. "You won't believe it! She's going to be shooting a movie in two months and has eight weeks to lose twenty-five pounds."

I frowned. "How's she going to do that here? We're known for our delicious cuisine."

"The agent has requested us to provide a trainer to stay with Valentina to keep an eye on her and to guide her physical training. Because the Beach House is known for assuring our guests total privacy, she figures the director and producer won't find out what shape Valentina is in before she loses the weight. Cool, huh?"

"I'm not sure." Vaughn, sweet guy that he is, had ranted and raved about Valentina's prima donna attitude on the movie set. He'd declared her self-absorption and her treatment of the people around her deplorable.

"It could be a bit tricky," admitted Rhonda, "but it's been a real slow fall season for us."

I couldn't deny it. In the past, we'd had a lot of VIP guests from the world of politics, but with the latest mess in Washington, they'd been forced to stay put. Not that I minded all that much. The pols were as egotistical as any movie star.

"Okay, let's call her back," I said reluctantly. Her visit could boost our cash flow, and who couldn't use a better bottom line?

On the way to our office, which sat behind the kitchen, I stopped and grabbed a cup of coffee, along with one of Rhonda's famous breakfast rolls. Sweet and buttery, filled with cinnamon and nuts, their enticing aroma filled the air. These breakfast rolls had been instrumental in promoting the culinary reputation of the hotel since we'd opened it a little over a year ago.

After sipping my refreshing hot coffee, I carried it and the roll into the office and sat at my desk. A sigh of pleasure escaped me as I bit into the soft, warm breakfast sweet.

Seated opposite me, Rhonda dialed the number she'd been given. I listened carefully as she informed Valentina's agent that we'd be delighted to have Valentina stay with us.

Rhonda stopped talking, then said, "Please hold. I'll check to see if we can make those arrangements." She turned to me. "Is it okay if I offer her the lower rooms at the far end of the hotel? If we give her rooms 101 and 102, Valentina will have the privacy her agent says she needs."

I busied myself checking our online reservations system. "How long does she want to use the rooms?"

"They want 'em for the full eight weeks, starting today. That takes us up to the Thanksgiving weekend."

I quickly looked at the reservations list. "We'll have to move a few people around, but we can do it." There were no full-house wedding weekends planned during that time. Only smaller groups.

After she assured Valentina's agent she'd take care of everything, Rhonda hung up with a sigh. "It sounds as if this situation hasn't been easy for anybody. Valentina is being put on a plane within the next two hours. We're to hire a personal trainer and meet her at the airport. She'll be traveling under the name Tina Marks, which I understand is her real name. And that's not all. I've agreed not only to provide special meals for her, but also to keep her out of the spotlight so no one even guesses she's here."

"Okay, that's settled then," I said, suddenly overcome by the horrible feeling that this might be one of the biggest mistakes Rhonda and I had ever made together. And there'd been a few.

◆　◆　◆

Tim McFarland, our young assistant manager, agreed to pick up Jerry Brighton, the personal trainer we'd hired through an agency, and to drive him in the limo to the airport to pick up Tina.

Rhonda and I stayed at the hotel to discuss the details of Tina's upcoming stay. Then I began my daily ritual of reviewing revenue reports, staffing schedules, and reservations to update my forecasts. The sales weren't as strong as I'd hoped, emphasizing for me how important Tina's stay was to us. I resolved to make her visit go well. In addition to paying for the rooms, her agent was paying a hefty price for the hotel to cook special, low-cal meals for Tina and her trainer.

I'd finished doing some financial projections when Tim called from the limo to say he was approaching the hotel with our guest. As part of our normal routine, Rhonda and I went to the front stairway to greet them. From the hotel's beginning, it was something we'd done as often as we could. Our guests liked it.

Rhonda and I were standing by the front door at our usual stations when Tim pulled the limo into the front circle.

"Here goes," Rhonda said, giving me a high five.

As the car came to a stop, we descended the stairs.

Tim got out and raced around the limo to open the passenger door.

A foot encased in a high-heeled gold sandal emerged. It was quickly followed by a young woman dressed in a denim skirt so short I knew she was wearing a thong. Her white tank top indicated she wasn't wearing a bra.

I lifted my gaze to her face. Large sunglasses hid most of it. Blue hair piled in a knot atop her head added a few inches to her height but couldn't help the fact that she was short and . . . well, wider than normal in places, for a movie star.

"Welcome . . ." I started my spiel.

"What a dump," Tina said, cupping her hands around her sunglasses for a better view in the sunlight. "I asked for a big fancy, glittery place if I have to do this stupid Hollywood thing."

Beneath her normal tan, Rhonda's face turned bright red.

I held my breath. Nobody bad-mouthed the hotel in front of Rhonda.

"That little brat," Rhonda murmured.

I grabbed hold of her arm. "Don't!"

She jerked her arm out of my hand and hurried down the stairway, her caftan flying behind her in a cloud of green.

Knowing what was coming, I raced past her. Tina might be a gigantic boor, but she was going to be properly welcomed like I'd been taught.

"Welcome to the Beach House Hotel," I said, elbowing my way in front of Rhonda.

A bald-headed muscular giant emerged from the car, looking like the smiling ad man on television who told viewers all about his cleaning products. Standing beside Tina, his bulk made her seem smaller than ever.

He smiled. "I'm Jerry Brighton, the one you hired to keep tabs on Tina." Turning to Rhonda, he smiled. "This place is beautiful."

The lines of distress left Rhonda's face. She returned his smile. "Thank you. I'm Rhonda DelMonte Grayson and this is my partner, Annie Rutherford. Among other things, the Beach House Hotel is known for great service; we're here to help you in any way we can."

"Great," he said.

Tina's red-painted lips formed a pout as she glared at us. "I don't need anyone watching over me. I can do this myself. And nobody can know I'm here at this fat farm," said Tina. "That would ruin me."

Rhonda drew herself up. This time I knew I couldn't stop her.

Hands on hips, Rhonda stared down Tina. "This is not a fat farm. This is a lovely place where guests can find some of the finest food in southwestern Florida." She paused for emphasis. "If they're allowed to eat it."

Tina gasped and stamped a sandaled foot. "That's it! I'm leaving!" The effect of her tantrum was ruined by her teetering on heels too high for her. She regained her balance and turned to climb inside the limo.

"Hold on." In one swift movement Jerry took hold of Tina's elbow to stop her. "Let's at least give this a try."

Tina's shoulders slumped in defeat, allowing me to see a vulnerability that touched me. I realized it couldn't be easy for someone so young to have so many demands made of her.

"Okay. I'll show you to your rooms," said Tim, who until then had been standing aside wringing his hands. He urged them forward.

After Jerry and Tina had followed him into the hotel, Rhonda gave me a sheepish look.

"I'm sorry, Annie, but that little brat deserves more than a scolding. She deserves a spanking."

"No wonder Vaughn found it so difficult to work with Tina," I said. "I hope this isn't how she's going to act for the whole eight weeks."

A frown creased Rhonda's brow. "We can do this, can't we? Keep Tina here and get her thin?"

"We're going to try our best," I said with determination, "but, Rhonda, she won't be our only guest. We'll have to keep everyone else happy too."

"Eight weeks seems like a really long time, huh?"

I nodded. "More like an eternity."

ABOUT THE AUTHOR

Judith Keim has loved stories and reading since she was a young girl. She spent hot summer afternoons lost in novels, traveling from her porch in upstate New York to far-flung fictional destinations. Her writing has been featured in *Chicken Soup to Inspire a Woman's Soul* and *Summer in Mossy Creek*, a Belle Books novel. She has been selected as a finalist in numerous RWA contests. Under the name J.S. Keim, she has also published middle-grade fantasy novels as well as short stories for children in *Highlights*, *Jack and Jill*, and *Children's Playmate*. Keim lives in Boise, Idaho, with her husband and their long-haired dachshund, Winston.